For those who love  **page-turner unveils the brutality of imperialism in Ireland and the Caribbean Island of Jamaica.**

A historical saga you will devour, pause to regroup, and never forget.

West Cork, Ireland, 1846: Desperate and half-starved, an Irishman boards a hurricane-battered ship to the Caribbean. But life away from Ireland is also bleak. The ship is attacked by pirates, his best friend is killed, and he arrives on a stunning, distressful, slave-scourged island.

Jamaica, West Indies, 1846 - 1849: Sean O'Sullivan barely endures his work as overseer for the cruelest British planter in Jamaica. Britain is forced to abolish slavery, but angry planters continue to brutalize and subjugate blacks. Rebellions erupt and activists are lynched.

O'Sullivan quietly resists planter abuse and creates thriving farming communities owned by his ex-slaves. How will he survive, as uprisings continue to flare and a well-respected human rights activist returns home to Jamaica; his name is Marcus Garvey.

Editorial Reviews

"...fascinating characters and events. ...a dramatic and heart-wrenching story of suffering, hope, and redemption. And freedom! Moving and inspiring. The worst and the best of us... I enjoyed this book very much and encourage all to buy it and be blessed."— *J. André Weisbrod, Financial Adviser, Speaker, and Award-Winning Author of Don't Ever Take Away My Freedom by Thomas Patrick Locke*

i

"Kudos to author Norma Jennings for writing this entertaining, essential, meaningful and historical account. This was like having spinach in your cake (if you hated spinach); you are not aware you are getting the well needed literary and historical nutrients, because it's sooooooo goooooood!!!!"—*Jeffrey Anderson-Gunter, Producer/Director/Actor/Founder and Artistic Director of The Caribbean American Repertory Theatre*

"... a fantastic page-turner of fiction embellished with facts. It was such a heartbreaking tale that I needed time to regroup after reading. Set in the mid to late 1800s, this book will appeal to historians and everyone who loves epic stories. This novel explored resilience, betrayal, selflessness, suffering, grit, survival, hope, and courage...Please, write more, Norma."—*Jennifer Ibiam for Readers' Favorite*

"... held my interest captive and left me with an impression that I was an active observer of the meetings and personal interactions which were happening. I almost felt as though I was eavesdropping on some of the conversations outlined...painstaking detail of the personal interactions...a must read..."—*Hilton Nicholson, JD*

"Sean O'Sullivan fled the devastation of the Irish Potato Famine of the 1840s, that caused more than a million deaths...to the island of Jamaica...O'Sullivan found work with the British elite [but] didn't shy away from helping to calm the turbulence of the years of slavery...a story of loss and redemption. Readers will get absorbed in its detail. Norma Jennings is the quintessential storyteller."—*Michael I. Blake, ABR, SRS, SRES*

THE IRISH CONNECTION

Norma Jennings

Moonshine Cove Publishing, LLC

Abbeville, South Carolina U.S.A.

First Moonshine Cove Edition Jul 2023

ISBN: 9781952439612

Library of Congress LCCN: 2023910419

Cover painting by Jerome Taylor; Cover design by Asha Hossain Design, LLC; interior design by Moonshine Cove staff.

About the Author

Norma Jennings, a four-time, award-winning author, was born and raised in Jamaica. Jennings often wondered how classmates who looked like her were named Gavin O'Connor and Olivia Murphy. After extensive research that gave birth to *The Irish Connection,* she boldly shares a piece of that history.

Jennings has a Bachelor of Business Administration degree, completed the Management Development Course at Harvard Graduate School, and has worked as corporate executive in the United States and Jamaica. She now lives in Florida and often visits her grandmother's old sugarcane plantation, Twickenham, in Jamaica. Her website is www.normajennings.com.

Jennings has presented at large events as an executive, at writers' conferences, at author conferences hosted by the Jamaican Consul General, and as commencement speaker at her Alma Mater in Texas.

After her first two novels, *Passenger from Greece* and *Daughter of the Caribbean,* Jennings was named one of the 50 Great Writers, in the 50 Great Writers You Should Be Reading Book Awards. *Passenger from Greece* was awarded finalist in the Best USA Book Awards, and in the Next Generation Indie Book Awards for Best Multicultural Fiction and Best Book Cover Design.

Jennings has completed her fourth novel, *Marooned,* about a woman Maroon warrior's vicious fight against slavery, leading to independence from the British almost 40 years before the U.S. achieved their own independence from England. *Closure, Interrupted,* Jennings' fifth novel in development, is a story of reclamation after the criminal betrayal of a loving husband.

www.normajennings.com

Author's Note

History will taunt us to relive painful memories of a society's atrocities against its poor and helpless, making the story of Sean O'Sullivan and his escape from famine-stricken Ireland, both pertinent and compelling. But escape could be relative, because, after feeding the starving and burying the dead during the Irish Potato Famine, O'Sullivan quietly joined the unrelenting fight for the rights of a brutalized people in Jamaica, the island to which he fled.

The Irish Potato Famine was a devastating period of mass starvation and disease in Ireland, which was then British territory. The Famine was caused by a blight, which infected and killed the potato crops. About one million people died of starvation or related diseases in Ireland, during that time.

The impact of the Famine was exacerbated by the British Whig government's economic policy of laissez-faire capitalism. Longer-term causes included the system of single-crop dependence by a poor, underprivileged people.

Absentee land ownership was popular, and many absentee landlords lived in England so most of the rent collected from impoverished Irish tenants went to England.

One of the most egregious facts cited by historians is that, throughout the entire period when people were dying of starvation, Ireland exported enormous quantities of food and supplies to England. So, the problem in Ireland was not a lack of food, which was plentiful, but the price of it, which the poor could not afford.

During the Famine, the Irish were encouraged to emigrate because of overpopulation concerns. Many evicted tenant farmers received free passage to the New World. About a million emigrated, and thousands made it to Canada and the United States.

Some Irish emigrants managed to get to the Caribbean; most went to Montserrat. But some got to Jamaica during wretched times, when slaves brought to the island from Africa worked the plantations under horrid conditions. Slaves were brutalized by

British planters with no relief, since the island was governed by the plantocracy. This was another tragic example of laissez-faire capitalism.

Britain eventually abolished slavery, but African Jamaicans were forced to fight for their rights against oppression by the plantocracy, whose only means of governing was by tyranny and brutality. But history has acknowledged the Irish for their silent support of Jamaica's brutal fight for freedom from slavery.

Those leading or participating in the fight for equal rights and justice were severely punished or killed. Prominent African Jamaican freedom fighters who got killed are now celebrated annually, on the island, as national heroes. They did not die in vain.

The Irish-Jamaican connection runs deep. Although the story in this novel takes place in the mid-1800s, history cites Irish slaves being brought to Jamaica and other Caribbean islands, to work on sugarcane plantations, under the English republic of the mid-1600s. According to Wikipedia, Irish people are the second largest reported ethnic group in Jamaica, after Jamaicans of African ancestry. Most Jamaicans with Irish ancestry also have African ancestry.

Strong Irish influence is evident in the names of some towns in Jamaica, including Irish Pen, Sligoville, Athenry, Bangor Ridge, Clonmel, Kildare, Belfast, Middleton, and Ulster Spring. Irish last names are also very common in Jamaica, including Burke, Clarke, Collins, Lynch, Murphy, Walsh, McKenzie, McDonald, McCall, O'Brien, O'Connor, and O'Hara. And there are even traces of Irish influence in the Jamaican accent itself.

Many prominent Jamaicans have claimed their Irish ancestry, including freedom fighter and national hero, Marcus Garvey, and Jamaica's first prime minister, Sir Alexander Bustamante, who had changed his name from Clarke. And, according to historians, the red, green and gold flag that Jamaica's Rastafarians now claim as their own, was put together by Marcus Garvey. At least one historian claims that, in August, 1920, Garvey explained that the color green in the flag represented solidarity with the Irish.

The Irish people spoke Gaelic, until the 19th century when English became dominant. The Jamaican people spoke patois in the mid-1800s, a language they created, which is an English-based creole language with West African influences. Patois is still spoken in Jamaica, along with 'the Queen's English'. Only small touches of patois are in this novel, to ensure its readability by everyone.

June, 1846, Bandon, County Cork, Ireland

Chapter 1

I burst through the front door and Mammy laid quivering on one side of the straw bed, her body a limp heap of bones. I flung myself to the cold mud floor next to her. D*ear God in heaven, the typhus has set in.*

My mother barely turned her head and stared at me, her eyes rheumy, her skin sallow, her arms unmoving. Holding her head in my arms, I said, "I have soup, Mammy. Open your mouth; let me feed you."

I yelled to my best friend, "Brian, grab a spoon from the table over there; left side of the wash pan." I dug the spoon into the turnip soup I'd just scrounged from the soup kitchen in Bandon, where Brian and I worked.

Mammy's lips trembled as she struggled to open her mouth. I got her to swallow half-a-spoonful. Heat from the fever seeped through her pores like poison, saturating the air around me. I fed her till she shook her head to say, no more. A vein in her neck quivered. Grabbing an old pillow case, I wiped away soup running down one side of her mouth.

My mother ate very little these days. Walking a tight-rope between starvation and typhoid fever had taken its toll on her bowel. *Dear Lord, help me. She's all I've got; just her and my beloved Ireland.*

My thoughts soon got interrupted. I swore I smelled the rotting flesh of the dead, just like I did when I hurried past the Bandon River earlier, on my way home. Struggling not to let this overwhelm me, I closed my eyes and opened my soul to better memories of my country before the Potato Famine.

Rolling hills once stood green and lush as far as the eyes could see. We sang till our throats grew sore, danced till our legs tingled, and guzzled stout at the end of every work week. Now, we suffered like lambs waiting to be butchered. *How much longer could we tenant farmers cling to life under these horrid conditions?*

Today, reality set in as I looked around. The mud floor of the cabin had started to crack. The front door had given way to rot, leaving us at the mercy of the elements. Old clothes stood piled in one corner, and the straw bed crumpled like hay in a barn full of famished horses. No table sat next to the bed, so the chipped cup of water I'd left Mammy earlier remained on the floor next to her head. It hadn't been touched. Her hand trembled too much to reach for it.

Holding my mother's head in my arms once more, I picked up the cup, "Try to drink some water, Mammy."

That day I walked away, fell to my knees and pleaded, 'Dear God, save us all; I beg you. Bring Ireland back to its simple beauty and warm living.' I whispered Psalm 27; 'The Lord is my light and my salvation, whom shall I fear ...' When I completed the Psalm, a calm washed over me and things seemed less unbearable.

Brian wrapped his arms around my shoulders, jolting me out of my misery. He'd stopped by the cabin earlier, propped Mammy's head up on the old bed pillow, and covered her with more old clothes. Old clothes helped shield her from the cold, since we had no blankets.

I stared into Brian's hazel eyes, which seemed to peer into my soul today. *Given his painful past, he must know what I'm feeling.* My six-foot, fair-haired friend wore his only pair of black pants, black sweater, and an old, gray winter jacket.

Brian had been an orphan. At only three years old, his father had been deported to Australia as punishment for a 'misdeed.' And his mother died one year later of a broken heart, according to the women nearby.

Brian never told me what 'misdeed' his father had committed, and I never asked. Why should I cause him more heartbreak, when it made no difference what his father had done? Better to just leave things alone.

Today, I could tell from Brian's stare that he felt my pain. That gave me enough assurance. Afterall, Mammy had been like a mother to him. And to me, he was the brother I never had.

"Let's head to the soup kitchen; get our hands on more soup or scraps of food after work. Better than nothing," Brian said.

"I'll meet you there. Want to make sure Mammy's all right."

"You taking her back to the fever hospital?"

"Waste'a time. Crowded, nasty; still can't get in. Mammy not strong enough for hours of waiting."

"And Dr. Barnfield up and died last month. Poor man," Brian said.

"Fever finally took him out. He'd treat her at home if he was still around, for sure."

I heard my mother wail, "Come here, Son." I hurried back to her bedside and knelt on the floor. She grabbed my arm with her trembling hand. It was hot and sweaty, but the rest of her body shivered from the cold.

"Thanks for taking care of me."

"Oh, Mammy, no need to thank me. You know I'll always take care of you." I tried to lift her spirits, but she just stared at me with those blue eyes that struggled to stay open.

"If you think I won't make it, leave on one of those big boats. Don't stay here and die, Son. Move on; you're twenty years old now. Just thinking 'bout your beautiful blue eyes and curly brown locks will make me go in peace. You're tall and thin, just like your Papa. I'm ready to join my sweet, hard-working Conan O'Sullivan, in heaven. I miss him so."

"Don't you talk like that, Mammy; you're not going anywhere."

"I love you, Sean."

"Love you too." Tears threatened to fall, but I held them back.

After my father died, I used to sleep with my back against hers so we'd stay warm in the winter. Nothing warmed the cabin, and freezing gusts of wind from the Bandon River often lashed us like whips hurled by an evil master. But Mammy now forbade me from huddling next to her. "You will not catch the typhus, not from me," she said.

So, these days, I slept next door in the mud cabin Brian shared with old man O'Brien and his son, Harry. Brian had lived there for years, and worked the fields with them before the Potato Famine devastated us all. Old man O'Brien had taken him in after his mother died.

"Be back soon with more soup," I said to Mammy before heading out. As I hurried along, my belly growled; I was hungry. But if I had to give Mammy my own soup to keep her going, that's what I'd do. Keeping her alive meant everything to me. Next, came my determination to help get Ireland back to the country we all knew and loved.

During this walk to the soup kitchen, I started talking to myself and wondering if I had gone mad. "Those damned Brits," I muttered. "Every potato farmer here is starving to death, yet all the food we produce, cattle, vegetables, grain, stocking salmon, sea trout and brown trout from the Bandon River, gets sent to England. They eat well, and still host their lavish balls and dinner parties. I swear, they must be punishing us for staying Catholic and not opening our arms to their Protestant churches. If that's not it, then why the Hell are they letting us starve to death?"

The wind blew colder, jolting me out of my wrath. I tugged the collar of my old jacket up and held it over my ears. Scurrying along as a freezing gust had me shaking like a leaf, I glanced up. The sky was blue; the sun shone brightly down. But the fields around me showed a pallid brown. And the stink of rotted potatoes polluted the air. I fought back vomit.

My mouth flew open as I approached Broad Street. Crowds of people stood lined up, waiting for the only food they'd have for three days, a cup of soup. Broad Street was almost a mile from the soup kitchen, yet they stood in line, shivering, quietly clutching their cups and waiting for the soup that would keep starvation at bay.

I walked along the lines for five blocks and finally got to Queen Street. Half-a-block more and I'd be at the kitchen. I stopped and looked back at those in line.

Sweet Jesus, they were all quiet, too hungry to utter a word, too cold to move, but for the shivering of their skeletal bodies. They huddled there in scanty old clothes, seizing warmth from anyone quivering next to them. I stared at those standing close to me. Over the past months, I'd learned what starvation looked like, large noses, big bellies, sagging flesh and jutting bones. Dr. Barnfield once told me that the nose was the only part of the face that didn't shrink from starvation.

I turned, entered the soup kitchen through the back door, and saw Brian scooping soup into cups with an old ladle. I grabbed the ladle next to him and got to work. Hundreds waited to be fed; we had to keep them from falling off a 'cliff' to certain death.

In the next two hours, I filled dozens of soup cups, collected one penny each from those who could pay, moved empty iron boilers aside, and scalded my hands while lifting boilers full of hot soup up to the table. I did all this, hurrying to keep the line moving. Brian's voice soon moved me out of my thoughts.

"Hey Sean, remember the first day the shock of the potato blight slapped you in the face like a cold, wet, rag?"

"Aye. Can't get it out of my mind, Laddie. I'd dug up a potato in the field behind my cabin, and as I tried to clutch and pull it from the ground, my fingers sunk into slime. I couldn't believe it! I kept digging and pulling more mess out of the ground. And the stench almost made my knees buckle."

"Big blow to me too. Just kept digging, hoping for better luck," Brian said.

"I finally gave up. Later, I watched Mammy throw herself to the ground, weeping, when I told her the news. She said, 'Sweet Jesus, all we eat is potato; that's how we pay the rent too. How in God's name will we make it through this?' Then she said, 'We're three shillings short on the rent money.'"

"'What, how did that happen, Mammy?' I'd yelled.

"'Had to save us from starving. Found turnips and some barley outside of O'Donnels," she'd said. I glanced at Brian; he listened closely.

"Your Daddy started working for the scheme right after that, didn't he?"

"Aye, but he had to walk two hours to and from that job repairing roads, with nothing in his belly, for days. Men were dropping like flies, dying from exhaustion and starvation."

"So sorry, Sean. Memories of the two of us picking him up off the ground at the corner of Duke and King Streets still haunt me."

"And after taking him home, we had to lay him down to die 'cause there was neither potato nor water to put to his lips."

"That day still torments you, eh?"

"Don't think the pain will ever leave. And it's worse with Mammy. I have to keep her alive, Brian."

"We'll do everything we can for her, my friend. By the way, you seen Cara lately?" Brian suddenly changed the subject, like he always did.

"Stopped by last week to check on her and her mother. Brought them soup."

"You two still together?"

"Nah."

"What the Hell happened?"

"Staying away."

"Why? Thought you two would be together a real long time. She's a pretty girl, Sean."

"You know she always called me a mammy's boy, right?"

"Yah, you are a mammy's boy." Brian giggled. I smiled and kept talking; didn't feel like taking that bait.

"Well, one night we were together and she looked me in the eyes and said, 'Mammy's boys make great husbands, Sean.'"

"You walked away 'cause of that?"

"Yah. She had that hungry, hopeful look in her eyes. I'm just not ready to be anyone's husband, Brian."

"Why didn't you just tell her that?"

I sighed. "Tell a woman that and all you get is a forever puss on her face. Better to set her free to find some fella open to husband talk."

We'd just emptied the last boiler of soup and I'd turned around to take it to the back of the kitchen, when I heard a commotion. I flung the boiler down and spun around.

"Sorry, no more soup. Come back in three days," Quaker Tomas, who managed the soup kitchen, shouted. Men yelled and women bawled. Babies screamed and puked. Some babies went quiet. One woman shook her limp baby, then she flung herself to the ground and let out a chilling wail, still clutching the baby.

"She's been clutching a dead baby and didn't know it," Brian said.

Oh, sweet Jesus, that poor mother. And that sweet, innocent baby. I'm going to be sick.

I grabbed my gut and ran back into the kitchen. Vomit threatened to erupt from my bowel. I bolted through the back door of the kitchen and clutched my throat as vomit spewed to the ground. I held my head back up, grabbed my sleeve, and wiped vomit from the side of my mouth. I breathed air deep into my lungs, over and over.

"You okay, Sean?" Brian asked, his head stuck through the back door. He hurried over and put one arm around my shoulder.

"Three more days with no food and half of them will be dead."

I held my head down; tears rushed down my cheeks and fell to the ground. My gut clenched, devastation threatening to overcome me. Brian shook his head and sobbed so hard his body trembled and he gasped for air. I tightened my grip around his waist.

"Take deep breaths, Brian; take real deep breaths."

I stood there for a while, my arm around my friend's waist as he breathed in and out, reaching for calm.

Returning to the kitchen later, I was just in time to see the Quaker turn and head in my direction. He paused, stared at Brian and me, and he started talking. I quickly wiped my eyes.

"Tomorrow, we take soup to out-of-the-way places. We'll be taking three horse carts. We'll have nine boilers of soup, three shovels, and an axe. Sleep good tonight and be here by five in the morning."

He paused and looked at me, and then at Brian. A sense of foreboding swept over me. After seeing that dead baby, vulnerability had taken over my emotions.

"Get ready to see dreadful things, but we need you to stay strong. We'll feed you real' good. Keep your strength up, or you'll be no use to those who are dying," The Quaker said.

I winced, but I knew I had to do it. I needed the extra work. We were still short on the rent and month-end drew closer.

I walked home that evening, clutching a small cup of soup that I'd scraped from the bottom of two boilers. Brian had also managed to scrape together two cups of soup for old man O'Brien and his son. We hastened along in silence, me dreading a sleepless night after seeing that dead baby. My heart still ached.

I whispered another prayer. *Please Lord, have mercy on the soul of that poor baby. And Lord, Mammy is depending on me; I won't let her down. If she knows there's a white cross of eviction on the front door of the cabin, it will kill her for sure. She has nowhere else to go. Mammy will never survive, crouched in a hole in the ground with straw over her head, like most tenant farmers live after the landlord burns their cabin down. If I have to serve soup to earn a few more shillings, I'll do it to keep Mammy alive. And I'll do it to help get Ireland back to the land of peace and happiness it once was.*

Chapter 2

It was only eight the next morning and I felt like I'd already done a full day's work at the soup kitchen. Working since before dawn, I'd cut and shredded cabbage, shucked corn, mashed tubs of boiled peas into a paste, blended oatmeal with cold water, and sliced a whole, skinned, cow head into small pieces.

Two cooks worked at the kitchen. One, a tall, lanky man named Art with a huge nose, and clothes that hung off of his bony shoulders. The other, a woman named Alma, wore frocks twice her size. As she stirred one boiler this morning with a long, rusty spoon, flesh swung from side to side under each of her arms; it was like staring at the necks of old turkeys on the run.

Come to think of it, everyone looked like those two these days. Starvation had taken its toll. But while this day offered up a cold and windy morning, the old wooden building that housed the soup kitchen buzzed with activity. Sweat ran down my back from the flurry, and the fires kept the air nice and warm.

I took a breather and stood next to Brian as the boilers bubbled away, aromas wafting through the air. Alma walked up and handed us each a cup of what looked like vegetable stock. Steam seeped into my nose, and the smell stirred my senses. Tomas followed close behind and handed me two thick slices of bread. Standing in front of me, Brian grabbed his bread and bit into it with relish. I was hungry, so I devoured my food in no time. Tomas began to speak.

"Three horse carts are waiting outside to take us to out-of-the way places. Some folks are too weak to come here, so we're taking soup to them. One horse cart is owned by Quakers at the soup kitchen in Cork, and O'Sullivan's Alehouse loaned us another. We needed a third cart, so we borrowed Darcy Hackin's death cart. Darcy fussed, but I convinced him that the dead could wait another day to be picked up and buried, but the starving needed soup now, or his work would double."

My gut stirred, but there was no time to be queasy. *Pull yourself together; stop thinking about that dead baby,* I thought. Then I stared ahead, as Tomas continued to speak.

"Our first stop should be Innishannon, but we'll stop along the way if needed. These are the strongest horses we could get our hands on. They'll have to haul heavy loads through rough roads and bushes. And you'll need to keep your strength up. We'll feed you again in a few hours. Now, let's load the carts."

I helped load the first two carts, each with three huge milk churns of hot soup. Brian and I grabbed a bundle of jute sacks, tore them open, and wrapped them tightly around the churns to keep the soup warm.

The death cart was the largest, so in addition to soup, I helped load jute bags filled with corn, grain, barley, a little boiled meat, firewood, and whatever else was left in the kitchen, just in case we ran out of soup and had to get to cooking on the side of the road. The three horse carts pulled away a little after ten in the morning.

We'd been traveling for over twenty minutes, the horses cantering along at a steady pace. Suddenly, my eyes almost flew from their sockets. Horror gripped me in the gut.

Two ravenous dogs, their tails wagging furiously, gnawed away at something on the road. We slowed down and moved closer. I grabbed my gut and retched, struggling to stay calm. The dogs tore away at the emaciated body of a dead boy. *Dear God, he's no more than 10 years old.*

"Son-of-a-bitch!" Brian yelled, grabbing a shovel and leaping to the ground. I grabbed the axe and jumped down behind him. Brian raised the shovel and hit one dog in the ribs. He leapt away, screeching so miserably my ears rang.

The second dog bared his teeth and snarled. I kicked him in the head with my boot. He howled and dropped to the ground, panting. Then he sprang up and bolted, whimpering all the way.

I jumped back on the cart, which had slowed and stopped. Struggling not to spew vomit, I sat, slumped over, clutched my belly and fought back tears. But there was no time to recover.

"We have to bury him," the Quaker yelled. "Leave him here and the dogs will be back."

Tomas threw a second shovel at me. Brian and I got to digging and shoveling dirt for what seemed like forever. A shallow grave soon stood in front of me. Tomas and Darcy lifted the boy's body and lowered it into the grave. I could not look. My gut churned. Brian's face lost all color.

Tomas grabbed the shovel from his hand, and he and I shoveled dirt over the body. I lifted my shovel and patted dirt into a mound on top of the grave. I helped pile dry leaves and branches on top of it.

Tomas jumped back on to the cart. Brian and I followed close behind. Tomas pulled the reins and the horses jerked ahead. All three carts continued on the journey.

My thoughts whirled, *Hell on earth, this is what you've become, my beloved Ireland. How do we stop this horror? How do we keep our people alive? Please show me the way, dear God.*

Minutes later, clusters of mud cabins in the distance plagued my eyes. I flinched. *Sweet Jesus, what horror is waiting there for us?* I glanced at an old wooden sign on a tree to my right. It said Kilbrittain. Slamming my eyes shut, I breathed in deeply ten times, trying to calm my nerves.

The carts approached a cluster of cabins. I whispered Psalm 27. As I got to 'I had fainted, unless I had believed to see the goodness of the Lord in the land of the living,' I stopped and stared, my eyes narrowed, my mouth wide open. A woman, looking half-starved, crawled out of a roofless mud hut.

"The landlords were here. See the white cross by the door heave?" Brian said. I nodded, sighed, and glanced at the half-rotted heave.

"Cruel, greedy bastards!" I said. Then I gazed, once more, at the woman crawling toward us.

Her face, filthy and withered, seemed riveted to the ground. She wore an old black frock that hung to the dirt from her emaciated body. She kept crawling, struggling to keep her shivering body from collapsing. Two shriveled breasts hung from her chest like strings, under the neckline of her loose, tattered, frock.

The woman's lips moved; they trembled so much she could barely speak. "Mmmy ... my baby."

Brian sprang from the cart and raced into the cabin. I grabbed a cup of soup and leaped to the ground. I held it to the woman's mouth. She guzzled it down. Then I heard Brian scream.

"Sean, in here, quick!" I dashed to the door. The smell of rotted flesh stopped me in my tracks. Slapping one hand over my nose, I glanced around. The bodies of an older man and woman laid there, partially decomposed.

"They're dead! Check the child over there while I run to the next room. I hear a baby wailing," Brian said.

I glanced to the left; a pale-faced young boy sat huddled on the ground. He looked around eight years old. He wore a big, blue sweater that must have been his father's, and tattered black pants. His bare feet, almost blue, trembled from the cold.

Rushing to the boy, I slapped one hand on his neck and the other in front of his nose. He breathed, but with bare consciousness.

"Water and soup," I yelled. Tomas stood in front of me in a flash. I put a cup of water to the boy's mouth. He guzzled it and tried to sit up. Holding his back, I steadied him. I fed him four spoons of soup as Tomas rubbed his feet with both hands. Color soon returned to the boy's cheeks.

Brian ran from the adjoining room with a baby girl in his arms. She seemed just over a year old, with droopy eyes. She wore a pair of old shorts, stained and stinking with pee and feces, and a tight gray top. Her belly bulged from malnutrition.

"More soup and water," Brian yelled.

The cook, Alma, arrived right away and fed the child water. Then she fed her soup. The child's mother stumbled in, looking stronger after gulping down a cup of soup. She glanced around, bawling and moaning. Then she wrapped her arms around her baby and rocked from side-to-side.

"We must bury the dead. Can't leave them here," Tomas said.

"I'll get the shovels," Brian said, rushing out the door.

"Everyone outside. Start digging." Tomas yelled.

We dug a large hole behind the first two mud cabins. Holding an old dish-rag I'd found in one of the carts, over my nose, I tied it behind my head.

I gingerly lifted the body of the old woman in my arms, hoping it would not fall apart. I refused to look at it and just kept moving, the fragile sensation of suffering and death in my arms.

The child's mother darted toward me, grabbed the old woman's hand and cried, "Mammeeeey!" Tomas wrapped his arms around her and pulled her away. I took the body outside. Brian hurried out with the old man's body, his face red, his brow tightly knitted.

"Let's put him in first," I said.

Brian sat at the edge of the grave with the man's body in his arms. Darcy held on to him, keeping him steady. He stepped into the grave and laid the old man's body on the earth below. Next, I sat at the edge of the grave and handed him the old woman's body. He laid it on top of the old man, face up.

Brian climbed out of the grave and I grabbed a shovel. Holding my breath on and off against the stench, I shoveled dirt into the hole. Brian and Darcy joined me. Soon, we patted down a mound of mud and dirt as the young mother clutched her baby and son, and wailed. The two children held their arms out and bawled.

Struggling to contain myself, I fought off nausea. *No time to fall apart – stay strong. Mammy is waiting for you at home.*

We hurried to the next hut. Things got worse. They'd all starved to death. We pulled two dead bodies out, a man and what looked like a teenage boy. We laid them next to the back door.

"More to bury. Dig bigger hole," Tomas yelled.

Brian and I glanced at each other, eyes wide, dumbfounded. I hurried behind the others to the next cabin; this time everyone stood armed with cups of soup and water. Four people sat around in that hut, all alive. We handed them soup and water and hurried to the other huts.

We moved back and forth, dragging five more bodies to the back of the hut where we'd left the other two.

"Shovels. A real big hole this time. Seven to bury before the dogs get here," Tomas yelled.

Air stuck in my throat. I gasped; I could barely breathe. I dragged the old dish towel down from my face and let it hang around my neck.

Grabbing a shovel, I dug and dug with the other men, till Tomas yelled, "Enough." I pulled the old dish rag back over my nose and helped roll bodies into the grave, one after the other. I shoveled dirt back in. Patting another mound on top of the mass grave, I heard Tomas shout, "Done for the day. Let's head back."

I sat on Darcy Hackins' death cart that evening as we headed back to Bandon. A horrible sickness ravaged my gut. I stiffened my body to stop it from quivering. Staring blankly ahead, I felt dumbstruck. *Dear God, help me to withstand this. Keep me strong. Mammy needs me.*

Finally, I glanced behind. Brian sat on the next horse cart, his eyes void, his face vacant. Shock and horror had taken its toll on us all.

At the soup kitchen that evening, we unloaded what we needed, washed the milk churns and turned them over on old dish rags in one corner, to dry.

Brian and I got ready to head home with four cups of soup scraped from the bottom of the churns, when Tomas called us to attention.

"Today was a tough one, but you were strong. I need you here again tomorrow by five in the morning, so we can get ready to head to four other towns. We need to save more lives." I glanced around. All faces looked empty and numb.

"Go home and try to get a decent night's sleep. See you early tomorrow morning," Tomas said.

A decent night's sleep? I thought. *That will not happen, anytime soon.*

I walked into Mammy's cabin with two cups of soup that evening. Suddenly, I stood staring, wide-eyed, at my ex-girlfriend, Cara. Kneeling at Mammy's bedside, she wore a loose gray frock, an old black coat, and black shoes and socks. As I approached, she looked up, eyes droopy, flesh sagging on the side of her face.

"Here, Cara. Have this cup of soup," I said, handing her the cup. Walking to one side of the room, I grabbed two spoons from the counter and handed one to her. I sat at Mammy's bedside and fed her soup from the other cup. Glancing over at Cara, I saw her slurp her soup down like she hadn't eaten in days.

"How you and your Mammy been holding up, Cara? Sorry I haven't stopped by lately, been working hard to make sure we don't get evicted."

"I know. Mammy's holding on, but I don't know for how much longer. She has the fever too, Sean."

"Sweet Jesus! Taking soup to out-of-the way places now. I'll make sure we stop by your cabin when we can."

"I miss you, Sean," Cara said.

"Miss you too. How'd you get here?"

"Walked. Wanted to check on you and your Mammy."

"Let me walk you home before it gets dark. You shouldn't be on the road alone."

I finished feeding Mammy her soup, covered the half cup of soup left behind, and handed it to Cara.

"Give this to your Mammy. Better than nothing."

We headed out and I wrapped my arms around Cara, for warmth against freezing winds from the river. Starvation and trauma had taken its toll on us both; we had very little to say. The trauma of the day had left me dazed. Silently, I swore I'd keep my promise to check on Cara and her mother, every time we headed out with the carts.

But as I hurried back home that evening, my tears flowed so hard I could barely see. Stopping two times, I held my head down and let my tears flow freely to the cold ground below. I took deep breaths, and I silently prayed to God for strength.

Chapter 3

Brian and I arrived at the kitchen ten minutes early the next morning. Exhausted and sleep deprived, rest had refused to come my way after walking Cara home. The death and mayhem I'd endured, plagued my thoughts the minute I closed my eyes. And I kept thinking about the skin and bones I felt when I wrapped my arms around Cara's shoulders. That poor girl. How long will she survive? How long will her mother last? *Dear God, please save us from this misery.*

But gratitude soon washed over me when Tomas handed each of us big cups of black coffee, chunks of cheese that looked like they'd been around for a while, and wedges of wheat bread. I gobbled my food and got to working the kitchen, like I did the day before.

"Brian, you notice only two horse carts outside when we got here?" I asked.

"Yah. Darcy must be running late, not like him."

Two minutes had barely passed when Darcy burst through the kitchen door.

"My horse! My horse is gone!"

"Gone? What you mean?" Tomas asked.

"The starving son-of-a-bitches ate my horse."

"What? Who?" Tomas yelled.

"The family two doors from me stole him last night. I'm sure of it. They must'a butchered him and sold the meat. No sign of him anywhere. Dear God, I could scream."

"You didn't hear anything?" I asked.

"Not one damn' thing. I was so exhausted and distressed last night, the minute I laid down, I was out cold."

"How'd you get here?" Brian asked.

"Walked. That's why I'm so late."

"Here, eat this. Make you feel better," Tomas said, handing Darcy his share of coffee, bread and cheese. He devoured his food.

"That old girl's been with me over six years. She was a strong and loyal friend. Sweet Jesus, I miss her already. And how the heck am I supposed to make a living carting the dead around, if I have no horse?"

"Work with us till you figure things out. We'll just use two horse carts today," Tomas said.

Darcy got to work. He seemed to have a hard time focusing, but the poor old boy worked like a stallion despite a few fumbles. He knew slowing down would bring him nothing but distress.

We headed out just after ten that morning. I saw the usual dried-out fields and destitution. But the sky boasted an azure blue; the beauty of it caught my eyes. Three crows hovered overhead, cawing expectantly.

Soon, trepidation set in; I straightened my shoulders. *It's going to be another horrendous day. Please give me strength,* I prayed.

About thirty minutes later, we pulled up to a cluster of cabins in a town near Cross Barry. We saw no one. *Jesus, don't tell me they're all dead,* I thought, tightness gripping at my chest.

I walked into the first doorless and dilapidated cabin. The smell of death hit like a poison dart. I gagged. Quickly backing to the door, I yelled, "Brian, two dead women in here. Help me get the bodies out." I grabbed another old dish towel from my back pocket and tied it around my face.

Brian rushed in. We dragged the bodies, one at a time, through the door. We laid them behind the cabin, just in time to hear Darcy yell, "Another cup of soup and water." Brian grabbed water; I filled a cup with soup. We darted into the next ramshackle cabin.

Brian held an old man by the shoulders on a straw bed and tried to feed him soup. The man refused to swallow. He stared at us, his eyes weak and rheumy, soup running from his mouth. His arms suddenly slumped to his sides. Then his eyes closed and his head dropped to Brian's chest.

"He's gone. Dear God, we're too late," I said.

"Let's try to save the woman. Give me water," Brian said, as a woman whimpered in one corner of the cabin.

He laid the man's body down, propped the woman's weak head up from the bed and held the cup of water to her mouth. She barely opened, then closed her eyes. She tried to swallow. Water came running down the side of her mouth. Brian shook her.

"Come on! Don't you leave us." But the woman was gone, too. Once more, we'd arrived too late. Brian and I lifted the bodies and laid them behind the cabin.

"We'll bury them before we leave. Let's head to the next two cabins," Tomas yelled. We had no time to ponder or weep; we had to move too fast.

Brian and I found a family of three in the third cabin, mother, father, and a boy around fifteen. Weak and feeble, they appeared in better shape than the others we'd just encountered.

"There are three here. Bring water and soup," I yelled.

Alma and Tomas responded. This family was strong enough to feed themselves. They guzzled water. They devoured the soup so fast, the young boy coughed and choked. But he paused and kept guzzling.

Tomas and I rushed to the next cabin. The dreaded white cross stood clearly marked on the rotted door jam. The landlords had arrived earlier. They'll burn this cabin down, leaving everyone inside to the elements.

In front of me, a young woman sat on the ground outside the cabin's door. Nose jutting out, her cheeks had no color. The old black frock she wore hung around her like a shroud. Her feeble eyes met my stare. A dark pit opened up in my belly. Before I could yell for help, Alma showed up with water and soup. The woman guzzled them down, slurping and groaning, her eyes like rabid slits.

"My husband, my baby," she said, pointing at the cabin.

Tomas and I rushed into the cabin, the woman stumbling behind with Alma by her side. Her husband's body laid on the mud floor.

The body of a one-legged baby girl sprawled on a mound of bloody straw nearby.

"What, what happened to the baby's leg? Don't tell me ..." I said.

"Sweet Jesus, no! Don't even think about it," Tomas said.

"Remember what we read in the *Irish Times?*" I said.

"The starving will lose their sanity. That poor woman and her family," Alma said.

A desolate howl came from my belly. I choked back vomit. "No more, please, no more."

Clutching my gut, I bolted out of the cabin. I stopped, bent over and retched. Minutes later I kept heaving, but nothing came up. Dropping to the ground, I felt weak and nauseous. I took ten deep breaths, my eyes closed, my soul in turmoil.

I wanted to cry; I wanted to wail and curse defeat. But I needed to get my strength back. There were seven to be buried. *Get yourself together, breathe, breathe.*

Tomas, Brian and I soon dug a mass grave, buried the dead, and patted the mound on top with our shovels. Standing over the grave with eyes slammed shut, I whispered Psalm 27, all of it, two times. Then I headed back out with the others, the vestiges of my sanity clutching fiercely at me.

In the hours that followed, we traveled to three other remote towns and served soup and water to dozens of starving people. What used to be small potato farms stood around us, dry and desolate, the stench of rot and death defiling the air.

I helped dig two more huge graves. We buried eleven more bodies. By the end of the day, I had helped bury eighteen starved or typhus-ridden Irish men, women, and children.

Devastation wrapped its arms around me and refused to let go. I felt like a spider that had just been swatted by the bottom of a shoe.

My blood ran cold; my belly clenched into knots so tight, if death had come for me that day, I would have welcomed it. Horror took over, then it gave way to numbness.

"No more soup," Tomas finally shouted, jolting me out of distress.

We turned the carts around at a cluster of mud cabins at Dunderrow, after feeding over twenty people there. Emaciated, half-starved men, women and children crept behind the carts. They pleaded for soup we no longer had.

I would take that memory to my grave; I just knew it. The dead baby with one leg lopped off, would also be seared into my consciousness. I looked up as two death carts cantered by.

Heading back to the soup kitchen, I sat in the back of the cart and stared ahead. I said nothing. I felt nothing.

I'd asked Tomas to stop by Cara's cabin on the way. As the carts approached, Cara walked to the door and I motioned for her to meet me at the cart. I handed her two cups of soup I had scraped from the bottom of two milk churns. I nodded, blankly, as she thanked me.

The carts turned around and continued the journey back to the soup kitchen. Brian and I walked home that evening in a daze, me with soup for Mammy, Brian with soup for old man O'Brien and Harry.

I entered the mud cabin and fed Mammy her soup. She quietly drank the soup and stared at me, sensing, in that moment, that I had become a shell of a man. I cleaned her and myself up and headed next door, still stunned, distressed, and exhausted.

Laying on the old straw mound next to Brian's, tears blurred my eyes as I sobbed in silence for over an hour. A surge of fear and dread made the blood in my veins run cold. I refused to close my eyes.

Chapter 4

Last night had become unbearable. I'd tossed and turned, horrors of the day attacking my senses as I cried, wiped my eyes, and cried all over again. Total exhaustion must have set in during the early morning hours, because next thing I knew, I'd jumped up in bed after the most frightening nightmare.

In my dream, the stench of rotting flesh tarnished the air, and deranged dogs snarled away at the foot of my mother's bed. Afterward, I'd refused to close my eyes. Sleep would have been too much of an ordeal.

Sitting up in bed that morning, I wiped my eyes with my sleeve. Then I hurried next door, looked in, and sighed with relief. Mammy laid there under the pile of old clothes, fast asleep, breathing deeply. Her face had more color than it did a few days earlier.

A little soup goes a long way, I thought, as I walked to the back of Brian's cabin. Outside, I paced back and forth, trying to pull myself together without waking the others. But Brian's voice soon moved me out of my misery.

"Didn't sleep either, did you? Barely a wink for me."

"Aye. Yesterday filled me with more horror than I thought possible. And it's about to get worse. The Brits don't give a damn if we all drop dead." I was mad as Hell now, pacing faster, back and forth, without pause.

"Never thought it could get this bad. Swore they'd give more help to the Relief Committee, more corn, more barley, scraps of meat." Brian said. He grabbed me by the shoulder from behind and slowed me down.

"Let's sit over there. Not enough in our bellies to waste energy pacing around. Don't want to see you hit the ground like Papa O'Sullivan did."

I sat on the ground and Brian lowered himself next to me.

"Breathe real' deep. Stop that heart from pounding so hard." I listened and took a few deep breaths.

"Yesterday was horrific, Brian. What we going to do? There isn't enough soup to stop some folks from starving to death. And the landlords are wicked bastards. They're evicting us left and right; they're burning our cabins to the ground."

"I heard Father Flannery and two of the top Quakers have called a meeting this morning with local landlords at ten. They're meeting outside the gates of Baldwin Estate."

I sprang to my feet. "Tomas doesn't need us at the Soup Kitchen till this afternoon. Let's go."

"Need to hear what those cruel bastards have to say," Brian said.

I hurried back to Mammy's cabin and peeked in. She was still in a deep sleep. Brian and I washed up with whatever cold water we could find and headed out on the eight-mile walk to Baldwin Estate.

A tough walk on an empty belly stood before us. But, as memories of the prior day haunted my thoughts, I moved faster.

The disaster around had me quickening my pace as we passed even more mud cabins burned to their foundations by landlords unable to collect rent, and starving people living in mud holes with straw over their heads. A funeral cart with four bodies cantered by. Hungry dogs on the hunt prowled, and the foul smell of human remains polluted the air.

Hell-on-earth; that's what I faced. I coughed to stop myself from choking. What, in God's name, could be done to bring Ireland back?

But the scenery abruptly changed as Brian and I got closer to Baldwin Estate. We approached communities of wealthy British land owners. Amazed, I now stared at castles and estates. I smelled no more stench. I saw no more crumbling cabins or large noses reaching for a cup of soup to dodge death.

Brian and I walked past a castle named Elderberry and I stared, almost having to pull my bottom lip from the ground. The castle stood tall and resplendent in its own grandeur, with an eight-foot fence looming high to keep paupers like us, out.

Soon, in the distance, I saw what looked like another castle on the east side of the road. A small group of people gathered on a vast, green lawn just inside the massive iron gates.

"That must be Baldwin Estate," Brian said. We walked faster.

It was close to 10 a.m. when I walked up to Baldwin Estate, Brian by my side. The opulence appalled me, especially when my mind flashed back to the horrors of the past few days. Poor Irish people dropped dead from starvation, yet Brits busily maintained their privileged lifestyles.

They owned everything, the best farms, the best homes, the best food and wines. Ireland had no lack of food, yet the poor could not afford to feed themselves. The cruelty grabbed me by the throat and refused to let go.

Baldwin Estate stood vast, surrounded by brick and stone, with well-manicured gardens and the soaring chimneys of three fireplaces. Laid out along the left side of the front lawn, lines of white, linen-covered tables with pots of coffee and tea, pastries and breads, blessed the eyes.

People began to help themselves to food. Father Flannery strolled up to us.

"Morning. Glad you came. Help yourselves to food, Laddies," he said. He didn't have to say another word.

I loaded up a plate and devoured it all. The growling in my gut came to a sudden halt; I hadn't eaten anything like this in years. I felt like I could now listen to whatever came my way.

"Look over there. Those two are the Harrises from Skidbourne Castle," Brian said, taking his final sip of coffee.

"Aye, they came to the soup kitchen early last week. I wondered why they'd bring nettles when what we really needed was meat. Unbelievable, given that they own the largest cattle farm around. They're the main supplier of beef to Brits in this area."

"Those two walking up to them are Lord and Lady Kensington of Kensington Estate. They're filthy rich too," Brian whispered, looking on without being too obvious.

Soon, he poked me in the side, "Look, there's Alroy Doyle, one of the local magistrates."

"Lots of big shots here today. Let's see what they have to say."

"Keep your mouth shut. We're barely keeping ourselves and those around us alive. Don't need no trouble," Brian said.

"I'll try, but if I hear too much malarkey, I might just explode."

"Stay calm, Sean. They'll ship you to Australia with other criminals, like they did Bertha Doherty's brother and father." Brian could be full of drama, but his words hit home.

"Ladies and gentlemen, time to get started," Father Flannery shouted, jolting me out of my reverie. Dozens of privileged Brits had arrived by then, and crowds of ordinary people had gathered around, mostly church members and Quakers. Everyone quieted down; all eyes focused on the priest.

"Before we get started, let me thank the Baldwins for allowing us to use their beautiful front yard for this meeting, and for providing pastry and beverages." Father Flannery paused as the crowd applauded.

"We're here today to discuss the horrible conditions our poor Irish people are suffering through. Hundreds have starved to death, and those still alive are barely making it from one day to the other. The potato famine has taken its toll on our tenant farmers, who are now surviving only on the cup of soup we serve every three days. And things are getting worse. Typhoid fever is attacking those too weak to fight. We are horrified at the state of affairs. Some of you have donated to the soup kitchens, and for that we thank you. But we need a lot more help."

"What you mean? We help!" One Brit yelled. A middle-aged man with graying hair, he stood, well-dressed in a dark gray suit, black vest, and a gray and black, striped ascot.

"Yes, many of you have contributed grain and barley to the soup kitchens, but more is gravely needed. The kitchens can't provide enough to stop hundreds of people from starving to death ..." Father Flannery said. But he was interrupted.

"What more do you want from us? England has taken a back seat on all of this, hoping it will work itself out," another landlord yelled.

"Ireland is over populated. Seems something should be done about that problem, don't you think?" Another Brit said.

"These are dire times. People are starving to death here!" One of the Quakers yelled.

"No one told them to lay around and breed like rabbits," another landlord yelled.

"Yeah. And what are we supposed to do about that?" A land owner said.

"You can stop evicting the poor, who can no longer pay their rent. For God's sake, gentlemen, tenant farmers can barely feed themselves and their children. The potato rot has devastated them all," Tomas said. He'd arrived right after I did.

"It's our land. The Queen of England gave us the right to own land here when Ireland became one of our territories. If tenant farmers can't pay the rent, the value of our land will plummet," Lord Kensington said.

"That's right. And besides, England is in great need of Angus beef and all kinds of vegetables and corn. We'll be much better off if we use our land for that purpose, instead of wasting it on tenant farmers," another Brit yelled.

"But people are dying in the streets and in their cabins, for God's sake! When did we become so merciless?" Father Flannery said.

"We can't feed every poor Irishman and his family. That is too much to ask. You're pinning their poverty on us. Seems to me overpopulation is the real issue here," Mr. Harris from Skidbourne Castle said.

"Indeed. I heard there are tons of acreage aching to be farmed in the New World. Maybe we should find a way to transport some of the Irish there. They'll find work, for sure. I hear England is considering paying assisted passage for those willing to go to those countries," another Brit yelled. A short, ruddy man with a bushy beard, he had a gut that clearly stated there was no starvation on his side of town. I did not recognize him.

"What countries you talking about?" Another Brit asked.

"Canada and America," someone yelled.

"Brits are in the Caribbean too. Sugar is big in that region. When the ships get to us with sugar, they usually look for people or cargo to take back. They call it ballast, used to stabilize ships on the journey back to wherever they came from. Maybe they could take men with them to help run the plantations?" The tall Brit to my left said.

"You have a point there, old chap. With less of the Irish to feed, we could grow what we want and not feel responsible for them and their problems," another said.

"But we need to feed the starving now. They continue to die. Help us help the dying. Agree not to evict them in their time of need. Please, I'm begging you," Father Flannery said.

Tomas sprang to his feet and shook his fists. "Give us more grains and a little more meat to help keep people alive. We can't ship them overseas if they're dead."

"Who's for continuing evictions and for putting our land to better use?" One landowner yelled.

The crowd shouted, "Yeah, yeah, yeah!"

I could listen to no more. I was about to cause a scene, so I spun around and headed home. Anger took hold of me. The landowners were only concerned about lining their pockets and continuing their opulence. They didn't give a damn that Irish men, women and children were dying of hunger. Brian caught up with me and we hurried along in silence. Not a single word left my lips till we were halfway home.

"Cruel, greedy bastards, that's who they are," Brian said. We kept walking along in silence. I finally spoke.

"We must come up with a plan, before we all drop dead from starvation. If I could just get Mammy well again, I'd be able to think more clearly."

Sweet Jesus, save my mother. Save Ireland, I prayed.

Chapter 5

In the days that followed, I helped prepare whatever provisions the soup kitchen managed to scrounge, mostly turnips, barley, bundles of dried nettles, corn, and finally, a cow head that Father Flannery got from a land owner. A ship had arrived with bags of grain from Massachusetts in America, so the kitchen received several jute bags of grain.

"More soup for the hungry. We can open the kitchen here tomorrow, then head back out on the road to far-off-places day-after-tomorrow. This time we'll head toward Timoleague," Tomas said, seeming hopeful.

But I just couldn't do it. Moving my soul from despair to hope had become impossible. More burial carts paraded the streets when I walked to the soup kitchen this morning, and the color that had returned to Mammy's cheek had disappeared.

Earlier, she looked really frail, and now my belly churned with both hunger and worry. Soup seemed to make little difference; she could barely eat a spoon-full or two in the last two days. Each time I put my hand to her forehead and listened to her sigh, I knew the fever had been relentless, refusing to let her go.

And, after attending that awful meeting yesterday, doubt began to stab at me. Would Ireland ever recover? Is there a future for us all?

"Sean, what you think about the landlords' idea to ship some of us on those boats to the New World?" Brian asked when we walked home that evening.

"My blood boils, just thinking about those greedy bastards. 'Breeding like rabbits,' they said. The nerve. The God damned coldness and cruelty."

"I know. Just trying to be realistic, though. We've been out there; this devastation will not ease anytime soon. I read in yesterday's *Irish*

Times that more than 500,000 tenant farmers and their families have already died from starvation or the fever. That's why we're seeing so many more burial carts on the road, Sean."

"I will not leave Mammy behind."

"I know. Just something for us to think about, that's all."

We walked the rest of the way home in silence that evening, glancing at burial carts on the move and skeletal figures hobbling by on the side of the road. When the cabin finally came into view, I hastened my pace and burst through the door to check on Mammy.

This time she just laid there, barely opening her eyes. Dropping to my knees next to the bed, I raised her head with one hand and put the cup of water from the floor, to her lips. She took two gulps and closed her eyes. I fluffed the pillow with one hand and laid her head back down. Then I gathered more old clothes from a corner of the room and spread them over her. A weak smile creased her trembling lips.

"I love you, Sean."

"Love to too, Mammy. Always will."

I stood there and stared at her, my heart broken. She went back to sleep. I walked next door, knowing this would be another sleepless night for me.

The next morning, I got up by six. I checked on Mammy and cleaned her up. A man should never have to clean his mother's privates of urine and feces. But Mammy needed me. She'd been too weak to move, much less clean herself.

Brian and I headed to the soup kitchen. As I approached, I saw dozens of starving people waiting, like they always did. Some lay on the ground in the cold, clutching their cups, too weak to sit or stand. Others stood close together, shivering, their cups and pennies in hand.

In the minutes that followed, Brian and I stepped over the weak and half-starved and made our way inside the soup kitchen. Those standing refused to move for fear they'd lose their place in line. I helped prepare, cook, and serve soup to hundreds of quiet, hungry people.

One young mother panicked when her two skeletal children screamed with hunger. The woman raced to the head of the line, clutching her children. She had to be held back and pacified by others around her.

Luckily, this turned out to be one of the few days we managed to feed every person in line, plus a few stragglers who arrived late. The grain shipment from America was a true blessing.

"We'll head toward Timoleague tomorrow. Plan to be here by five so we can start preparing," Tomas said that evening.

I felt my gut clench with bile at the thought of another dreadful trip. The horrors of finding, moving and burying dead bodies hung over me like a black veil.

But I had no choice; I had to do the work. Landlord Doherty had shown no mercy when I delivered the rent money, two shillings short, last evening. I needed to find the rest of the money to pay him. I refused to let him throw Mammy out and burn our cabin to the ground. I had nowhere to put her. *Sweet Jesus, please help me!*

Brian and I headed home that night, the trip to Timoleague haunting my thoughts. As always, we had cups of soup for those at home.

But, as I came closer to Mammy's cabin, I stopped dead in my tracks. There it stood, the white cross, clearly drawn on the half-rotted door jam. *Dear God, Mammy will be out in the cold.* I slammed my eyes shut and struggled to pull myself together.

Then I thought, *first things first.* I hurried into the cabin and grabbed an old spoon. I fell to my knees and got ready to feed my mother. I touched her shoulder.

"Wake up, Mammy. I brought soup." She did not move. I shook her by the shoulder. She did not move. I kept shaking her. Nothing.

"Aaaah, aaah!" I screamed.

Flinging spoon and soup to the ground, I grabbed Mammy's hands. They felt stiff and cold. Burying my head into my mother's cold, bony hands, loud wails erupted as sorrow and foreboding overcame me.

I wasn't sure how long I knelt there bawling, when suddenly, a hand clutched me on the shoulder. I raised my head. Brian stood over me, his eyes red and moist.

"Mammy's gone, Brian. She's gone."

"Oh, my friend, I'm so sorry."

"I must bury her. I refuse to let the dogs gnaw at her flesh. Dear Lord, not the dogs."

"We'll bury her together. Move fast before landlord Doherty gets here. I'll be outside digging the grave. You stay here as long as you want. We'll get through this."

Brian rushed out and I soon heard him behind the cabin, dragging the shovel. Then reality set in as he began to dig and throw dirt around.

I quickly slapped the tears from my eyes. Strength washed over me like a rogue wave over a ship in the deep, blue, turbulent ocean. I didn't know where the strength came from, but I was resolute.

"Okay Mammy, let me get you ready for a good sendoff. There's no coffin, but I'll fix you up real' good," I said out loud.

I moved the old clothes away from my mother's body and stripped it naked. I threw water from the cup next to her bed on a piece of soft, white, cloth and wiped her face. I threw more water on the white cloth and wiped her privates free of urine and feces. I soaked the other side of the cloth and wiped her bottom really clean.

I rummaged through old clothes hanging on a line in one corner of the cabin. I found an old black frock she liked to wear to church. Walking back to the bed, I opened up the buttons on the frock, rolled Mammy's body to one side, laid the frock down, and rolled her back over. I tore the sides of the frock, making it easier to get her stiff arms into the sleeves. I tied its sash to one side and put a pair of old black socks on her frozen feet, which were turning blue.

"Brian, bring me those jute bags I brought home from the soup kitchen last Saturday."

Brian stopped digging. I heard him fling the shovel down and rush to his cabin. Grabbing the old horse-hair brush, I combed my mother's graying hair back, away from her face.

A sudden calm came over me. She seemed at peace.

"Here," Brian said, handing me the empty jute sacks. "I'll be through with the grave in a few minutes."

I grabbed the only sharp knife in the cabin and slit the jute bags open. I wrapped Mammy's body in jute, feet first. When I got to her shoulders, I took one last look at her thin, peaceful face and kissed her on the cheek, "Goodbye Mammy. God be with you." I wrapped her head and shoulders up in the last jute bag and laid her down.

I walked outside. Brian stood in the grave, shoveling dirt up and to the side.

"Let me help, Brian. Give me the shovel." I got ready to jump into the grave.

"I'm almost done. Just get your Mammy ready. Go back to the cabin and take anything you want to keep; take it to my cabin. Take all your clothes; take something to remind you of your Mammy."

I ran back into Mammy's cabin, grabbed my few pieces of clothes and an old floral frock Mammy loved to wear. I took them over to Brian's cabin.

It was after 6:30 the evening of December 31, when I lifted my mother's body, wrapped in jute from head to toe like a mummy, and carried it to the grave behind the mud hut.

"Get all that straw over there, Brian. Lay it at the bottom of the grave."

Brian did what I asked. I handed Mammy's body to him, jumped into the grave, and held my arms out to take my mother's body back. I laid her body on the straw and climbed out. I stood over the grave, closed my eyes, and repeated Psalm 27, two times.

Standing next to me, Brian had his eyes closed. Grabbing the shovel, I dug it into the mound of dirt and mud. I threw the first shovel-full of dirt into my mother's grave, my heart broken, my eyes a river of tears.

Brian hurried to his hut for the other shovel and helped me fill the grave with dirt. Shoveling more soil from the yard next door, I built a mound on top. I reached up and picked a dry branch that looked like a crooked cross. I dug it into the mound above my mother's head, before covering the dirt with leaves and branches.

My aching heart had my mind conjuring up a few beautiful memories. Before the famine, my mother was a pretty, petite, blue-eyed woman who took really good care of me and my father.

Like other tenant potato farmers, we didn't have much. But Mammy always had hot food on the table every evening when we got home from the fields. She made the most divine colcannon potatoes with cabbage. When friends asked for the recipe, she'd say, "Only God knows what I put in these potatoes."

She always worried about us. "Don't forget to lift from the knees. Take care of that back," she'd say as she served us oats porridge for breakfast. When I tried to gather the dishes for washing, she'd say, "Stay put, Laddie. You'll be working hard all day. Let me take care of those dishes."

And my father loved her so. Each time I saw his loving stare I swore that someday, I'd marry a woman who looked at me that way.

But my beautiful mother had now surrendered to disease and starvation, and I'd have to walk this earth without her by my side. The pain had become unbearable.

Brian picked up the shovels and took them into his hut. I stood there, looking at my mother's grave, tears flowing, sorrow washing over my soul. I sang softly, between gasps as I caught tearful breaths, "Amazing grace, how sweet the sound, that saved a wretch like me. I once was lost, but now am found, was blind but now I see." When I was a boy, Mammy loved to sing that song in church.

But the peace that washed over me when I sang Amazing Grace did not last. Heat and light jolted me out of my reverie like a fatal flash of lightening before a thunderclap.

I remembered that it was New Years' Eve, but I knew, for sure, this was no celebration. I spun around, slapped my hands to my face and gasped. I screamed and bawled till my throat stung. It was over! The mud cabin of my birth and rearing had suddenly erupted into flames.

Chapter 6

Mammy had died, the cabin that had been my home since birth no longer existed, and Ireland had sunk to a far greater depth of wretchedness than I could ever have imagined.

I sat on the earth next to my mother's grave, staring ahead, my mind in a haze. Before me, ashes of old wood that once housed a family of three, who only wanted to work hard and love each other, blew around in the cold wind. Tears flooded my eyes and ran down my cheeks once more. I couldn't stop crying; I could barely breathe. My heart ached. Sorrow and pain threatened to devour me.

I leaned over and buried my face into the branches and leaves over my mother's grave. What do I do now, without Mammy? Who will watch out for me? Who will love me?

Help me, dear God. Give me the strength to survive this sorrow. Mammy had said, "If I look like I won't make it, leave on one of those big boats." Rescue me, dear Lord.

"Come inside, Sean. Try to get some rest," someone said, tugging me out of my mournful thoughts. Brian held me by the shoulder and yanked me up.

"Rest? How can I rest? I have no one, now."

"You have me, old man O'Brien, and Harry. Come inside and lay down, Laddie."

I brushed leaves from my face and shirt. I turned and walked next to Brian into the cabin. Harry and old man O'Brien were not yet home from work. Laying on my straw mound with Brian next to me on his, a calming silence surrounded me. Brian broke the silence.

"We have to go back to the soup kitchen tomorrow."

"Oh, Jesus, no! I can't face it."

"No traveling around, remember? Just preparing and serving soup to those in the area. It'll take your mind off your sorrows."

I stared up at the ceiling; I did not respond. Brian and I stayed silent for hours till I heard Harry and old man O'Brien at the front door. I listened to small talk from the three of them, and thanked them for words of sympathy.

Numbness had now set in. The hours dragged by, with me sobbing quietly. I must have fallen into an exhausted sleep, because next thing I heard was Brian's voice.

"It's 'round half past five. Let's head to the kitchen. Keep busy, take your mind off things."

I rose, washed up, got dressed, and we headed out. As always, the line to the soup kitchen stood almost a mile long.

Brian had been right; keeping busy did take my mind off my sorrows. As I got close to the head of the line, someone shouted, "Sean."

Cara stood there, looking even thinner and more drawn. She wore a knee-length, black, cotton frock and old black shoes that looked more like they belonged to her mother.

"Cara, give me some time. I'll bring soup for you and your mother as soon as we're done."

"Just for me, Sean. Mammy died three days ago. The fever finally took her." Tears welled up in her eyes.

"So sorry, Cara. Fever took my Mammy last night too." I fought back my own tears.

"Oh Sean. My heart aches for you. I'm leaving Ireland next week before death knocks at my door, too."

"Where you going?"

"Across the channel to England; one of my aunts lives there. You must save yourself too, Sean."

"I will. Glad you have someone to go to." I handed Cara a cup of soup and hugged her goodbye.

Later on, sorrow kept creeping back as Tomas and the other workers voiced their sympathies over my loss. I thanked them and kept working.

By the end of the day, I had helped cook and feed soup to hundreds of men, women and children. There was enough soup to feed everyone in line, and I was grateful. A decision had been made not to go on the road for the next several days, because the food lines had been so long.

We began cleaning up and preparing for the next day, when Tomas called us to attention. I wiped my hands with an old dish rag and stood still, listening as he spoke.

"My dear friends, you have done a stellar job in this kitchen. Your strength and hard work have saved hundreds, if not thousands of lives. For that, you will receive God's abundant blessings. As Quakers, we are fortunate to have the ears of governments and the wealthy, all over the world. With their contributions of money and food, we've been able to save lives and ease a lot of pain."

Tomas paused, and my mind went to dark places. *What's this talk about? Is something about to happen? What's that look on the Quaker's face?* I didn't have to wonder much longer.

"Despite our hard work, my dear friends, we've come up against some tough realities. The government has shut down most of the work schemes, so now, there will be more people to feed. We've applied for added assistance for the kitchens, but that has been denied. From now on, we may have to limit our efforts to the old and very young."

The room erupted with angry shouts and fist slamming. Tomas yelled, over and over, for quiet. Then he continued.

"I feel your pain and frustration. Take comfort in knowing that the Quakers continue to fight for the cause. But we're now faced with tons of paperwork from the Relief Commission. They insist that this paperwork be filled out before soup can be dispensed. No money will be issued to us to feed the starving until the paperwork is done correctly."

"What in God's name does this all mean? Will we have to stand by and watch more people die?" Alma, the cook, said. The room erupted once more. Tomas yelled for silence, then he continued.

"We Quakers are doing everything to fight this. In the meantime, we may have to make our soup with grain, Indian corn and cabbage; anything we can get our hands on, till the government figures things out."

Brian and I walked home that evening in silence, till he could be quiet no more.

"The bastards are making it harder for us to keep people alive. They are Devils, I tell you!".

"I ... I'm almost without words. How could human beings be so harsh? Ireland is supposed to be a sovereign state."

"One way or another, they will pay for what they're doing to us."

In the days that followed, we ran out of meat and, as anticipated, resorted to making soup with grain, oats, meal, Indian corn, and cabbage.

The starving soon complained, rejected the food, and said that we should give them uncooked food that they could prepare at home. They came close to rioting, and Tomas said this had made things worse.

The government became more difficult. They began to give even less toward the cause, claiming our people were not destitute enough if they had the strength to riot.

A few days later, I read in the *Irish Times* that demonstrations had erupted in Tipperary against how the soup kitchens were being run. An innocent woman who worked in one of the kitchens fell victim to that hungry mob's anger.

The newspaper cited thousands being fired from soup kitchens across the country. Reasons? The government wanted to save money, and they wanted to force labor back to the cultivation of food for the winter ahead.

But they did not provide enough money for seeds needed for planting. Starving people had eaten their seed potatoes earlier in the year, to keep themselves alive.

Tomas called us together for another meeting a few evenings later. Dread wrapped around me like a cloud before rain. *What is it now?*

"Thank you all once more for the hard work and patience. We have another problem. How many of you have heard the term 'souperism'?"

Baffled, I glanced around. Everyone looked puzzled. Tomas glanced around and continued.

"Not surprised none of you have heard the term. What it means, my friends, is that the government now demands that in return for soup, everyone must prove that they've become Protestants. Their church believes that what starving Catholics need is not food; they need the Bible. This Evangelical crusade has been going on in other parts of the world, in countries colonized by the Brits. Now they've brought it here, to us."

The room exploded with gasps and curses, drowning out the Quaker's final words. I struggled to tune out the mayhem. This had gone way too far.

Brian and I got ready to walk out of the kitchen and head home, when we saw three men, including the cook, Art, and the death cart driver, Darcy, huddled in a corner. They were talking quietly and intensely. Art called us over.

"When was the last time you read the *Nation*?"

"That paper created by the Young Ireland group? Haven't got my hands on one in a while," Brian said.

"Young Ireland. That's the group that rejects the right of Brits to rule over Ireland. They think Ireland should be under self-rule. They've been touting our history and heroes in their newspaper. I heard they also think we should return to only speaking our old language, Gaelic," I said.

"Exactly. Things are so bad, they're getting ready to launch a movement," Darcy said.

"I hear Brits are nervous. They've asked the group to sign some kind'a oath that there will be no physical force under any circumstances, as they rally for independence," Alroy, the other kitchen helper, said.

"Don't tell us they signed that oath," Brian said.

"They didn't. They said they were planning no physical force, but wouldn't rule it out either," Darcy said.

"I'm ready to join the group. Who else is ready?" Art asked.

"I'm ready. Time to fight to free our people from starvation and disease," Darcy said.

The two men looked from me to Brian, and then to Alroy.

"Brian and I will talk it over and let you know tomorrow," I said.

"Tomorrow for me, too," Alroy said.

As Brian and I walked home that evening, the Young Ireland group stayed heavy on our lips. We'd both reached our limit with the soup kitchen issues. News that starving people had to pledge to be Protestants in exchange for soup, had pushed me over a cliff.

"Emigrate or stay and fight for freedom from cruelty and starvation. Those are our choices now, Brian," I said.

"A tough decision. Hate to leave Ireland, but we can't go on living like this."

"You ready for rebellion?"

"I'm ready. But I heard that the Young Ireland group is disorganized and incompetent. The thought of them hauling me off to prison in Australia, like they did my father, makes me cringe," Brian said.

"Aye. Let's sleep on it and decide on our way to the kitchen tomorrow morning."

"Good idea, Laddie."

"You know, I've been thinking. What is my purpose? My first purpose was to work hard and keep my home going. Then it was simply keeping Mammy alive. After losing both Mammy and my home, I thought I should focus on helping keep Ireland afloat. But listening to the 'souperism' malarkey has me giving up on that goal. What am I living for?"

"Oh Sean, sometimes you can be so intense. Hard for me to think purpose when we're all struggling to dodge starvation."

I fell into a troubled sleep that night, and I dreamed. In my dream, a bright summer day surrounded me as I walked along the bank of the Bandon River, enjoying the breeze. Suddenly, in the distance, I saw my mother strolling toward me.

She wore a knee-length, blue, summer frock, a pair of strappy white sandals, and a beautiful, white, straw hat. She looked young and vibrant, her cheeks flushed from the sun. When she got closer, I held my arms out but she hurried past me. I turned around and saw her strolling up to a huge boat. Before stepping on to the deck, she turned around and motioned for me to join her.

As I started hurrying toward her, I heard someone calling my name and spun around. No one stood behind me. Turning back around, I saw the boat sailing away in the distance with my mother on board. Mist and fog soon enveloped it; I could see the vessel no more.

I awoke that morning, my soul washed in a wave of tranquility. At least I had Brian, now.

I knew what I needed to do.

Chapter 7

The large, imposing vessel stood there, belching smoke into the air like an expectant beast. Its menacing 'tentacles' reached out to me with a call of fear and anticipation. Anxiety gripped me in the gut like sharp claws. I'd embarked on a journey to the unknown, because the life to which I was born had become unbearable.

After seeing Mammy in my dream, I'd decided to get myself on one of those 'big boats.' Brian insisted on taking the trip, too. I'd been forced to walk away from everything I knew and loved.

Fear gnawed at me as my mind flashed back to the 'coffin ships' I'd read about in the *Irish Times*. The *Times* reported that many of the ships heading to Canada and America were unseaworthy, over crowded, and had inadequate amounts of drinking water, food and sanitation.

Most passengers on those ships had fares fully paid for by their landlords. 'They can no longer pay rent, so it's cheaper to get them out of Ireland and put our land to better use,' the landlords had said.

By the time I began reading the *Times* articles, passengers on those ships were said to be 'fleeing from one form of death to another,' and hundreds of bodies had to be buried at sea.

I'd read this, slapped my hands against my temples, and said, "Brian, I'll starve to death and be buried in Irish mud next to Mammy, rather than have my body devoured by sharks."

But when Brian and I let Father Flannery in on our thoughts about leaving, the old priest came through for us. He told us about a boat heading to the Caribbean from Liverpool, England; the boat was sailing to Jamaica.

He said the boat had just delivered sugar from the island, now known as the 'sugar capital of the world.' It needed a few passengers to act as ballasts, to help keep it steady on the voyage back. We'd have to pay half the fare to get across the Irish Sea, from Dublin to Liverpool, and half the fare for the journey to Jamaica.

So now, here I stood, staring at the huge vessel in front of me, thinking this was my only escape. Leaving Ireland was devastating, but I refused to give up on her. One day I would return to help bring her back to where she once was.

I glanced over at Brian, his eyebrows knitted with an anxiety he struggled to hide. Before leaving Dublin, Brian had paused, spun around, and waved a somber farewell to old man O'Brien and his son Harry, who'd refused to leave Ireland behind. After waving goodbye, Brian had slapped a rogue tear from his cheek and just kept walking.

But today, I faced a gloomy, cold, morning at the port in Liverpool, England. There was enough fog to make the blind stumble.

Hoisting the jute knapsack over my right shoulder, I walked up to the vessel. With Brian by my side and my journey to Jamaica about to begin, I stared up at the ship, in awe.

"Aye, my friend, time for a new life. Not sure whether to clamor or cry, but let's get the heck out of here," I said.

The name *Brig Watchful,* scrawled across the outer deck wall of the huge, rusty, old galleon, threatened to increase my anxiety. And the boat looked like it had seen better days, had sailed to many destinations in rough seas, and had weathered many storms.

But Brian and I stepped onto the gangway and courageously walked on board. I stared around.

My eyes rested on piles of fraying ropes, grungy old tarps, rusty metal lockers and containers, corroded anchors and shovels, machetes and goulashes of all sizes, and raggedy rain gear. More clutter could be seen in other corners of the ship's deck.

"What you doing?" Brian asked.

"Guaranteeing survival," I narrowed my eyes and whispered, shoving one of the machetes into my knapsack.

"Survival? From what—waves and seagulls?"

"We left the Devil behind in Ireland, but I learned over the past months that death could knock at my door any minute. If I can protect myself against it, that's what I'll do. I plan to sleep with one eye open to anything that stirs around me on this ship."

Before Brian could respond, I jumped.

"Over here, mates. Let's see your tickets," someone yelled.

Brian and I spun around as a deckhand approached with his hands outstretched. The man, dressed in a pair of old khaki pants scuffed at both knees, a worn gray sweater, and a thick black, hooded jacket, had eyes that seemed red and shifty. His skin looked wrinkled and leathery-brown from exposure to sun and sea.

"I'm Jack McFarlane, deckhand," he said, hands still outstretched. Brian and I handed him our tickets. *Cruel landowners got rid of us, and here I am, facing another Brit.* I took a deep breath, trying to remain calm.

"You two will share a bunker with two berths on the lower deck. Although you paid a small fee for your tickets, there are no free rides on this ship. We all work hard. You'll have to work for food and lodging. Starting tomorrow, you'll be assigned chores, from mopping deck floors to hoisting sails. Let's get you going, then."

Brian and I hurried across the deck and down ten steps to the lower level behind McFarlane, saying hello to two other deckhands along the way.

"This 'old girl' has taken many brave young men like you on the four-week trip to the islands. They were all seeking a better life for themselves. She's also taken back to the islands, tons of cargo, like crockery, pots and pans, wines, bedding, and other wares. We sell these to plantation owners at each port. She's a good old girl," McFarlane said. He opened the door of one of the bunkers and let us in.

I looked around the dark and gloomy room; compared to the mud cabin in Ireland, it was a palace. I immediately shifted my focus to a new life in the West Indies. This ship provided a means to an end; that was all.

"This will do," Brian said, flinging his knapsack on the berth closest to the door and glancing around. "It's a bit gloomy, but there's always the upper deck for fresh air."

The deckhand disappeared, closing the door behind him. I looked around once more. Small and windowless, the bunker had a berth in each corner, two old metal containers to store clothes and shoes, and an empty old box that could be used for garbage.

"Oh yes," I said. "I have a feeling we'll crash here and pass out every night after they work us hard. But anything is better than what we just experienced."

"For sure."

"Glad we're taking this journey together, Brian. Don't know if I could have done it alone. Sometimes I worry about what's waiting for us in Jamaica, but if we learned anything in the past months, it's to be brave."

"Couldn't have done it without you either. Friends forever, you and me. Let's swear to make it through this ride and whatever's waiting for us in the islands."

"Yes indeed," I said, stuffing clothes from my knapsack into one of the metal containers.

"By the way, how you feeling 'bout leaving Ireland right after your Mammy died?"

"Mammy was a great mother and the kindest woman I ever knew. I would've done anything for her. And my beloved Ireland, the devastation ..." I fought back tears.

"I know. She was like a mother to me too. And being forced to leave the place where I was born and raised is a blow."

"After losing Mammy, I had to fight to keep myself going, Brian. Don't get me wrong, I missed my father too. But at least when he died, I had Mammy."

"We have each other now."

"You think we'll sleep better on this boat? I haven't had a good night's sleep since I saw those horrid sights."

"Just thinking about them makes my gut clench. And the landowners; why were they so cruel?"

"England should have stepped in, instead of hoping things would work themselves out."

"It's a matter of kindness to other human beings. Why is that so hard? I hear slaves brought to the islands from Africa are treated better."

"Aye. That's not because of kindness. It's because plantations can't survive in the islands without slaves working them."

"You're right. Wonder how they'll treat us?"

"Guess we'll find out soon. Can I talk about purpose now?" I asked, changing the subject.

"Better time for that conversation, Laddie. What you have in mind?"

"My purpose is clear now. Suffering has seen to that."

"Okay, let's hear it."

"At first, I thought I'd work like Hell in Jamaica, hoard my money, and live like a king with slaves tending to my every need. Afterall, I deserve it. But you know I'm not the self-serving type. I plan to take some of that money back to Ireland and help with its recovery."

"What you going to do with the rest of the money?"

"Use it to make a difference in Jamaica, while I'm there. Been doing some reading. Slaves receive terrible treatment on the island. They need to be freed from the plantocracy that's been oppressing them. I want to be a part of that movement, Brian."

"Wow, sounds like you've given this lots of thought. What a purpose that would be; helping to free slaves. You'd really go back to Ireland after that?"

"In a flash, when I'm not so helpless and can make a difference. How 'bout you. What are your plans?"

"Not sure. Leaving Ireland behind and being anxious about the unknown, has me in a muddle. Need more time to figure things out."

Brian and I worked for nine hours the next day, cleaning the galley, scrubbing floors on the top deck, repairing sails, painting gangways, and storing cargo. By nightfall, I flung myself on my berth, exhausted.

"Jesus, I thought working the soup kitchen was tough. This is backbreaking work," Brian said.

"Focus on what's ahead, Laddie. In another few weeks we'll be off this floating den and on to bright sunshine, palm trees, sugarcane plantations. Let's hope for the best after that."

"Trying not to let my imagination run away with me, but I heard the Brits are desperate to have more whites on the island. You know what that could mean?"

"Yeah. We could be foremen or overseers in no time. When the trip gets tough, let's focus on that." I laid on my back with both arms under my head.

"Can't wait. Anything's better than what we've been through." Brian sighed, closed his eyes, yawned, and succumbed to darkness.

In the weeks that followed, this became our daily ritual. But I had nothing to complain about. We ate a decent breakfast of porridge or eggs, bread, and tea, each morning. And dinner usually included beef or fish, rice, and vegetables like corn or sweet peas. All this, after surviving for months in Ireland on a cup of soup per day and a piece of bread here and there.

Guilt tried to take hold, but I fought it off. I needed to feed my body to withstand the back-breaking work expected of me on this ship.

But, as the ship sailed closer to the Caribbean, uncertainty began to haunt me. I had very little money after paying part of the fare. Where would Brian and I live? How long would it take me to find work? Would my body adjust to so much hot weather? What if I caught one of those deadly tropical diseases I'd heard so much about?

To calm my fears, I looked back at what I'd left behind and thanked God for health, strength, and food.

Chapter 8

The hurricane roared in like a venomous beast. I sprang from my berth to sounds of ear-piercing screams and the foot-pounding of men on deck as they struggled to align order with chaos.

Bolting up the steps, I heard Brian's footsteps following close behind. I flung my body against the door to the deck; it did not budge. Brian lunged forward, crashed against it and almost sent me hurling back down the steps. The door did not move.

Fear gnawed at my insides as I listened to the wind howl and roar like a freight train from Hell. Then it paused. I glanced at Brian as it changed direction. Suddenly, the door flew open and the wind leapt at us, whining like a ferocious swine.

I clutched the deck walls with both hands and looked around, rain lashing at my face. Brian raced over to two men holding a mast that threatened to snap.

The sky to the east turned crimson. A menacing darkness shrouded the ship.

'Crack!'

A splintering sound jolted me out of my frightful reverie and I looked up. Bolting over to Brian and the other men, I grabbed on to the mainmast that held the shuddering mainsail, which threatened to crack in two. Every man panted and groaned, bolstering the mast with pure muscle and adrenaline.

The wind howled louder and louder, flinging down harsh, blinding rain that seared the flesh of everyone in its path. The sea's rage clashed against the 'whoosh,' 'whoosh' of the sails. Rising to terrifying heights, the ocean seemed ready to swallow everything, like a vengeful serpent.

The ship moaned upward, struggling to climb a gigantic swell. Then it started to keel.

More men raced about, trying to hold down anything that moved. I gripped the mast, my feet struggling to remain grounded. And my thoughts wandered, turbulent, like the howling wind.

Holding on for dear life, I tasted blood as my teeth sliced through the inside of my lower lip. Then, out of nowhere, determination took hold of me.

I will hold on and never let go. This is a minor setback. I will ride this through, then life will be better. Nothing will stop me now.

My skin stung, as wind, rain and ocean water lashed me, over and over.

After what seemed like a horrifying eternity, the ship began to steady itself and move to a wobbly sail. The rain soon halted, and a consistent, gusty, drizzle ensued. The wind ceased howling, but sporadic gusts threatened to stir the wet hair over my forehead.

Wiping water from my eyes, I glanced up. Huge black clouds gradually moved away and headed west. My heart almost leapt out of my chest.

We survived. Thank you, Sweet Jesus, we pulled through!

Sunday night finally came and all went quiet; a welcome change. Sitting on deck with Brian, I breathed in fresh air, grateful to be alive. We began to share our aspirations.

"Oh my God, Sean, can you imagine us becoming overseers right away?" Brian asked.

"It's so exciting, I can almost taste it, Laddie."

"We survived a hurricane; we've made it through the worst that could happen. It's up hill now."

"Aye! Let's turn in and get ready for tomorrow," I said, a yawn taking over.

We headed to our bunker around ten that night and got our work clothes ready for the next day.

Brian flopped down on his cot and promptly began a quiet, steady snore. I turned the lamp down, leaving enough light, just in case.

I laid there thinking about what the future may hold for me in that land called Jamaica. The sugar capital of the world, indeed! Would I find work quickly? Would I, one day, have a sugarcane plantation of my own? Would this new life change me for the better, as I pursued my purpose to help others? Seems like it took a hurricane to have me thinking more positively about the new life ahead.

I sighed, closed my eyes, and fell into a deep, restful sleep.

Chapter 9

My body jerked. Plops of thick, warm liquid landed on my face and neck. Harsh noises corroded the air. Bayonets exploded. Screams of obscenities disturbed the darkness around me. I heard a frightening clamor, "Pirates!"

I shot a glance over at Brian. *Sweet Jesus! He's sprawled on the berth. God of all mankind, the blood!*

My heart pounded with terror and rage. He's my *only friend and brother; has he been taken from me?* Panic gripped me in the gut and reality crashed down like a ton of rocks.

Grabbing the machete from under the berth with my right hand, I sprang to my feet on top of the berth with a jerk. My mind conjured up traces of Brian's blood splattered all over my arms, face and neck. If I didn't act fast, I'd also be dead.

A figure with the face of Lucifer suddenly appeared in front of me. He lunged at me with a sickening thrust. Eyes red and bulging with wrath, his grubby, gray shirt flew wide open. It swung around him like the cape of the Devil. In the dim lamplight, I barely saw my attacker's gape as he let out a thunderous, "Aaaah!"

My body flew off the berth as I swung the machete. Landing on both feet, I swung a second time. Then I swung a third, fourth, and fifth time, metal to metal as my arm reverberated against the clang, metal to flesh as blood splattered, metal to bone with a grotesque hack. Madness had invaded my very soul.

A machete flew through the air. I surged and grabbed it with my left hand. I swung and hacked with both machetes as more blood flew through the air and a body tumbled to the floor. Nothing moved.

I glanced around, staring in horror at what was left of my friend's mangled body. I turned and glimpsed at the torso sprawled on the floor beneath me. Bile plundered my throat. I choked. I stood, unmoving and my body began to shudder.

Dear God, Brian is gone. We made it through Hell together, and now he's gone. I couldn't save him. Why am I still here? Why didn't they kill me too? My mind raced. My body fought off more nausea.

I quickly wiped sweat from my temples with the back of one hand, as the ship swayed around me. I whirled my blood-splattered body around and raced up the steps to the upper deck. The roar of an explosion almost deafened me.

The ship veered and swayed even more as I sprang out on deck. I crouched, desperate to hold my footing. Then I saw four unfamiliar bodies sprawled out on the deck floor, hacked or shot to death. Close to one of the port holes, I watched the captain level his bayonet and poke a body on the planks beneath him.

The stench of spilled blood, gunpowder, and death wafted through the salty sea air, bringing more sickness to my gut. Deckhands scurried about, machetes and bayonets in hand. They surveyed the grotesque scene, staying alert to more invaders.

I stared out at sea and saw a battered old galleon named *Devil's Whore* sailing away. One blood-splattered man sporting a long, black beard, stood at its helm.

Reality suddenly hit me like a brick in the face. I let go of the bloody machetes and dropped them to the deck floor. Tears stung my eyes; shock and despair washed over me like liquid poison.

In the midst of it all, my friend and brother laid dead. Please tell me he got killed instantly. Please tell me he didn't suffer too much pain. My beautiful, young friend showed me nothing but love and loyalty. Sweet Jesus, how will I survive in an unknown land without Brian?

Late that night, I got moved to another bunker, which I shared with the deckhand named Abe. I laid in the bunker that night, pain and sorrow crawling up and down my spine. My heart ached, I cried and sobbed. Sleep refused to come my way.

Drowning myself in grief and sorrow, I could not raise my head above the flood of my tears. Abe stayed quiet as I hummed "Amazing Grace", over and over.

* * *

The time had come to bury my beloved Brian. It was two in the afternoon, and the ocean gaped at me as I stood over it on the aft deck. I stared down in a stupor, watching the sea swell and retreat.

Six deckhands stood next to the captain, their faces showing sorrow for the loss of the 'spirited, hard-working young passenger who only wanted to escape the horrors of the potato famine'. But that passenger meant the world to me.

My bowel clenched. Anguish choked me as I tried to swallow. The captain yelled something unrecognizable. I tried to focus.

"Dear Lord, take this innocent soul out of its watery grave and up to Heaven ..." I heard, or something of the sort. I stood there, transfixed, and I watched, sorrow digging a black hole into my very soul.

Two deckhands swung Brian's body, wrapped in dingy, white sailcloth, and tossed it overboard. Numbness threatened to take over. I stared down, as my friend's body carved a neat space into the deep-blue sea. It sloshed through the swell, and then it got sucked into the ocean, never to be revealed.

I howled and screamed, my voice raw with agony. Everyone spun around and stared at my face, which felt hot with wrath and defiant pain.

"Stupid sod! Son of a bitch! You're the only one who got your ass killed! Why'd you leave me ... why?"

Insanity suddenly took over. I bent down and grabbed everything I could get my hands on. I flung them overboard. Two big deckhands approached with ropes; they were about to restrain me. I held my palms up as if to say, 'back off, I'm all right.'

Breathing in and out, I struggled to regain control. I closed my eyes and whispered, "The Lord is my light and my salvation; whom shall I fear? The Lord is the strength of my life; of whom shall I be afraid? When the wicked, even my enemies and my foes, came upon me to eat up my flesh, they stumbled and fell ...." I took solace in Psalm 27, like I always did. And, like Brian, I slapped two rogue tears from both cheeks and stared ahead, my insides wounded and raw.

The captain told me to take the next day off, and I laid on my berth, unmoving.

"Come with me on deck, Bloke. Get some fresh air. Do you lots'a good," my new roommate, Abe, said. I could not move.

"Can't face deck right now, Abe. Listening to the waves will bring back horrid memories of Brian's body being tossed overboard. Can't face the waves; just can't face the waves."

"So sorry, Sean."

"You go. I need some time alone."

"Want me to bring you a little breakfast?"

"Can't eat; thanks, though."

I laid there, alone, tears flowing so hard they soaked the pillow. All those years that Brian had been there for me came rushing back. I began to talk to the Lord.

Thank you, Jesus, for sending a brother into my life. You've taken him back, so I know you have bigger plans for him. Rest his soul in peace, dear Lord. And when that's done, come back and protect me from any evil coming my way. Amen!

I spent the rest of the day in the dark, crying, praying, singing 'Amazing Grace,' and repeating Psalm 23 and 27.

They say only time heals the wounds of grief and sorrow, but it will take a whole lot of time to heal these wounds. They also say that grief is love that has nowhere to go. I will depend on the Lord to guide me to a place, where my love can be in the service of a greater cause.

Two days later, another reality hit me like as rock in the chest. I stood alone now, no friend, no family. It was just me, the elements, the deep-blue Caribbean Sea, and the most stunning sunlight I'd ever felt warming my face and hands as I walked on deck.

The deep-blue Caribbean Sea, Brian, old chap, we finally made it to the Caribbean. Good-bye, my brother. I'll miss you for sure. You were a great friend; loyal and kind. Why am I the one still alive? I can hear you now, saying, 'Chin up, Laddie. Use my murder as fuel for the journey ahead.'

One question remains, though. What the heck will I do in Jamaica without you? I don't want to be there. I want to turn this ship around.

But what would I return to? There's nothing and no one left for me in Ireland right now. I've always believed everyone has a purpose. God must have a bigger plan for me. He's taking me to Jamaica, alone. I will keep hope alive, and well.

* * *

Dawn took the distant horizon into its arms as I rushed up on deck the next day, to sounds of revelry and guffaws. I stared beyond the din and gasped.

Never had I seen anything as stunning as what laid in front of me. The water had gone from deep blue to an exquisite, sparkling, turquoise. In the distance laid an imposing mass of land, rising like a phoenix out of the sea. It soared up toward pale-blue skies, dotted with plump puffs of white clouds.

As the ship sailed closer, I stared down at the crystal-clear turquoise water. Tropical fish of all colors 'danced' gracefully around. A team of dolphins playfully disturbed the peace, darting up and down, in and out of the water as if both taunting and welcoming me.

Never, in my entire life, had I seen, smelled, or sensed anything so magnificent. Yet, I wanted to jump overboard and end my misery. But I didn't. I thought I heard Brian say, "Don't be a bloody coward. Pull yourself together, Laddie, for God's sake."

A voice on a megaphone jolted me out of my agonizing reverie.

"Gentlemen, welcome to the latest jewel of the British crown. Welcome to the sugar capital of the world. Welcome to Jamaica."

I took a deep breath. Surges of sadness, grief, anxiety, and excitement pulsated through my veins. I'd finally arrived in Jamaica, and though I wanted to jump overboard and join Brian in the belly of the deep, blue sea, I held my head up high. I breathed deeply, in and out, over and over.

I have a purpose; Brian was very impressed with my purpose, as he struggled to find his own cause. Suddenly, I swore I heard my friend and brother say, "Heads up, Laddie. Jamaica is waiting. Purpose, remember?"

Chapter 10

I strode anxiously down the ramp of the Brig *Watchfull*. Standing in stunned silence, I shifted, as the weight of the jute bag dug into my shoulder. I stared down at the ocean that had not only swallowed my best friend, it had conspired with the wind to put an end to my life, and had forced me to murder a man. Pain and fear stabbed at my gut.

What do I do now? I have no one. My money is gone, stolen by the son-of-a-bitch who escaped after attacking us at sea. There's nowhere else to go. Be strong; try and make this work. Mammy is gone; she wanted me to take this trip. My mind whirled; my heart ached for Mammy and Brian. I felt lost in a haze of uncertainty.

Finally, I steadied myself and looked at the scene in front of me. This was no bustling port like the one in Liverpool.

Four white men signed papers and issued orders to a group of Negro men. The men rushed to lift huge bags and boxes of goods on to raggedy pulls, which they dragged to the dock's entrance.

I stared through the entrance. Sunshine lit the elements like brilliant rays of hope. The sky was the most beautiful blue I'd ever seen; there wasn't a single cloud above.

I backed off my deck jacket and looked down at my short-sleeved, open-necked cotton shirt and khaki pants. My shirt clung to me, and I felt sweat meandering down my back. *God, it's hot!*

As I moved closer to the dock's entrance, my senses got hit with a cacophony of bright colors ... endless shades of greens, yellows, bright oranges, and reds. Exiting the dock's covered area, I saw palms, thatch, and flowering hibiscus. Crotons grew wildly, enhancing the sun's rays with exotic tropical hues. I'd only seen drawings of this foliage in books about the Caribbean.

In the distance, lush, green mountains towered up to the skies. Tropical birds flapped their wings and chirped melodious songs. This was the most beautiful place I'd ever seen.

My thoughts returned to Brian. *Sorry you're missing this, Laddie. Here's hoping for great sceneries for you, too.*

Sadness threatened to overcome me once more. I kept it at bay and held my head up to the sun. My eyes watered. I wiped them dry with my handkerchief.

"Hello, I'm Clinton Vassell." A strong British accent interrupted my sad and anxious thoughts. The man approached with his right hand outstretched. Tall and tanned, his thin blond hair looked like it needed a good trim. He wore a pair of dusty old, brown, work boots and khaki shirt and pants.

"Sean O'Sullivan is the name." I said, shaking Vassell's hand.

"You'll be looking for work then?"

Brusque and undiplomatic, he stared me in the eyes. There was no 'welcome to Jamaica or 'how was the voyage.' Vassell only thought about business, as far as I could see, and he was well aware that any white man who had braved the long journey across the ocean must be looking for work. *Another Brit, arrogant and to-the-point.*

"Yes. Need work right away. I hear —"

"Good then. We should talk. I own Havendale, a plantation six miles from here. I need an assistant overseer. Ever done this kind of work? You sound like an Irishman. I hear things are tough in Ireland these days."

"Yes, I worked a potato farm for years before the famine hit."

Anger threatened to take over as I struggled to subdue my thoughts. *You hear things are tough in Ireland these days? Your countrymen are starving my people to death. And here I am, on the other side of the world, having to deal with you.*

I took five deep breaths and calmed myself down. I stood alone, with no money, in unfamiliar territory; not smart to go on the attack.

"Very good; no potato farms here. Come with me, then. I'll give you room and board till you get up and running. One of my overseers will show you the ropes."

"That quickly - remarkable," I said, walking next to Vassell as he approached a cart hitched behind two mules, and tended by an old Negro man.

I had never seen a Negro before. Dressed in a pair of tattered old short pants and faded blue shirt, he stood there, barefooted, bridle and whip in hand, his face glum and expressionless.

Must be a slave, Sweet Jesus, how do I survive here without being sucked into the mistreatment of slaves? I'd find a way. I have a purpose, remember?

Vassell sat in the front of the cart, and I heaved my sack, then myself, into the back.

"Glad I waited for the Brig Watchfull to dock, Old Boy. I just knew a white bloke or two would walk down that gangway, looking for work."

The whip cracked and the mules surged forward. Dust rose from the horses' hooves as they broke into a spirited trot. *A white bloke or two. Yes, there were two of us,* I thought. I struggled, once more, to push down mournful thoughts of Brian.

"Hard to find workers here?" I asked, fighting to focus and take my mind off my losses. I thought I heard Brian say '*Get it together; Laddie. What the Hell's wrong with you?*'

"Not enough whites on the island. Most don't have the courage for a long boat trip to the unknown."

I remained silent for the rest of the ride. We galloped along a rough stone road. A lush, tropical forest loomed on one side, and on the other side laid sloping valleys covered with blankets of green grass, and adorned with patches of colorful foliage.

We entered a dark, winding gully. The temperature immediately dipped. I looked up and around; some kind of tunnel? No. Sweet Lord in Heaven, it's a rainforest!

Lush green ferns stood everywhere, and plants with huge leaves grew out of limestone walls. They looked like ornamental fans displayed on the wall of an elaborate home.

Huge tree trunks sprung out of the earth and walls, like aliens, spreading their tentacles into the air and exploding into luxuriant greenery that loomed above like canopies.

Long, hanging vines threatened to brush my scalp, and wild orchids dotted the landscape, some growing from trees, in purple, yellow, and pink. And the red birds of paradise and rainforest lily leaves were a remarkable sight. Ireland had nothing like this, not even during good times when the hills were covered with lush greenery.

The slave pulled the reins, and the mules slowed to a steady, rhythmic trot as we coasted downhill to a large, open cavern. Then the driver yelled "Yah," and the horses galloped through the rainforest's exit.

Beautiful, bright sunlight embraced us once more, and I glanced to the left at the turquoise Caribbean Sea. It was as if it followed us around, enhancing the landscape at just the right time. I imagined Brian, treading water, craning his neck and shading his eyes from the sun with one hand, watching and making sure I was okay.

A small island loomed out of the ocean off the coastline, and sand, as white as fresh fallen snow, blanketed the shoreline. I looked to my left and there they were again, those lush, green mountains reaching up to the skies in all their splendor.

I think I died and went to Heaven. Brian, my boy, I hope you're in Heaven too. I didn't want to be here without you, but this is one stunning place.

Twenty minutes later, the gates of what looked like a huge estate dotted the distant landscape. As the horse cart drew closer, I saw a gilded crest the shape of a tropical dove with outstretched wings, hanging over two large, iron gates. I narrowed my eyes; the crest said Havendale Plantation.

The cart soon came to a halt. Two male slaves opened the gates, and the mules trotted in. I stared at the two slaves.

Their skin looked so dark, they seemed permanently sun burned. And their faces looked almost blank. I couldn't read them. What were they thinking? How did one communicate with them? I'd read that the Brits thought of them as barely human. I couldn't imagine the treatment they got, given that the Brits turned a blind eye as Irish humans died of starvation and disease.

I glanced ahead at an enormous one-story great house made of tan and white stones. A huge, wrap-around verandah encircled six-foot tall, elegant windows that sported white lace curtains on the inside, cinched on each side to let sunlight in.

Looking around, I saw sugarcane fields stretched into the distance. Slaves armed with machetes worked the fields in the boiling tropical sun. The men, mostly shirtless and barefooted, had bodies black and glistening with sweat, and scarred backs.

My thoughts began to whirl. *Sweet Jesus, those scars must be from the whip. What did I get myself into? How should I deal with this?*

Most of the slave women, also scantily dressed, wore burlap. They stood around large drums mounted on piles of hot coals and wood. Some stirred laboriously with long wooden sticks, while others tended the fires. My thoughts suddenly got interrupted by Vassell.

"Welcome to Havendale Plantation."

Jumping off the cart, he held his hand out for my jute bag.

"Wow! This is quite a place," I said, holding one palm out to say 'I'm all right,' and tossing the bag over my shoulder. I jumped down from the cart and steadied myself.

"Yes, one Hell of a place, indeed." His words came with a major emphasis on the 'Hell.'

A white man walked by, of medium height, sun tanned, big floppy canvas hat almost concealing his eyes, whip in hand. I stared at him.

'One Hell of a place,' indeed. Why did I get the feeling this would also be one heck of a journey? Then I thought I heard Brian say, "Don't be a damned coward. Keep it together, Laddie."

Chapter 11

"This is one of the overseers' quarters," Vassell said that afternoon as I walked briskly behind him into a small cottage, the second one from the entrance of a cluster of cottages.

I looked around; a small living area stood before me. Two burlap bags filled with straw sat in one corner, and an old wooden table in the other. I glanced up. Made of thick thatch woven in and out of rows of wood, the roof looked brand new. The floor, made from some kind of red clay, glistened under my feet. I followed Vassell into another room.

"You'll live here for the time being. An assistant overseer named Fleming lives in the other room. He's working the fields right now, but he knows you're here," Vassell said.

"Thank you."

"There's an outdoor toilet, bath pan, and coal stove outside that door. Make yourself comfortable, and come to the fields with Fleming in the morning at seven."

After Vassell walked out the door, I had a chance to really survey the place. My room had a straw bed on a wooden frame on one side. An old wooden box turned upside down next to it, served as a table. In another corner, twine stretched stiffly across the room, attached to two sides of wall. I could hang my clothes there. Under the clothes line stood another wooden box, open on top, for clothes. An old wooden chair sat close to the foot of the bed.

I eased my shoulders out of the straps of my jute bag, and continued looking around. Loneliness threatened to take over, but I shrugged it off and busied myself. I hung two shirts on the clothes line and packed the rest of my things in the old wooden box. This was much better than the mud cabin at home, and I was grateful.

Exhaustion took over, so I laid on the bed and closed my eyes. The room swayed from side to side, just like it did on the ship that brought me here. I must have dozed off, because next thing I heard was a knock at the door and a man's voice.

"Hello Bloke. You there?"

"Aye. Come in," I said, sitting up in bed, my feet on the floor, still wearing my shoes and socks.

"I'm Fleming," the man said as he walked in, his hand outstretched. I stood up and shook his hand.

"Sean O'Sullivan. Pleasure to meet you."

"An Irishman! What you doing here?"

"Long story. Let's just say I barely escaped starvation, the typhus, a hurricane, and pirates."

"Good God, Old Boy. Glad you made it. Here, I brought you dinner from the overseers' commissary." Fleming handed me a small jute bag with food.

"Thanks. You already ate dinner, then?"

"Yes. Vassell said you'd be here, so I packed you some food."

"I am hungry. Grab a seat." I pointed to the chair as I opened the bag of food and pulled out a sandwich, and a covered cup of liquid. I devoured the sandwich and washed it down with fresh fruit juice.

"What's the juice? It's delicious."

"Mango juice. The mangos on the island are sweet and delicious. Glad you like it."

My mind wandered to dark places. Brian should have been my roommate, but my best friend was gone. *Here I am sharing space with a Brit, working for Brits. They're everywhere. But I need to get along with them if I'm to survive here. Help me, dear Lord.*

"How long you been here?" I asked.

"About six months. I came here on the *Flying Flamborough* from Portsmouth, after my father threw me out of the house. Had nowhere to go, so I decided to start a new life for myself."

"How's it been so far?"

"Tough. The island is beautiful, but plantation life can be brutal. Don't think it's worse than where you came from, though."

I left that comment alone, not wanting the vein by my temple to start thumping.

"What about Vassell? What's it like to work for him?"

"Sometimes it's like Hell on earth. You have to keep your shoulders to the wheel and work your backside off. That's the only way to survive around here."

Fleming's voice took on a quiet tone as he responded to my last question, almost as if he feared someone might hear him. Guess I'd learn on my own.

Later that evening I fetched water from behind the commissary, cleaned myself up, and retired early.

The blast of a horn had me springing up in bed the next morning. A little disoriented, I cleaned myself up and got dressed. Fleming and I walked to a common area nearby. There were two lines of slave men and women, waiting for food. They ate quickly, some still standing, some sitting on the ground. Soon, they hurried to the fields.

Fleming and I walked to the commissary for breakfast. I had cornmeal porridge, a thick chunk of bread, and a cup of hot cocoa. Afterward, I headed to the fields next to my roommate.

Chapter 12

In the months that followed, Vassell directed Fleming to train me. The sun blazed down day after day, the heat, unforgiving. But mornings emerged beautifully, with cool breezes and tropical doves cooing melodiously to start their day. And I always started work on a full belly, which I saw as a blessing.

Fleming taught me to protect myself from both sun and slaves, how to communicate with the slaves, how to get them to work, and how to never, ever trust them. I listened and watched my tutor closely. I cringed as I witnessed one of those brutal lessons.

"Lazy nigger bitch. Pick up that bundle and throw it into the drum, now!" Fleming yelled, standing over a slave woman, brandishing his whip.

The woman seemed confused - she looked up, her eyes squinting against the sun. Three other slaves stood next to her, busily chopping cane. Sweat ran down their backs and under their arms, but they held their heads down and kept chopping.

"Yessa," the woman said, stooping to pick up the bundle. She groaned with pain; there was some kind of injury, but that didn't matter to Fleming.

The whip cracked and echoed as it crashed down on the slave woman's bare back. I watched it curl around to her gut. Blood spewed as it opened old wounds. And blood splattered on my light-blue shirt.

"You heard me. Pick up those bundles of cane and throw them into the molasses drum, right now."

"I tryin' sah."

"No back talk." Fleming whipped her again. The woman collapsed into the dirt.

"Get her up and back to work," Fleming yelled to the slave next to her. "Be quick!" The man scrambled to help the beaten woman, and they took the bundle to the drums together.

"You got to lash them to get things done?"

"You don't lash their backsides; things never get done."

"They that stupid?"

"They're not stupid. That's how they get by; they call it 'playing fool to catch wise.' They play slow and dumb so less is expected of them. You have to keep lashing them."

Sounds like they're pretty smart to me, just plain defiant, I thought.

"You're sure they're doing this on purpose?"

"I know they are, and you'd better get used to it. When they play around, I let the whip take care of their backsides. Got to keep them in line."

"Good to know." *Good ole Brits. They'll get what's coming to them one day.*

Fleming then said, "You don't brutalize them, they'll rise up and kill you. They could kill us all. It's strike, or be struck."

"What you mean?"

"You haven't heard about the Maroons? They've been attacking our plantations for years, with the help of runaway slaves."

"I did hear about them from a deck hand on the ship. How'd they end up living free in the hills?"

"Long story. Suffice it to say we had to sign a peace treaty with those beasts to keep them quiet. Now they think they can get away with anything."

Several months after training I got promoted to overseer at Havendale, but uncertainty continued to gnaw away at me. I must have done well as assistant overseer, because Vassell introduced me around, and whites in the area immediately welcomed me into their small group. It didn't matter here that I was Irish. All whites stuck together for survival.

But my thoughts took me to places of doubt and confusion. *Am I up for the job of overseer? Will I get used to whipping slaves for malarkey, like petty thievery and working too slowly; for anything Vassell thought was deserving of a beating? Can I whip another human being with as much viciousness as Vassell and his overseers?*

I know they're human beings. That blank look in their eyes when they're being whipped, it's belligerence. Or are they just resigned to the abuse?

They're obviously not stupid. Their brothers built free communities in the hills and have fought like panthers against the system. Oh, Brian, please help me understand all of this, I pleaded. *And Lord, help me to fulfill my purpose.*

But life was much better here than what I'd left behind. I ate well and made good money. *Fleming was right. Life on this beautiful island could be challenging and intimidating. Spring ebbed into summer and winter. The heat and mosquitoes were relentless.*

But I must survive and adjust. I must do this quickly so I can quietly save enough money, make a difference here for these suffering people, and help bring Ireland back to prosperity.

"Your ship docked in Jamaica years after the damned Maroons attacked us," Vassell said one morning as he and I sipped tea, in a meeting in the dining room at Havendale's great house.

The room boasted an ornate, oblong, wooden dining table with eight beautifully-tufted blue chairs, and walls painted a deep tan. The dried head of a crocodile hung over a matching cabinet filled with crockery; it stood in the left corner of the room.

"Aye, I heard that earlier. How were slaves able to escape to the hills and form free communities?"

"We were too busy fighting the Spaniards off and taking over the plantations to see what the heck was going on under our very noses."

Ah the Brits, always too greedy for their own good, I thought. But I kept my mouth shut.

"We brought hundreds of Africans here. I've often wondered if this was a good idea, but we don't really have a choice."

"Why wasn't it a good idea?"

"The Negroes have outnumbered us. The Maroons are dangerous; they could rise again and kill us all."

"Why don't we go after them, capture them and bring them back in chains?"

"Ha! We tried that, all right. But they've become vicious bush warriors. Most whites on the island are terrified of them. Didn't you hear? They used guerilla war tactics to kick the asses of the British army. We even brought Spanish slave hunters with their 'hounds from Hell,' from South America, to kill off the black bastards. But they kicked their backsides too. That's how they ended up with the peace treaty." Vassell paused, sighed, and then continued.

"To make things worse, many whites have been beaten down by mysterious tropical diseases like dengue fever and malaria. And there's more bad news; the damned slaves are furious because some of us brought diseases like syphilis with us, and have infected many of their women. They claim that we rape their women, or use them as sex slaves."

"Jesus! Is that true?" I asked, unable to hide my alarm.

"Yes. But how do you rape them if you own them?"

Good God. You own them, so forcefully bedding them wasn't rape? That was one heck of a concept. It was atrocious! I knew the Brits were cruel bastards, but were they sexually depraved too? I've often wondered how they got their needs met around here. I took a deep breath and stayed calm. I refocused on Vassell. He continued to talk.

"The Maroons are even bolder now that they have their peace treaties. Part of the treaties say they're to help us capture runaway slaves. But most of the times, they don't return those slaves. Damn them to Hell."

"I've seen horror in the eyes of overseers when they talk about the dreaded Maroons. Is there nothing we can do to get this under control?"

"More Negroes on the island than whites, remember? We can only control those on our plantations; and we have to be brutal to do that." Vassell stared into my eyes as if to make sure I clearly understood what he'd just said.

I kept the conversation going. "I've watched slaves who tried to 'pull foot and bolt,' like they call it, maimed and burned at the stake by overseers, as an example to others. Is all of that necessary? Can't we find other ways to punish them? Maybe if we treat them better, they won't try to escape."

"Other ways to punish them? You obviously don't know what you're dealing with. As dumb as they act, they're secretly vicious and will attack or flee if you give them the slightest opening. They cannot be trusted, and don't you ever forget that. It's either them or us. It's strike, or be struck. If we don't control them, they will destroy us all."

There's that 'strike, or be struck' saying again. Maybe if we Irish had been strong enough to put the fear of God in them, like the Maroons did, less of us would have starved to death. But we were too hungry and sick to fight back.

"Jesus! How did we get ourselves into this predicament?"

"We were stupid and greedy, that's how. We had to bring the biggest and strongest Negroes here from West Africa, because we thought we could get more work out of them. Some of them had already hunted, killed, and captured whole villages where they came from. I don't know why the Hell we thought we could control them here."

"So, you're saying brutality is the only way for whites to survive on the plantations?"

"Yes, and if you're some weakling, you'll get us all killed. You cannot be weak and an overseer; the two don't go together. The time is coming when you'll be tested. If you fail, you're better off boarding that ship, returning to Ireland, and starving to death. If you succeed, there's lots of money to be made, and a good life to be had here. But it won't come easy. You'll have to hold your nose and do what it takes. It's survival of the fittest."

I did not sleep that night. I laid in bed, my mind frantically wandering to dark places. *How do I survive here without turning into a cruel, greedy Brit? Was Vassell right that it's either strike, or be struck? Will I be able to strike in the ways he wants me to?*

Oh Brian, please show me a sign. But Brian stayed quiet; I did not feel his presence. I no longer imagined hearing his voice.

Vassell soon began to show me his strength. He performed several lashings in front of me, and I laid in bed at night trying to justify those actions. If I didn't do what he did, I would be out of a job, for sure. And no one would hire me as overseer if I refused to perform slave punishment. So Vassell may have been right. It was act like a cruel Brit, or be out of a job. How would I survive this?

Soon, I watched Vassell perform one of the most brutal slave punishments at Havendale. One of Vassell's house slaves, Marva, had been caught leaking information to one of the Maroons, who secretly came to the plantation at night. After she was discovered, a trusted overseer had caught Marva trying to escape through the woods behind Havendale.

"Shackle her!" Vassell yelled. I stared at Marva's face. The slave's eyes welled up, but she looked resolute and fully aware of the horrible fate that awaited her. I saw no fear on Marva's face. Instead, I saw pride and defiance.

These people refuse to cower or wring their hands. They defy you, and then they take their punishment like brutes. Their women are the same. They are human beings, all right, and they're strong and ferocious. What would the Brits have done to us Irish if we were able to stand up to them like this?

Rage seeped out of Vassell's pores. "Take this as a lesson if you plan to survive in this treacherous place," he said, turning to me.

"I'm about to exercise real brute force now. They're all liars, cheats and animals who can never be trusted. I will stretch her at the wheel, then I'll chop her head off and hang it in the town square for all to see. Bring me the wheel." He spun around to overseer Ian, who stood behind him. "Bring me the damned wheel."

"Why not just give her a good lashing?" I asked, nausea beginning to gnaw at my gut.

"Because she was a trusted house slave. She knows many of my secrets, personal and business. To have that leaked to the Maroons cannot be taken lightly. It could cost me my life; it could cost you your own life."

Soon, I heard a clang as overseer, Ian, stood the contraption called the wheel in front of Vassell. He stared me dead in the eyes and screamed, "Bring that betraying bitch to me!" The overseer grabbed Marva and dragged her to him. Vassell ripped the slave woman's frock from her body and threw it to the ground.

As he was about to lay her on the wheel, she arched her head like a snake and spat into his face. "Aaah! Backstabbing bitch," he yelled, lifting the hem of his shirt and quickly wiping his face.

Vassell secured Marva's neck and arms to the wheel himself. Overseer Ian did the same with her feet. *My God, this is like when they nailed Jesus to the cross,* I thought, my gut in a knot. I saw Marva's eyes slam shut as Vassell grabbed the handle of the wheel and turned it. I heard bones crack. I cringed.

Marva barely moaned, as tears flowed down her cheeks. Slave women forced to watch the slaughter held each other and bawled. Slave men just stood there, motionless, jaws clenched, silently gritting their teeth. Vassell turned the wheel one more time. Now, not only did I hear bones cracking, I saw the woman's hip bones move down the side of her gut.

I looked at the slave woman's head, collapsed to one side, her mouth half-open. Consciousness had left her. Vassell turned the wheel one more time. I stared at him, my heart filled with disgust. I swear, he looked like he had suddenly grown fangs.

Unable to bear anymore, I lowered my head. This cruelty had become a canker; it needed to be stopped. Trepidation began to eat me alive. The past stood in front of me, like an infected sore. Anger and detestation unfurled like that of a charging bull after someone had flung the gates of the ring open. I retched. That sickening feeling washed over me; the one that overcame me when I killed the pirate. But if I didn't kill him, he'd have killed me, just like he'd killed Brian. But, oh, Jesus in Heaven, this was wrong.

"Chop her head off!" Vassell screamed, jolting me out of one misery and flinging me into another. Torment swept over my very soul. I slammed my eyes and fists shut. I heard bizarre sounds as they moved Marva's body from the wheel. Then I heard an axe doing its work.

"Hang the bitch's head in the town square. Throw her body in the bushes for the crows to devour," Vassell yelled.

I did not walk into the town square next to Vassell, Marva's head on a large platter perched on his right shoulder for all to see. But overseer Ian did, and later described the debacle to me. I'd refused to go to the town square to see Marva's hanging head. I was sickened by the thought of watching Vassell toss her brutalized body into the bushes 'for the crows to devour.'

Confused thoughts haunted me once more. *Should I sell my soul, stay here, make tons of money, or pack up and go back to starvation-ridden Ireland? Sweet Jesus, did I sell my soul to the Devil when I killed the damned pirate? There had to be another option. Please tell me there was another option.*

And, like a miracle, I thought I heard the Lord's voice say, 'yes, there is another option. Like your friend, Brian, once said, "Your purpose, remember?" You'll stay here and silently help remove slaves from the brutality you just witnessed. Start making a plan, man!

Chapter 13

At dusk one Wednesday, I walked into the compound at Havendale, where all the slave huts stood. I stared ahead, perplexed. There stood this man, surrounded by three slave men, a package in one hand and another under his arm. He wore burlap from waist to just below the knees and his feet spread bare. He had very short hair; no whip marks wailed his back.

The other men wore tattered slave clothing, old pants that hung halfway down their calves, some with frayed hems, ragged old shirts that were almost threadbare, and they all stood bare-footed. Their backs bore scars from the whip.

Sounds of children caught my attention. I glanced to my left and saw three slave children prancing around and giggling. Focusing my attention back to the men, I listened as they talked aggressively in Jamaican patois, which none of us whites understood. They seemed to be bartering. The slave men soon exchanged packages with the man in burlap.

I walked up to them. The three slave men lowered their heads and walked away. But the man in burlap just stood there, unmoving.

He stared me in the eyes. He did not blink. Searching his eyes for clues about his thoughts, I came up with nothing. This man stood and stared like he saw me as an equal, or, if anyone was less of a man, it would have been me. In my time on the island, no slave man or woman had looked me in the eye.

"Who are you?" I asked.

"Bene Olumbo," he replied, his head held high, his stare unwavering.

"Why are you here?"

"To trade boar meat for cloth and salt."

"Where did you come from?"

"New Nanny Town."

"What's New Nanny Town?"

"My Maroon village."

"You're a Maroon?"

"Yes."

"Why are you here to trade meat?"

"Maroons been tradin' meat for dry goods with plantation slaves for years."

"They say you're free. Why not buy your goods in a local market?"

"We do dat sometimes."

"You're not afraid to be seen around here?"

"No. Maroons not 'fraid of anything." He continued to hold me in a dead stare. I believed him.

"You don' talk like Brit. Who you? Where you come from?" he asked.

"I'm overseer Sean O'Sullivan. I'm from Ireland."

"Ire ... land? Where that?"

"It's an island off the coast of England, where the Brits came from."

"Brits bring you here?"

"No. I came on my own."

"Why?"

"To escape starvation."

"Who starve you?"

"The Brits."

"So, you come here to help them starve my people?"

"Not really. Long story," I said. He turned to walk away.

"You come back again?" I asked. He turned and stared at me, disbelief in his eyes. He spun around and disappeared into the shadows. Afterall, I was the enemy. I was a white man.

But fascination overcame me. I'd heard so much about the Maroons and their vicious fight for freedom. Brits spoke about them with dread, about how they fought like bush warriors from Hell, how they'd slashed and burned the plantations for 85 years, and would not stop until the Brits offered them a peace treaty ... and on and on.

Maybe I could partner with this Maroon and fulfill my purpose, to help remove slaves from the whip of the planters; to help them get their freedom. How I wished we Irish had half the strength of the Maroons.

Smart and brave, they took advantage and bolted to the hills when the Brits stayed busy fighting off the Spaniards to take over the sugar trade. It was then, that they became known as Maroons. And they fought like lions to get and maintain their freedom.

Stories about how they tore the British army to shreds got told by whites around the island, with dread. Whites described them as uneducated yet shrewd, brutal, and afraid of nothing, including the white man.

How did slaves, who were constantly beaten, maimed, and worked almost to death's door, gather the strength to escape, build free communities, kill their hunters, and hunt down their abusers? What kind of mind-set made these people fight to the very end? Awe began to play with my senses when I thought about the Maroons.

That Friday night after I'd met the Maroon, Vassell hosted a dinner party at his great house. He invited all overseers and four local plantation owners, and their overseers. Two cooks from plantations next door prepared food.

It was a feast to remember, with rum and wine, and a five-course meal of steamed vegetables, soups, fresh breads, curried goat, beef pies, stewed boars' meat, potatoes, yams, and desserts with plums and pineapples, creams, flaky dough, and honey.

Conversations about the dreaded Maroons, and British and local politics, filled the air. I wished I could have slammed them about the cruelty that had my Irish brothers and sisters starving to death, but, as usual, I kept my mouth shut. I stood outnumbered. This territory belonged to them.

But I will find a way to quietly avenge African Jamaicans before I return to Ireland. That's my purpose here. That's the other option I prayed for. I couldn't save my fellow Irishmen, but I could help free African Jamaicans from the scourge of slavery. Brian used to say I was too intense, but I've always needed a purpose. There had to be a reason God put me on this island.

An Irish accent pulled me out of my thoughts. I couldn't believe it. Looking to my right, I saw a tall, brown-haired man talking with two Brits. I walked over to them.

"Hello, allow me to introduce myself. I'm Sean O'Sullivan. I work here."

"You're Irish too! Howya doin,' Laddie? I'm Gavin Ryan from Toco Plantation. Pleasure to meet you," the Irishman said, shaking my hand with gusto.

"And I'm Derek Shaw and this is Ian Martin. We're from Coco Plum Plantation too," the Brit standing next to Gavin Ryan said.

"Aye, good to meet you all. Gavin, where'd you come here from?" I asked, focusing on the Irishman. I'd never been so excited to meet a man in my entire life.

Another guest approached and took Shaw and Martin away with a conversation about the Maroons. Now, just me and Gavin Ryan continued talking.

"From Ballingarry, South Tipperary. Parents and sister starved to death. You?"

"Bandon, County Cork. Mother died from the fever. Thought about joining the Young Ireland group, but ended up here."

"Good choice. You hear what happened to that group?"

"No."

"They rebelled, hoping to finally take control of Dublin. Rebellion took place near my town. Articles appeared in the Nation, urging us to build barricades around the city, and giving instructions on what we should do to make an insurrection successful."

"You were still there? Did you take part? What the heck happened?"

"I was in Ireland during the rebellion. The group was not very organized. To make things worse, the Brits had disarmed us all several months earlier, because they were afraid that we'd rebel. I laid low, hoping for peace. But there was none."

"What finally happened? Tell me."

"Turnout was lower than expected. Villagers who showed up were ready to fight, but they were badly armed. They had no military training; only had stones and pikes. By this time, ten thousand British troops had already been sent to Ireland."

"Sweet Jesus."

"Villagers were chased to a cabbage patch and surrounded by police and soldiers. They were easily defeated."

"Was anyone killed?"

"Not really. The Young Ireland leader, O'Brien, who led the rebellion, quickly called an end to the confrontation."

"I won't even ask what happened to him."

"Sent to exile in Australia. So were many of the other Young Ireland members."

"That's why I didn't join that group. After surviving starvation and the typhus, I'd be damned if I was going to end up in prison in Australia."

"Me too. No way was I going to give the Brits that kind of satisfaction."

"Sad. Look at the way the Maroons fought here for their freedom. Why couldn't we have done that to save ourselves and our people?"

"Sean, those of us who survived were too hungry and downtrodden to win any rebellion. The Brits would have killed us all."

"Aye. Let's get together soon, Gavin. I could use a friend."

"Me too. When's a good time to visit?"

"I'm off on Sundays. How 'bout this Sunday afternoon."

"Perfect. See you then."

Chapter 14

That Sunday, Gavin and I got together and strolled the grounds of Havendale. The stunning afternoon had sun peeking out from behind puffs of white clouds, against a back-drop of pale-blue skies.

Aromas of thyme, scallions, and curry wafted through the air as slaves, on their one day of rest, cooked whatever they got their hands on, be it small pieces of cured fish or chicken back and neck.

Gavin and I sat on two rocks under a huge lignum vitae tree close to my quarters. We talked for hours about the tragedy in Ireland. I talked painfully about the attack on my best friend and my slaying of the pirate.

At one stage, we both fought back tears as we reminisced about the lives we'd left behind. We had come together as Irishmen, grieving our losses and trying to find solace in a country we still struggled to get to know. When I finally pulled myself back together, I said.

"I've come to a decision, Gavin."

"What's that?"

"See how brutal the Brits are to the slaves? They treat them like animals."

"Yah, they claim it's the only way to survive around here."

"Don't you see? They need the slaves to work the cane fields. So, they feed them just enough to keep them going. They'd starve them to death if they didn't need them, just like they did our families in Ireland."

"Probably right. Where you going with this?"

"After coming here to escape the horrors of Ireland, I feel the need to help slaves escape the brutality of plantation life."

"Mmm. How you plan to do that?"

"Don't know yet. But can't you see? You and I were brought here for a bigger purpose. Neither of us want to become a cruel Brit, beating and maiming slaves. If the Maroons were able to fight like panthers for their freedom, I have a feeling the time will come when other slaves will do the same. Maybe we could help them get freedom and justice. God knows, we were not able to do that for our own people."

"Damned right, Laddie. I, myself, been wondering what the heck I'm doing here. This could give me purpose. It could give us both purpose. Let's talk about this more and come up with a plan. But it must be a real strong plan, or we could get ourselves killed."

"Aye. We survived Ireland. We can survive here."

Gavin listened, staring out into the distance before responding.

"All those nights I laid in bed, beating up on myself for abandoning Ireland, for not fighting harder to help our people. You're right, Sean. Maybe God had a reason for sending us here."

I knew, there and then, that he was my kind of Irishman; he was kind, fair, and socially conscious, always wanting to do the right thing. He reminded me of Brian.

Thank you, Jesus, for giving me another friend. We've both been to Hell and back. But we'll make it here. We'll help the slaves get their freedom; I can feel it. And Brian, rest in peace, my friend and brother. I plan to make you proud.

"I can feel change in the air, Gavin."

"Yah? What you mean?"

"After Vassell brutally murdered the slave, Marva, I sensed nothing but anger and unrest among the field slaves. I get the feeling they're just waiting for a chance to wreak havoc."

"You're probably right. I wouldn't blame them one bit."

"Let's work hard but keep our heads down and listen to the slaves. They already know we're different from the Brits. We could probably earn their trust."

The next Saturday afternoon, Vassell sent a house slave to the fields to get me. I walked with her to the great house, and Vassell asked that I go to the market to buy boars' meat, seasoning, and provisions.

"Here's three shillings," he said, handing me the money. "Usually, I go myself, but I need to stick around today. Slaves acting up. Take my horse cart."

Heading out the gates of Havendale in Vassell's cart, I remembered that Toco Plantation was along the way. I decided to stop there and pick up Gavin.

A few minutes later I drove through the gates of Toco. As I approached the entrance to the cane field, I asked for Gavin. An overseer told me to wait, before rushing off to get him.

"You off your shift soon? Going to the market. Want to come along for the ride?" I asked, as Gavin approached.

"Love to, Laddie. I'll be off shift in ten minutes. Can you wait?"

"Aye. I'll wait here."

Fifteen minutes later Gavin and I headed to the market, chatting away about our day. After arriving at our destination, I jumped down from the cart and tied the reins to a tree at the side of the road. Gavin and I walked into the market.

I stared around; the scenes were startling. Never before had I seen so many African Jamaicans, and they weren't working the fields.

There were women of all sizes, dressed in big cotton frocks, most of them with colorful scarves tied around their heads. Some women had braids sticking out on the sides of their heads or hanging down their foreheads.

Most of the men were bare-footed, wearing short-sleeved cotton shirts and knee shorts, or old pants that hung mid-calf. They chatted away in patois, laughed, and gestured with their hands as beads of sweat gathered on their foreheads.

The cacophony of smells, sights, and sounds aroused my senses. I smelled fresh fish and meat; I smelled curry, cumin, and other exotic seasonings. The crisp odors of onions, thyme, and garlic had me sneezing. It was a magical taste of local life I'd never experienced before.

Gavin and I walked slowly around and I took in more of the scenery. Mangos, yellow and orange and lusciously ripe, were piled into heaps everywhere. Breadfruit, and other tropical provisions I didn't recognize, were displayed on make-shift wooden tables, partially covered with old crocus bags or raggedy burlap.

Tables with mounds of yams, potatoes, cassavas and other provisions that looked like they had just been pulled from the ground, stood all around. I breathed in, smelling yams and the pungent tropical earth.

Raggedy old tables packed to the hilt with small bags and pans of seasonings, stood in front of me. Two men raised machetes and chopped away at big slabs of meat on tables ahead, chatting and guffawing. Skinned carcasses of wild boar and fowls hung from ropes and wires overhead.

Women bartered with black and white buyers, after boisterously asking them to stop by and look at their goods. I glanced next to me and saw Gavin staring, his mouth open.

"Yam, Massa?" A large woman asked, jolting me out of my reverie. She wore an old blue frock with a light grey scarf wrapped around her head.

"How much?"

"'Tuppence' a pound. Real good an' fresh."

"Give me four pounds."

I did no bartering. The way I saw it, these people worked like mules in or outside of the cane fields, and the food was really cheap. They deserved every 'tuppence' they could get their hands on.

I was about to finish shopping when I felt someone's eyes on me. I glanced around — no one. Then I stared ahead and saw Bene Olumbo, the Maroon I'd met at Havendale.

"Why's that man staring at us?" Gavin asked, catching sight of Olumbo.

"Let's go talk with him," I said, moving in Olumbo's direction.

"Why? You know him?" Gavin followed closely behind me.

"Met him at Havendale one evening."

"Who is he?"

"A Maroon."

"You know a Maroon?"

"Not yet, but I'm about to."

"Bene Olumbo, meet my friend, Gavin," I said, stopping in front of the Maroon and lifting my eyes up to meet his.

"He ... hello there," Gavin said.

"You Ireland man too?" Olumbo asked.

"I'm an Irishman, too."

"Ah, Irishman, that what you call yourselves. You run from starvation too?"

"Yes, lost my whole family to it."

"Brits, they real cruel. Thought they only starve black people. You here to help them starve our brothers in cane field?"

"No, I'm here to help your brothers when I can," Gavin said. I was surprised. He must have given deep thought to our conversation earlier. Either that, or he was too scared to say anything else.

"Where did all these free African Jamaicans come from?" I asked.

"From all ova' the island, to sell goods," Olumbo said.

"I mean, how come so many of them are free to sell goods in the market?"

"Some'a them born here of parents from Sierra Leone in West Africa."

"Sierra Leone? Why there?" Gavin asked.

"Ah, Irishman. You don' know that the Brits tried to send us back to Africa?" Olumbo said.

"What ... what you mean?" I asked.

"One day I tell you all 'bout it. But I must go now. Family waitin.' You lookin' for boar meat?"

"Yes," I replied.

"Buy it from Ibu over there. He Maroon hunter. Sell best meat."

"Next time you're at Havendale, ask a slave to come get me. I'll make sure you get whatever goods you need," I said. Olumbo stared

92

at me like I had two heads, then he took off into crowds of buyers and hagglers.

"See that look? They do not trust a single white man."

"Can't say I blame them."

Gavin and I had a lot to talk about on our ride back to the plantations. After we opined about what better shape the Irish would have been in, had they chosen to grow more than just potatoes, the conversation changed to Olumbo and the Maroons.

"I need to be around when Olumbo tells you about Sierra Leone," Gavin said. "Have a feeling that will be one heck of a story. What's it all about?"

"Don' know, but I'm going to find out."

"Looks like the Brits tried to get rid of them, just like they did us."

"They got rid of us because they wanted less of us to feed. They tried to get rid of Africans because they were scared shitless."

"Yeah, after the Maroons kicked their backsides, they probably figured the less blacks around, the better. But blacks continue to be in the majority here."

"Fascinating! Can't wait to get more information on that Sierra Leone story," I said, as I pulled the horse cart through the gates of Toco Plantation and let Gavin off. I turned the cart around, jerked the reins and yelled 'Yaa,' sending the mule into a brisk gallop toward Havendale, my head filled with more questions than answers.

Chapter 15

"Please, Mas Sean. I can talk to you?" The slave woman pleaded as she walked up to me and stared into my eyes. Something must have been terribly wrong; slaves never looked white men in the eyes. I was close to my quarters. She must have followed me there.

"Yes, of course. You're Zoya, right?"

"Yes, sah."

"What's wrong?"

"House slave Zane is my cousin, sah. This mornin' she hear Massa Vassell say he goin' to sell my son at slave trader' market."

"You have a son? How old is he?"

"He five. He all me have."

"Why the massa want to sell him?"

"Massa sell slave chile all the time, when he want to buy older slave to do field work. Please sah, I beggin' you to help me."

"How can I help?"

"Zane hear the massa say he goin' to send you, me, my son Uma, and the obeah woman, Miz Ada, in cart to meet him at slave trader' market. He love to see mother and anyone close to her, beggin' and moaning as he sell child."

"Dear God!" That was all I could muster when I listened to this other level of cruelty.

"I kill myself if they take my son, sah. Nothin' else to live for."

"You must tell me how I can help."

"I send message to Uma father. He meet us at foothill leadin' to Maroon village."

"Why there?"

"He Maroon, sah."

"You have a son for a Maroon?"

"Yes, sah. Uma father is Bene Olumbo."

I paused, and then I pulled myself back together. This revelation was astonishing. Zoya must have noticed, because she spoke once more.

"Some'a us have children with Maroons, sah. They here at night a lot, tradin' goods. Please, Mas Sean. You a good white man. If they sell my son, I never see him again."

She was almost on her knees now, sobbing. I looked out into the distance, trying to get some perspective. She continued talking.

"Massa don' know who Uma father is. Those of us with Maroon children keep it real quiet. If massa and overseer know, they beat us read bad."

"All right; I'll help. No one must know, though. You hear me?"

I had a small cabin to myself now that I was no longer an assistant overseer. So, I wasn't concerned that someone could hear me from inside.

"No, sah. Ah promise, no one will ever know."

I wasn't in my quarters for long that evening when one of Vassell's house slaves knocked on the door.

"Is Jafari, sah. Massa Vassell send for you," he yelled.

"Tell him I'll be right there." I put my work boots back on and headed out the door.

Walking toward the great house, I stared at the lush, tropical landscape around me, highlighted by a brilliant full moon that just began to shine its beams on everything below.

Beauty and cruelty; they just didn't go together. But I forced myself to link them in this place; like wrapping a barb wire fence around a stunning estate. After talking with Gavin, I'd become more convinced I was sent here to help stop the cruelty.

The great house soon came into view. This time, I dreaded the mere sight of it. I gathered all the courage I could muster and walked up to the verandah. Before I got to the top of the steps, Vassell's voice resounded in the balmy evening air.

"Ah, Sean. Just the man I want to see. Grab a seat over there. Want a drink?"

"No drinks tonight, thank you."

"I need one. Be right back," he said, walking back through the front door.

Vassell returned with his drink in hand and sat on the verandah chair in front of me. He took a long sip and looked past me.

"Hard to get labor these days, need more workers in the fields. You're a man who reads the papers. Britain has just made it illegal for us to bring Africans into the island. Those idiots have stopped the slave trade in its tracks," he said.

"I didn't know that. When did this happen?"

"Word came to our local government yesterday."

"Did they abolish slavery?"

"No. They just stopped us from bringing slaves in from Africa." He paused, then he continued.

"I'm going to have to sell a few slave children, and buy men from across the island, who can work the fields." He stared at me. I did not respond; I kept a straight face.

Sweet Jesus, Zoya was right; he's going to sell her child. But, bigger question; if Britain just stopped the slave trade from Africa, were they getting ready to abolish slavery all together?

"Tomorrow morning, I need you to meet me at the slave traders' market with the slave Zoya and her son. Take the obeah woman Ada with you. Those two are friends. I need to teach her a lesson too."

I continued to keep a straight face. Finally, I was able to comment.

"Which one of the slave markets, the one in town or the one close to the dock?"

"The one in town. Take the two-mule cart. Make sure you shackle the two women's feet to the cart. Leave their hands free to hold the child."

"What time should I meet you there?"

"Nine thirty in the morning."

I bade him goodbye and left him sitting comfortably on his lovely verandah, sipping his drink. *Cruel bastard!*

I barely got to the door of my quarters when Zoya's voice came from behind a clump of bushes, making me jump.

"What time we leave tomorrow morning, sah?"

"At nine. Let Miz Ada and the child's father know," I said.

I kept walking, opened the door to my quarters, walked in and locked the door behind me. I was grateful to be alone. I needed time to process all of this. Then I'd try hard to get a decent night's sleep.

I put the horses in a steady gallop the next morning, Zoya and Miz Ada behind me, their feet shackled to the cart. Zoya held her son tightly as we exited the gates of Havendale.

Another cool morning wrapped itself around me, the sun bursting through puffs of white clouds in the distance and taunting me. Beauty and cruelty, together again.

"Where we goin', Mama?" I heard Zoya's son ask.

"We jus' goin' for a little ride, Son," his mother answered.

I cracked the whip and the horses moved to a spirited trot as we headed toward town.

We'd been traveling for a few minutes, when I pulled the reins and slowed the horses down. We approached the foothills of the mountains at the bottom of the Maroon village.

Suddenly, Olumbo stepped out from behind the bushes. He was on Zoya's side of the cart. I'd made sure of that when I shackled her. I slowed the cart down more, as we approached.

Olumbo grabbed his son and disappeared into the forest. I cracked the whip and we galloped ahead to the slave trader's market. Zoya sobbed behind me. She soon went quiet, but not for long.

I heard the women shuffling and glanced around. They looked like they'd been in a fight for their lives. They had tousled their hair, and their clothes looked disheveled and slightly torn.

Several minutes later, I pulled the cart up to the slave traders' market. Vassell hurried out to meet us, and looked from me to the women, questioningly. Zoya sobbed really loud, now.

"Where's the boy?" He asked.

"We were attacked by Maroons. They snatched the child and vanished into the forest. I tried to go after them, but they were gone," I said.

"You can't catch no Maroon. When, in God's name, did they start snatching children?" Vassell yelled.

Zoya sobbed even louder, "My baby ... they take my baby."

"Shut that bitch up and get back to Havendale. I'll have to sell another child. Next time we'll travel to the market with guns cocked."

I drove back to Havendale in silence. Not a word was uttered by the two women in the back of the cart. As we got close to the plantation, I slowed the cart down and glanced back. The women sat there with blank stares.

After we entered the gates, I unshackled their feet. Zoya walked to the fields in a daze. Miz Ada headed to her hut. Obeah women didn't work the fields; they cured the sick and sometimes they predicted the future.

I took the cart up to the great house's verandah and tied the reins to a tree. That day in the fields also had me stunned and off balanced, but I forced myself to get through it.

It took a while for me to fall asleep that night. Although I'd experienced far worse in my country, I, too, felt traumatized.

But I couldn't let this place of beauty and cruelty get to me. I needed to stay strong. And now, the need to help African Jamaicans fight for their freedom had grown stronger in my gut.

Vassell said Britain was no longer allowing planters to bring slaves here from Africa. I will quietly work to help make the abolition of slavery their next step. Not sure how I'd do that, but there had to be a way, and I planned to find it.

African Jamaicans have been treated like animals; enough is enough.

Chapter 16

"Toco Plantation's owner has invited us all to an event there this Saturday afternoon. It's a chance to break bread and discuss issues. Coco Plum's owner and overseers will be there too," Vassell said. Friday evening had come, and overseers had gathered at the great house to collect their pay.

The next afternoon, I arrived at Toco Plantation with overseers Jack Turner and John Billingsworth. We rode in Vassell's large cart, pulled by two mules and guided along by an old slave man. We'd been following closely behind Vassell's cart, driven by a young slave man. We cantered through the front gate of Toco.

The great house stood huge, with a veranda that wrapped around the three sides of the house I was able to see. Orange, yellow and green crotons bordered both sides of the entryway. The front verandah boasted polished, wooden lounge chairs with green cushions. Two huge, dark brown, iron horses stood at each side of the steps to the verandah. It was quite a sight.

Two young slave women greeted us as we approached the steps to the verandah. They led us up the steps and around the right, to a side entrance of the backyard.

There were tables and chairs set up on the well-manicured back lawn, facing a line of tables being prepared with platters of food, by three young slave women. One table had already been set up with cups, glasses, pots of tea, carafes of cold beverages, and bottles of rum.

Opulence amidst cruelty and suffering, I thought, as my mind flashed back to the land owners' meeting in Ireland when the Brits said it was our fault we were starving to death.

Keep yourself together, Sean. Don't let bad memories pull you down.

"Please take a seat, sah," a young slave woman said, jolting me out of my thoughts.

"Thank you. Know where I can find overseer Gavin Ryan?"

"Yes, sah. Want me to sit him wit' you?"

"Yes, please; that possible?"

"Yes, sah," the girl said, before walking away.

Minutes later she returned with Gavin by her side. Before I could rise, he plopped down on the chair next to me and happily shook my hand.

"Good to see you, Laddie," he said.

"Good to see you too." I lowered my voice. "Know what this is all about?"

"Massa really nervous about the state of affairs here because of changes happening in Britain. This should be a very interesting meeting," he said, referring to his boss like a slave would.

Two other overseers introduced themselves and joined us at the table. Looking around, I saw that most tables had already filled up. Soon, one overseer began to talk.

"Welcome to you all. I'm overseer James from Toco Plantation. Please help yourselves to drinks before we get started." He pointed to the drink table.

Men rose and headed to the table. Gavin and I joined them. I noticed a head table where another man and Vassell sat huddled together, talking quietly. I assumed the other man was the owner of Coco Plum plantation.

Pouring myself rum with a dash of pineapple juice, I walked back to the table behind Gavin, and sat down.

A man and woman strolled up to the head table and sat on the other side of Vassell. A well-dressed woman also arrived and sat next to the man huddled next to Vassell. Gavin and I made small talk and sipped our drinks for several minutes. Things got started.

"Welcome, friends and neighbors. It's a pleasure to see you. I'm Ian Chambers, owner of Toco Plantation, and sitting next to me is my wife, Mary. To my left is Clinton Vassell, owner of Havendale

Plantation and Basil Walker, owner of Coco Plum Plantation, and his wife, Sybil. We're here to break bread, and discuss important matters about our current state of affairs. I invite you all to help yourselves to the spread in front of you, and afterward, we'll get started with our discussions."

Gavin and I helped ourselves to food and more drinks. We ate and exchanged small-talk with the others at the table.

Glancing around at one of Jamaica's stunning afternoons, I watched the sun slip slowly into the horizon behind puffs of white and light gray clouds. Orange and yellow rays lit up the skies to the west, and a nice cool breeze kept things comfortable. No mosquitos buzzed by my ears this evening.

About forty minutes later, dishes clanked and silverware tinkled as the tables were cleared and we got invited to help ourselves to another drink before things got started. I settled back into my chair with another rum and pineapple juice, and waited. I didn't wait for long.

Chambers said, "Gentlemen ... and ladies, I called you here to discuss the current state of affairs in Britain and how it's affecting us in Jamaica. Those of you who read the local newspapers know that our dear homeland is now going through an industrial revolution. Poor Brits are working in factories to make a living, and there are disturbing reports about child labor. According to reports, the working class has started to rebel over working conditions at the factories."

"We've all read the reports. How does all that affect us here?" One overseer behind me asked.

Walker said, "Oh, it affects us all right. The British working classes are now comparing themselves to slaves in the West Indies. This is making the government really nervous."

"Why are they so nervous?" another overseer asked.

"Think about it, man. If working class Brits start rebelling, it'll encourage the slaves around us to rebel, too. Have you forgotten stories we've all heard about the Maroons kicking the backsides of our army? We had to sign peace treaties with those beasts to stop them from destroying us all, and our plantations."

"Yes, but that was years ago. If slaves were going to rebel, wouldn't they have done this sometime ago?" Another overseer asked.

"There's been slave unrest in the past, and we were able to get things under control. But don't forget that many of the slaves can now read; they're much smarter ..." Chambers said.

"Yeah, thanks to the damned Baptist priests who are all over the island, preaching, 'the time has come for all men to be free.' Since they landed here years ago, they've been haranguing about the injustices of slavery and how it goes against God's wishes," Vassell said. "They're the ones teaching the slaves to read."

"We should not have let them into the country. But it's too late, now. That first black preacher who came here from America appealed to England, and next thing we knew, white Baptist preachers were swarming in," Walker said.

Chambers said, "There are so many of them around now, I could puke."

"And the blasted revolutionary hymns they sing in their churches. I'll never forget the day I sneaked up on a group of slaves in the fields, and heard them singing 'we will be slaves no more, since Christ has made us free.' They were singing while they worked, and I lashed their behinds to make them stop."

"Britain should never have stopped the slave trade," an overseer to my left yelled.

"Yeah, ever since they did that, the damned slaves think they actually abolished slavery. All Britain did was stop us from bringing more Negroes in from Africa," another overseer yelled.

"Don't even mention abolishing slavery. Can you imagine those beasts being free to roam the streets? They're our property; they wouldn't know what to do with themselves. Either that, or they'd kill us all," Chambers said.

This was familiar, same accent and attitude, different place. My mind did another flashback to that landowners' meeting in the old country. Instead of helping the starving, I had to listen to 'no one told them to breed like rabbits. We can't be responsible for feeding them.' *Good God, the more things change, the more they remain the same.*

"Good for us to vent, but what we going to do about things. With the industrial revolution now raging in England, we're being pushed aside," Vassell said.

"And with other islands in the sugar business these days, there's less business for us," an overseer to my right yelled.

"We may all soon have to start growing bananas," another overseer said.

Vassell said, "Let's focus on safety. Keep your ears peeled to any sign of insurrection. Share this information so we're prepared and can help each other out. If things get really bad, the governor says there's a contingent of marines at Port Royal, that can be transported here quickly on the *HMS Sparrowhawk.*"

Sighs of relief echoed around me. A few more minutes of venting took place, till the meeting finally came to an end.

In the minutes that followed, tables were cleared and the group milled around, chatting away and taking their last sips of drinks. Darkness began to wrap around us, and a cool breeze blew wisps of hair over my forehead. I heard the crickets beginning to hum their happy nighttime tune. Gavin and I huddled in a corner.

"They're running scared, Sean."

"I know. After the way Vassell brutalized one of his slave women, he needs to be scared. But you and me, we're going to be all right."

"You seem sure of that. How come?"

"Slaves are no fools. They know we're different. Besides, I've built relationships with many of them. I get them to work hard by using subtle kindness, no brutality. I'm about to build a bridge with some of the Maroons too. Vassell and Chambers may have to run for their lives and leave us behind. We have nowhere to run to right now, so we must survive here. I know we can do it. And besides, don't forget our plan to help with the fight for freedom. Let's get together and come up with a strategy."

Gavin slowly nodded and stared off into the distance. He was on board; I just knew it.

Chapter 17

"The dressmaker is Miz Muncie, sah. Wan' me to take you to her?" Zoya asked.

"Would you? I need some cloth. Think she'll sell me a few yards?"

"Yes, sah. Come with me."

We walked along a path to the dressmaker's hut. Mango and plum trees lined the path, loaded with ripe fruit. Jamaica had some of the richest volcanic soil on this earth. The fruit was the sweetest I'd tasted, and there was an abundance of it.

But the slaves could not eat any fruit from the trees. They ate basic foods, like bean stew, just enough to keep them working the fields, not a spoonful more.

I glanced up as I walked along. The end of the work day had come, and the sun hid itself behind dark, gray clouds. Looked like this night might be a rainy one. Zoya picked up her pace. I kept up with her.

"Thank you, Mas Sean, for sendin' food to our huts in the evenins' when you can. Sometimes we real hungry, and we get to cookin' right after the food reach us," Zoya said.

"No worries. After burying my mother in Ireland, I'm not about to starve anyone around here."

I tried to limit as much cruelty around me as possible. *I wasn't able to free my people in the old country, but I'll be damned if I'm going to stand by and watch these people suffer.*

"You a kind man, sah. We not use to no kind white man 'round here. Why your mama die?"

"We Irish only grew and ate potatoes. When the potato famine hit, we had nothing else to eat."

"No other food in Ireland, like corn ... grain?"

"There were."

"Why you not eat them?"

"Had no money to buy them. They were shipped away."

"Where they go?"

"To England."

"You mean they starve white people too?"

I didn't respond to Zoya this time. No need to cause more discontent. She had enough to deal with.

We got to a clearing and three old huts came into view. Each stood surrounded with wattle-and-daub, and the thatched roofs needed repair. The three huts had no doors. Raggedy burlap blew from the doors as a gust of wind rustled leaves and swayed tree limbs.

But these huts looked better than the mud cottages in Ireland. And no cold-weather suffering existed here. Only the beating and maiming made survival so unbearable.

"Miz Muncie hut over there," Zoya said, pointing to a hut in the middle of the three.

We approached and I knocked on the wall to the right of the front door. A hand quickly swept the burlap curtain aside. A woman stepped out. She stopped in her tracks and glanced at me, wide-eyed. Then she stared at Zoya, a bewildered look on her face.

"Miz Muncie, Mas Sean lookin' for cloth. You have any to sell him?" The woman's face became less tight.

"Yah man. Jus' got mi' hands on some blue cotton I was goin' to use to make frocks," Miz Muncie said.

"Mind selling it to me? I could pick more cloth up for you next time I go to the market," I said. She glanced at me once more and held her head back down.

"Is all right, sah. I know where to get more cloth. I pay one shilling for this piece," she said.

"I give you three shillings for it. I know you'd make more if you used the cloth to make and sell frocks."

"Yes, sah," she said, more disbelief in her glance.

She went back inside the hut and returned with the cloth, all folded up. She handed it to me and I gave her the money. Zoya and I thanked her and walked away. I felt her eyes on us as we headed back up the path.

A few evenings later I walked to my quarters after a day in the fields, and there he stood, Bene Ubote, walking up to one of the huts with a young slave man. Ubote had two crocus bags in his hand, filled with goods.

"Hey, Ubote! Was hoping to see you here again," I said.

The slave man next to him lowered his eyes, and attempted to walk away. Ubote told him not to leave, then he looked at me.

"Ah, the Irishman." I wasn't sure whether he was smiling or smirking.

"I have something for you," I said, looking him in the eyes.

"That new, a white man with somethin' for me and it's not whip or gun pointed at my head." The young slave kept his head down.

"You wait here. I'll get it from my quarters. It's cloth." He looked at me, incredulous. I turned and hurried to my quarters.

"Here, get some frocks made for your woman," I said, returning quickly and attempting to hand Ubote the cloth. He stared at it, then held his hand out with one of the bags he had brought with him. I refused to take it.

"I take nothin' for free; I pay you. This good boar meat from Maroon hunter. You not take it, I not take cloth." I took the crocus bag and handed him the cloth.

"I give this to my sista' so she can make new frocks. She be real happy." Ubote said. I looked at the young slave man standing with us.

"What's your name?"

"Kali, sah," he said, his head still down. I tried to hand him the crocus bag.

"Here, take this to your hut so your woman can make a good dinner for the family." He finally raised his head and looked at me, disbelief in his eyes. I kept holding the bag out to him.

"Take it, man. Have a good dinner tonight."

"It's all right; take it," Ubote said. The man took the bag.

"Thank you, sah!" He said. "I not forget this."

"We not use' to no kind white man," Ubote said, staring me in the eyes, like he always did.

"I want to visit your village. Want to hear the full story about how Maroons got sent to Sierra Leone," I said.

"You don' have to come to village for me to tell you that. Tell me the truth, why you really want to come there?"

"Not only do I want to hear that story, I want to see how your people live. I'm completely fascinated with your people. You fought like panthers and defeated the Brits. God knows, my own people were too starved to fight back." Ubote's face softened.

"I think 'bout it. I go now," he said. He turned and walked into the hut behind him, the young slave following close behind.

I hurried back to my quarters, my mind in a flurry. I needed to know the Maroons. I wanted to learn more about their fighting spirit and bravery. This would help me survive here. And it wouldn't hurt to have friends in free villages nearby. This could provide support to Havendale's slaves. Somehow, I saw tough times coming. I wanted to be prepared.

Chapter 18

In the days that followed, the fields took on an uncomfortable aura. Slaves gathered around bundles of sugarcane, whispering. They quickly scattered when I approached. I didn't lash them for small things, and they knew it. But a few men glanced at me with their eyes narrowed, their mouths slammed shut, their teeth quietly grinding. Passive defiance saturated the air. If a fight for freedom was looming, I needed to know so I could quietly support the cause.

One day, I heard women singing a suspenseful song as they dug away at sugarcane roots;

Talla ly li oh

Freedom ah come oh!

Talla ly li oh

Here we dig, here we hoe,

Talla ly li oh ·

Slavery ah gone oh ...

And although I didn't understand patois, I often heard them refer to someone named 'Daddy Sharpe.' I needed to find out what, in God's name, was going on.

That Sunday, I decided to show up at the Baptist church service on site. Baptist preachers spread all over the island now. Planters griped that Protestant preachers from the homeland knew how to 'keep the slaves in line.' They preached that 'slaves should do the work on this earth and they would be rewarded in the Lord's heaven.'

But Baptist preachers harangued about the horrors of slavery. Their proclamations said, 'No one has the right to enslave human beings.' They told slaves to do what it took to survive under the brutal conditions of their lives.

So, slaves survived by creating dance, songs, and the drama of masquerade. One celebration was called John Canoe. A slave woman once told me that John Canoe included a street parade with music, dance and costumes of West African origin.

"This how we keep we African roots alive. We refuse to let brutality and hardship break our spirit. The mask of John Canoe heal' our spirit, and the obeah woman heal our body and soul," the slave woman had said.

I hadn't yet watched the magic of John Canoe. But the experience awaiting me must have come close. It jarred me into believing freedom would come to these people, but it would come at a huge cost.

That Sunday morning as I walked up to the clearing at the west end of the plantation, I stared ahead and around, my eyes wide. Slaves stood everywhere, dressed up for worship. They raised their voices and sang so loudly, my ears stung. They clapped their hands and stamped their feet. They slammed their eyes shut and smiled, in a trance-like state. I took a deep breath.

The smell of fresh dew on trampled grass played with my senses. A beautiful yellow and purple butterfly flitted by and disappeared, as the singing and clapping intensified. The throng gradually quieted down.

A voice roared, "Brothers and sisters, blessings to you on this beautiful morning as we gather to praise the Lord and lift our spirits above sadness and cruelty."

Before me, a tall, robust, black preacher stood. Dressed in a long, white robe over black pants and black boar-skin shoes, he had short-cropped, black hair, high cheek bones, and sharp features. There was no patois; he spoke perfect English, like a learned and intelligent man.

The slaves stared at him, enthralled. They latched on to every word coming from his lips.

The black preacher held his arms out to the throng and continued to spread the gospel. He belted out words about the Lord.

He roared words about the Devil. He hollered words about how to worship one and turn your back on the other. He shouted words that stood as an affront to slavery. And, he rallied in favor of brotherhood.

All this, as slaves thrust trembling hands up to the skies and screamed, 'Amen, Brotha! Yes Lord! Help us, Jesus!'

I'd heard that white Baptist preachers Britain sent to the island were going door-to-door, trying to convert blacks. But this man was another story; he stood, commanding. His words landed with power and passion.

Did Vassell know this? Had he attended any of these services? I would not be the one to tell him.

I soon refocused on the preacher's next words, and they echoed even more compelling to the ears. Preacher man now stood armed with a big, black bible. Moving the pages from chapter to chapter, he harangued about armies of the oppressors being swept away by the waters of the Red Sea. He screamed about David aiming his sling shot and slaying Goliath.

The crowd yelled, "Amen! Halleluiah!" He preached in a passionate trance about Daniel in the Lion's den, about a valley of dry bones resurrected in Ezekiel's vision, about a bush that burned but could not be destroyed.

"Halleluiah, Amen, yes Preacher!" The throng shouted, over and over, totally mesmerized. Then they broke into hymns of joy and deliverance.

Hide me, Oh, my savior, hide,
Till the storm of life is past,
Safe into the haven guide,
Oh, receive my soul at last
Soldiers of Christ arise
And put your armor on.

My mind went to dark places. I just couldn't help it. Vassell will throw a tantrum when he hears about this. No wonder the planters felt so threatened by the Baptist preachers.

Their message railed against plantocracy. Slaves listened and became more empowered by the reality of their own strength. The rallying cry of every Baptist preacher egged them on. Sweet Jesus, this will not end well.

It didn't take long for the alarm bell to start clanging. Two days later, I got called to Vassell's great house for an 'urgent meeting'. When I got there, I saw that all overseers at Havendale were in attendance.

With no food or drink at this meeting, I stood around with the others, waiting for Vassell to take his place at the table up front. He soon arrived and began talking, his voice low, his stance rigid.

"That Baptist preacher will not be allowed back on my property. Damn him! Because of him, my slaves are all worked into a frenzy. I am a good, loyal Englishman. Those beasts are mine, my property." His voice rose to a louder, more vicious growl.

"Ever since the Brits ended the trading of slaves, everyone here thinks slavery has been abolished. Nothing we tell them sinks in. They insist that Britain has freed them all. How the Hell can we free those beasts? They'll run around like animals, destroying everything and everyone." Vassell slammed both fists on the table and continued his tantrum.

"You must whip their backsides at the slightest sign of lollygagging. The only way to control them is with brutality, you hear me? Brutality! Never forget that. We must strike them before they strike us. If you cannot be brutal, you don't belong here," he yelled, his voice rising to new heights.

But most of all, his voice echoed with fear. Sweat ran down the sides of his face and dripped on his crisp, white shirt. And the underarms of his shirt showed round, wet circles of sweat.

I walked to my quarters after the meeting, my mind working overtime. Vassell had been right. Slaves seemed ready to make their demands for freedom. But beating them to death was just not the answer.

Why couldn't the Brits negotiate a peace treaty with them, like they did with the Maroons? What am I thinking? I know why. Ubote said the Maroons fought 85 years for their freedom. They had to kick the asses of the British army in order to get it. Determination and brutality had gotten the Maroons that far. I'm afraid the same may be coming for the slaves.

"Been waiting for you, Sean," a deep voice moved me out of my torrid thoughts.

"Gavin, what you doing here?"

"Came to see you, Laddie. Got a minute? Need to talk."

"Sure, let's sit on the rocks over there. What's going on?"

We sat on a large rock under a mango tree. Dusk had arrived, the sun sinking slowly into the horizon. A white tropical dove swooped by above our heads, signaling the end of another beautiful day.

But the mood around us was far from beautiful. Fear, anticipation, anger, and hope, all mixed into one hot brew, corroded the warm, tropical air.

"You been saving your money?" Gavin asked.

"Every penny. Why?"

"I've been saving real' hard too. Good thing for both of us. Chambers been panicking. He thinks a slave revolt is coming."

"Vassell's panicking too. The way he's been treating those slaves of his, he does need to panic."

"For sure. I was thinking; why don't you and I put together and buy our own place? We're just not built like the Brits. We don't have it in us to beat and maim. If freedom is coming for slaves, I think they'll work for us. And we'll be better able to help with the fight for justice if we have our own place."

"Great idea, Gavin. I've been saving to return to Ireland and help rebuild the country. But you know, I've been thinking that maybe God sent me here for a reason. Helping African Jamaicans find their way out of hate and brutality is that reason. The more I think about it, the more I believe that's why I'm here."

"You think Ireland is ready for rebuilding?"

"Not yet. Rebuilding will probably begin in a few more years."

"Why wait that long when we could make a difference here, in a land that's quickly becoming our home?"

"If the two of us put together, we could make things happen around here real' fast. And you're right, the struggle for justice and freedom could use our helping hands. I think you have something there, Gavin."

"We could buy a place and start paying blacks to work the fields. No slavery. I think a lot of them would welcome the idea."

"Aye. There are already free blacks, and Maroons too, who may grab the chance to work for pay. Hopefully, our people here will have their freedom by then."

"Let's get together soon and plan this out. Got to go, now," Gavin said. I bid him good night and watched him disappear into the darkness.

I barely slept a wink that night. Lying in bed with my eyes closed, the conversation with Gavin replayed over and over in my head. He was right; we could make a big difference here.

Unlike the other overseers, I'd been kind to the slaves. I did not fear them, and they would do me no harm. Besides, I'd been developing a relationship with one of the Maroons. This could work. But will we find a place we could afford?

Get some sleep, Laddie. Tomorrow is another day.

A good night's sleep always cleared my mind and helped me find answers.

Chapter 19

I turned around and there he was, Ubote, this time with a crocus bag slung over his shoulder. Hurrying to my quarters, I returned with a bag of pumpkin seeds I'd bought at the market two days ago. I caught up with Ubote just as he hurried to enter Miz Ada's hut. Miz Ada had the reputation of being the best obeah woman on this side of the island, according to Zoya, and the Maroons often traded fresh herbs with her, in exchange for her potions.

"Hey, Ubote. Got something for you," I said.

"Irishman, you always catch me sneakin' 'round. What you got in bag now?"

"Best pumpkin seeds for planting. I hear the biggest pumpkins come from these very seeds."

"I takin' this boar's head and some herbs to Miz Ada. She make soup for old slaves with little in belly. I have nothin' to trade you for seed today."

"I make a deal with you."

"Oh no. White man deal not good for African." A smirk on his face said he was not that serious. I'd learned to read his facial expressions, which was a good thing.

"I want to visit your people. Take me to your village. That will be payment enough."

"What you want with my people, Irishman?"

"Want to get to know them. They fought the Brits and won, when my people couldn't. I need to learn what motivates them."

"We not no teacher. We jus' surviving."

"You are the best survivors I know. And things about to get tough around here. There's talk about slave rebellions and all."

"What that have to do with me?"

"Who knows. One day we may need each other when times get really tough. Besides, I want to see how your little boy's doing. I told his Mama I'd check up on him."

"You only good white man 'round here. Slaves say you kind to them. I think 'bout it. You got any more cloth? My sister loved the blue cloth. I like seeing her happy."

"Tell you what, I'll get more cloth if you take me to the village."

"You drive hard bargain. I come back Sunday when slaves off work. I meet you down-hill when sun just come up. Same place where you drop Uma off that day headin' to the slave traders. If you don' see me, that mean ah not coming."

"All right, I'll be there."

That Saturday, I went to the market and found the most beautiful cotton cloth, light powder blue with large pale-yellow hibiscus flowers. I also bought some seeds to grow beets.

But I had trouble falling asleep that night. *What the heck are you getting yourself into, Sean? Brits say Maroons are beasts, but you're cozying up to them? What if they kill you? No one would have a clue, because you can't let anyone know where you're going. Have you lost your mind?*

My mind kept racing here and there. I drove myself close to exhaustion, till sleep finally knocked me out.

I was up before dawn the next day, rearing to go. I'd survived starvation, the fever, and buried dead bodies in Ireland. I'd prayed last night, and trusted that God would keep me safe.

I washed up and got dressed in khaki pants and shirt, a floppy hat, and my walking boots. I paused, repeated Psalm 27, and pulled myself together. No time for breakfast.

I stopped by Zoya's hut, knocked at her door, and whispered my whereabouts to her after she stepped out the door. Her eyes widened when I said I'd check on her son and bring her news. She said she'd tell Gavin where I'd gone, but only if I didn't return that day.

I hurried to Havendale's back gate holding a crocus bag with the cloth, and a small bag of seeds.

The sun barely peeked out from behind puffs of light gray clouds, and a cool breeze fanned the air. Sounds of the night, like whistling crickets and tree frogs, had just retreated for another beautiful day. Walking to the back gate, I told the guard to let me through. After giving me a questioning look, he opened the gate.

I walked quickly up the path for several minutes, and then I slowed down. I heard Ubote say, "Psst, this way Irishman."

I turned left into the bushes and took several steps, my boots crunching away at dry tree limbs and pebbles. Soon, I was face-to-face with the Maroon.

"You smart white man. You dress good for journey. We go now."

Ubote moved quickly through the forest, but there was no path. He raised his hands and slapped away bushes in front of us as we hurried along. I did the same.

He seemed to take a round-about trail. My guess is, he did this to make sure I couldn't take the journey without him. I asked no questions, focusing instead on keeping up with him. I wondered how, in God's name, he could trudge through this much bush barefooted.

We continued along the journey for close to half-an-hour. Then we started climbing up hill, where things became even more dense. Sunlight occasionally hit my face as we made our way through thick forest.

"Stay close to me. Don't want you to get killed."

"What you mean?" I asked, breathing hard and almost talking patois. I clutched the bags and kept his pace.

"Traps on ground everywhere to stop invaders. We gettin' close to village."

He didn't have to repeat that instruction. I was on him like sap on a tree. Finally, we stopped climbing and stood facing a small clearing. The welcoming smell of freshly-cooked food wafted through the air.

"Village over there."

We walked across the clearing and back into more bushes. The most amazing sight suddenly blessed my burning eyes.

Looming in front of me stood a village of at least fifty wattle-and-daub huts, each standing a good distance away from the other. The roofs, made of glistening thatch, boasted well-painted walls in sparkling white below.

All huts had gardens of beans and provisions out back, that looked healthy and well cultivated. Some cabins had large rocks in front under big Poinciana trees, with bursts of red and yellow flowers overhead, which looked like colorful umbrellas. Others stood surrounded by red, green and yellow crotons. What an amazing sight to see.

"I take you to family hut. Follow me."

We walked through the village. Maroons began stirring for the day, and many greeted Ubote as we hurried along. They all gave me questioning or suspicious looks. Two women wearing colorful cotton dresses walked by, each carrying a bucket of water on their heads.

Three bare-chested men wearing tattered old pants walked past us, carrying tools. One had a shovel, one an axe, and the other, a machete. A young mother with two simply, well-dressed, children walked toward us. The woman bowed her head and the children, one around eight and the other around ten, said, "Mornin' sah,' as they passed us by.

Soon, we approached a large hut with freshly-woven thatch on top. There were two windows on each side of the front door. Clean, white curtains blew out of them, and a gust of wind had me grabbing my hat.

Ubote knocked on the door-jam of the half-closed front door. A woman's voice shouted, "Coming."

A young woman opened the door and stepped out.

"Ah, it's you, my brother."

She stared at me with the brightest, hazel eyes I'd ever seen. I'd never seen such eyes on a brown-skinned woman. She continued to stare at me, looking puzzled.

"I bring friend to meet you and Papa. This Irishman Sean from Havendale Plantation."

"Pleased to meet you, Irishman Sean. You're here, so my brother must think highly of you. My name is Asha."

The young woman spoke perfect English, with a slight accent that I could not place. She had smooth, light-brown skin and a dark-brown mop of hair that hung to her shoulders. Her smile showed full lips and white teeth that glistened. I didn't want to look her up and down, but whatever she wore was sleeveless, and it hung over broad shoulders and thin, muscular arms.

"Pleasure to meet you too, Asha," I said, staring into her eyes. She smiled. Ubote looked from her to me, then back at her. A deep voice from inside the hut soon broke into my uneasiness.

"Who's there?"

"It's Bene and his friend, Sean, Papa."

"Invite them in, will you? We have breakfast," the man said.

Asha led the way into the hut. Ubote and I followed closely behind.

I looked ahead and saw an older man sitting around a hand-carved, wooden table with four wooden chairs. The man stood as we approached. He looked tall, of medium build, with hair graying on the sides of his low-cut, black hair. He smiled.

"This is new, a white man comes to visit?" He glanced at Ubote.

"Papa, meet Sean from Havendale Plantation," Ubote said.

"Ah, the kind man from Ireland. My son mentions you quite a bit."

With a stronger accent, the older man's English sounded almost as good as his daughter's.

"Come, sit down and have some breakfast. Want some tea?"

"Thank you, sir," I said, sitting in front of him. Ubote and Asha sat on either side of me.

I heard a child running toward us, yelling "Papa!" It was Zoya's son, Uma. He scampered up into his father's lap. He seemed happy and playful.

"The 'sir' is much appreciated, but you can call me Ode if you'd like. I'm Ode Ubote," the older man said. "Let me get the tea and a few cups." He rose and walked away.

Ubote opened, one at a time, then closed, three covered platters on the table. Tempting aromas wafted through the air.

"Mmm, salt mackerel in coconut milk, dumplings, and cassava. I'm starved," he said.

"Me too. I'll get plates," Asha said.

Ode returned with a pot of tea and four slightly rusted tin cups, which he held by the handles in one hand. He poured us each a cup of tea.

"Help yourselves to food," he said, as Asha returned with five tin plates and a cup of what looked like juice. She put a plate and an old fork on the table in front of each of us; she put a spoon in front of Uma.

"Here, Uma; your favorite juice, pineapple." The boy took a sip of juice, his eyes gleaming.

"Thanks for sharing your breakfast with me. I brought you these," I said, handing Asha the bag with cloth, and Ubote's father the smaller one with seeds.

"Thank you, Sean, I'm so grateful!" Asha said.

"Much appreciated. We open gifts after breakfast?" Ode said.

Ubote dug into the platter with mackerel and passed it around. Then he grabbed the other platters and did the same. We all helped ourselves, with Asha putting small portions on Uma's plate and using her fork to dig into his mackerel and search for bones.

Ode soon grabbed the hands of those next to him, bowed his head, and said, "Mighty ancestors, bless us as we join hands to thank you for this food. Amen."

I took a bite of mackerel; simply delicious. We devoured everything in front of us while making small talk. Then Ode rose and began picking up the dirty dishes.

"Can I help?" I asked.

"Oh no," he said. A woman will come to clean up. I have more pineapple juice. Let's sit outside, enjoy, and have a chat."

We headed outside with cups of juice and sat on rocks under a blooming Poincianna tree. Ubote sat next to me on one rock, and Asha and her father got comfortable on the other. We sipped our juice.

Uma ran around the tree, picking up flowers and rocks. He soon sat on the ground and started playing with his loot.

"What a beautiful morning," Ode said, looking up at bursts of yellow blossoms above. A nice, cool breeze wrapped itself around me, and I stared ahead as a magnificent blue and yellow humming bird paused in mid-air, sticking its beak out at a burst of red hibiscus flowers in front of us.

"It sure is. And your village is wonderful. The fruit trees and flowers are stunning. Thanks, so much, for this experience," I said.

"We work hard to keep things going and in great shape. Now that we're not fighting off constant attacks from planters and the British army, we can focus on building our community," Asha said.

"And we have best hunters 'round. They make sure we never run out of fresh boars' meat. And a team of our men rear pigs and chickens, while another team fish in the rivers," Olumbo said.

"I see well-kept provision grounds in back of the huts, too," I said.

"Oh yes. Families grow their own provisions. We're never out of food," Asha said, then she paused and looked at me.

"Can I open my gift?" She asked, changing the subject. She'd been carrying the crocus bag around ever since I handed it to her.

"Of course," I said.

She opened the bag and retrieved the cloth. She unfolded some of it and looked back at me, her eyes beaming.

"I love it. Thank you. Another beautiful dress for me."

"Your bag has seeds for planting beets," I said, looking over at Ode.

"Thank you. I'll get to planting in back later on."

We fell silent for a moment and watched Asha touch and feel her cloth. Then I broke the silence.

"Who runs this amazing village?"

"We have a Maroon Chief and a head of community affairs. And we still have a chief warrior, just in case the white man decides to go against the peace treaty we all signed years ago," Ode said, giving me a glance. I ignored the comment.

"Asha, I was wondering. How come you speak such perfect English?" I asked, glancing at the beautiful young woman sitting next to her father.

I could take a closer look at her now. She wore a short, yellow, summer frock and light-brown hemp sandals. The morning sun shone beams around her face, through wisps of curly, brown hair.

"My brother didn't tell you? I was born and partially raised in Halifax, Nova Scotia, and then in Freetown, Sierra Leone." I couldn't believe my ears.

"Nova Scotia? That's Canada! The Brits shipped my Irish brothers and sisters to Canada too, during the potato famine. They called us breeders and said the less of us they'd have to feed, the better."

My ugly past had come rumbling back at me like a freight train from Hell. But those sitting next to me were far from shocked. They'd had their share of abuse.

"They deported us from Trelawney Town, which had the largest Maroon community on the island at the time, with a false claim that we had breached the peace treaty. This was after the second Maroon war. My father was one of the Trelawney Town Maroons and I was just 15 years old, but I was already a father. I took my son sitting next to you with me, to Halifax," Ode said.

"Sweet Jesus, sorry, I should say Sweet Ancestors." I tried to digest this fascinating story. I soon found my voice once more, "How did you end up in Sierra Leone?"

"We stood up for ourselves in Canada too; we rebelled. So, they shipped us off to Sierra Leone, to get rid of us. Asha was eight years old at the time. She never saw her Canadian mother after that," Ode said.

"To quote Christians, we 'raised Hell' in Sierra Leone too. Many of us built businesses there, and some of us got into politics. But it was jus' not Jamaica," Olumbo said.

I moved my head slowly, from side to side, "So, you found your way back here? How?"

"We put together a Jamaican Atlantic Crossing, no chains, no laying in our own shit. Just joyfully huddled together on a boat ride heading for home," Ode said.

"That's the most remarkable story I've ever heard. You are true fighters. I'm humbled to be here with you."

"Yah man, and the fight continues," Olumbo said.

"Let's take a walk through the village," Ode said.

We rose and strolled up the path away from the hut, Uma skipping along next to us. I looked around. Mango and plum trees grew everywhere, laden with fruit not yet ripe.

The village had come alive now, with Maroon men, women and children walking about, minding their own business. They were all neatly dressed and cheerful; after all, it was Sunday.

Then I heard drums, pounding away. The beat sounded infectious; the rhythm rang sweet in my ears. I began to move my head from side-to-side. Apart from listening to slaves singing, it had been years since I'd heard music, just before the Irish famine.

"Oh yes, we celebratin' the first Sunday of the month," Olumbo said.

"Just Sunday?" I asked, my head still moving to the drums. I just couldn't stop.

"Indeed. Maroons love to celebrate. The ancestors taught us to celebrate everything, to the beat of the drums. That's how we survived all these years," Ode said.

I looked in the direction of the music, toward a clearing. Two musicians pounded their drums and Maroon men, women and children looked on. They moved their hips and behinds to the rhythm. I'd never seen people move their bodies like that.

"You must move your hips too, Irishman ... like this," Asha said, as her body gyrated to the music. Olumbo and his father joined in, their hips and behinds gyrating to the rhythm.

I stood next to them and jerked my hips from side to side. I couldn't get my body to move like theirs, but it sure was liberating. I felt free, I felt powerful. Now, I knew why the drums kept them alive and hopeful.

That afternoon, I bade goodbye to Asha, her father, and little Uma. Olumbo and I headed down hill and through bushes, as he led me back toward Havendale. I didn't want to leave.

How I wished Havendale allowed everyone to plant provisions behind their own huts, so they could feed themselves. *That will never happen with Vassell around.*

Pushing Vassell out of my mind, I kept moving my hips and legs as the rhythms of the drums echoed, quieter and quieter, in my ears. Soon, I heard them no more.

Sometime later, Olumbo stopped walking and looked me in the eyes, "We close to Havendale now. Jus' head west over there. You be at plantation in no time."

"Okay. Thanks so much for showing me your world. I'm a better person because of it. Hope to see you again, soon."

"Not before I tell you this. Remember you tellin' me you wanted to know my world, 'cause we might need each other one day?"

"I believe that."

"Slave uprising comin.' Lay low; let slaves help put out fires, if needed. They talk to me 'bout your kindness. Obeah woman, Miz Ada, and Zoya, you can trust them. Zoya never forget how you save her son."

"How do you know about the uprising?"

"Brits call on Maroons to help round up rebelling slaves. All part'a peace treaty we sign years ago. Most Maroons see it as blood pact. But my Maroon Chief refuse to help Brits."

"Slaves fighting for freedom, Olumbo. They've had enough abuse. I plan to stick around and quietly help them. They deserve a better life."

"Slave not Maroon; they can't fight like us. When they escape and come to us, we teach them bush warfare so they fight like Maroon. Careful, Irishman, things going to get tough."

"I know, but I'll do everything in my power to support them."

"You good man."

"Can I call on you for help if needed?"

"Peace treaty say Maroon not help slave rebellion. But I give quiet help if needed. Stay safe, Irishman." Before I could respond, he vanished into the forest.

Turning around, I trudged my way through bushes to the west and I prayed, *Sweet Jesus, please let Havendale survive whatever is coming its way. And give me the strength needed to support the cause.*

Chapter 20

Havendale wrapped itself into a cloud of uncertainty. Drastic changes loomed; I felt it in my bones. Slaves worked the fields at a slower pace, and they constantly took lashings. But they just stood there and took the beatings, 'like lashing dead horses,' one overseer said. And with their backs bloody and sore, they'd simply show up at the obeah woman's door. She'd make them numb or heal them with bush medicine. Then they'd return the next day for more slow-downs and beatings, their wounds opening up, over and over. Never, in my life, had I known people to take abuse with such relentless defiance.

I quietly stayed clear of the abuse. I'd slip away with whip in hand when other overseers doled out lashings. I'd talk silently to the next group of slaves about picking up the pace. They'd look at me and obey, but their gazes said 'only because it's you, Mas Sean.'

The middle of December soon came upon us. Were the slaves just tired and preparing for the measly two-day Christmas holiday, which they had to fight for like bulls? After abolishing the slave trade, England had ordered that Christmas vacation be increased from one to two days.

But the planters fought to deny this time to their slaves. Vassell still fought to deny them the extra day, before I talked him into giving up. As things escalated; I urgently needed to have a talk with Zoya.

"Zoya, I hear a slave uprising is coming. That true?" I asked, walking up to her as she headed home alone from the fields one evening.

Zoya raised her head and glanced at me, eyes wide. She did not answer.

"I'm trying to protect all of us, Zoya. Please tell me what you know. I've heard the slaves talking about a Daddy Sharpe. Who is he? Is he the one leading the rebellion?"

"Yes, sah, is Daddy Sam Sharpe. He a Baptist preacher with his own church, and he watch out for us all."

"Is he plotting to kill all whites?"

"No, sah."

"What's he trying to do? Tell me."

"We think British government free us, but massas don' want to let us go."

"Zoya, the Brits have put a stop to the slave trade; that means the massas can't bring any more slaves here from Africa. But they didn't abolish ... they didn't get rid of slavery."

"Tell that to other slaves 'round island, sah. They think the Brits free us all."

"Okay, you said slaves not trying to kill the white man. What are they planning to do?" I asked. Zoya glanced up at me once more, her mouth slammed shut.

"I promise not to tell anyone, especially Vassell. If you tell me, I can work around Vassell to make sure our people here are safe. I've decided to help you fight for your rights."

"We plannin' to stop workin' sah. We already slowing down."

"What is it that you want when you stop working?"

"We want pay. We not workin' no more without pay. And we don' plan to take any more beatins.' So, it's goin' to be war."

"When will all this happen?"

"Can't tell you that, sah." She glanced up, then quickly walked away.

I didn't follow Zoya; I turned and headed to my quarters. I got her message, loud and clear. I must keep this quiet as promised, or she would never trust me again.

But I must also plan ways to survive this. God knows, I'd suffered through the savage task of burying the dead, over and over. Having to do that here, too, would destroy me.

Besides, a deep need inside me said I must protect these people. It's called recompense, for what I was unable to do in my beloved Ireland. I needed to quickly put a plan together.

Vassell called a meeting with his overseers next evening after work. I'd never seen more fear in the eyes of a man who'd been so brutal, I often questioned his own humanity. As soon as we all got to the meeting, he began to rant.

"I just read in the *Cornwall Courier* that a party of marines will be heading here after Christmas, on the *HMS Sparrowhawk*. They'll be led by General Sir Willoughby Cotton, commander of the British forces in Jamaica. You know what the Hell that means?" Vassell stared around, wide-eyed. No one responded. He continued to yell.

"It means those beasts are getting ready to rebel, and we won't stand for it. So, get your whips and bayonets ready. You, at the front and back gates, let no one in you don't know. And no one must be let out after 6 in the evening. We will shoot any slave or intruder who disobeys this order."

"What kind of rebellion we expecting, sir?" An overseer asked.

"Don't know, but get your guns ready. The idiots think Britain has freed them, and no matter how we try, they think planters are the ones holding them back. We all know that Britain didn't free them; they just stopped the slave trade. They were a bunch of asses to do that, but here we are, stuck with it." Vassell paused, and continued.

"Slaves are beasts, but they're no Maroons. They don't have the fierceness or bush warfare skills. Unfortunately, many of them can now read, thanks to the blasted Baptist preachers and their church schools. So, they read what's going on in the papers, and pass the word around. They know about the working class rebellions going on in Britain that have caused empathy for slaves here in Jamaica. Also, I hear a few of them know how to use guns, so we have our work cut out for us. But I bet most of them will be armed with machetes, pitch forks, shovels, and sticks. A bullet will take care of those fools."

"Maybe we should stop beating them for slowing down, sir. That may be making them even more angry," another overseer said.

Vassell slammed both fists on the table, "I don't give a damn about their anger. We need the work done, and if they don't do it on time, keep whipping their backsides."

I laid in bed that night, my head filled with complex thoughts. Here I go, again, dealing with people who valued property more than the lives and the welfare of human beings.

Brits viewed slaves as property, to be controlled and brutalized, just like they did when they stood by and let us starve to death. The cruelty will only end when these people are free.

* * *

"... Oh receive my soul at last

Soldiers of Christ arise

And put your armor on ..."

I heard those words as I approached the clearing the next Sunday morning.

The same tall, black, Baptist preacher stood before the throng, delivering his message to the souls of those in front of him. Slaves stood shoulder-to-shoulder and rocked from side-to-side, singing joyfully, their eyes slammed shut.

Today, preacher man stood, dressed in black from head to toe. He wore a black, short-sleeved shirt, black pants, and a pair of black shoes. He belted away at the song, his throng now singing passionately along.

When the singing died down, preacher man opened his big, floppy Bible and hollered, "Today, let us turn to Galatians 5:1."

"It is for freedom that Christ has set us free. Stand firm, then, and do not let yourselves be burdened again by a yolk of slavery." The preacher paused, stared at the crowd in front of him, and looked back down at his bible.

"Let us now turn to Lamentations 3:25 – 27."

"The Lord is good to everyone who trusts him, so it is best for us to wait in patience; to wait for him to save us. And it is best to learn this patience in our youth."

"Amen, halleluiah!" Slaves chanted, their eyes closed, their arms raised high.

Suddenly, screams befouled the air. A huge, red-faced overseer bolted to the stage, grabbed hold of the preacher, and dragged him to the left front corner of the clearing. The overseer clutched the arms of the kicking man and held him to the ground. Another overseer began to rip the cloths off of his body.

Before I could move, Vassell approached with a bucket. Steam rose in the air from the bucket. He threw the contents at preacher man.

Overseers close-by scattered. The crowd gasped; hot tar flew through the air. The preacher let out a chilling wail as the liquid scalded his body. The smell of burning flesh polluted the elements. The preacher's body shuddered. Then it moved no more.

Slave women screamed and clutched one another. Slave men stared on in horror, grinding their teeth.

Vassell quickly retreated and returned with another rusty old bucket. He stuck his right hand into the bucket and came up with a handful of what looked like fowl feathers. He looked down, grunted, and flung feathers all over the preacher's body.

One overseer tried to turn the body over but couldn't; it stuck to the ground. Vassell turned the bucket upside down and emptied all the feathers on top of the preacher. He screamed at the slaves, his voice a trembling howl.

"Damn you all to Hell. Do your work, or that's where you'll end up, in Hell!" Looking like Lucifer, he glared at the throng of slaves in front of him, turned, and stomped toward the great house.

I stood there, dumbfounded, unable to move. Vassell had tarred and feathered the preacher. Overseer Basil rushed over.

"Help me clean up this mess and remove the preacher's body for burial."

I held my gut, bent over, and vomited, right in front of him. This time, I'd have to help scrape the body of a murdered man of God from the ground, and bury him? No way in Hell.

Repulsion washed over me. Someone else would have to help right now. I kept heaving, till nothing came up. I hurried into the bushes and bawled like a child, my gut ravaged, pain digging itself into my soul. No God-given strength could have helped me.

After that, I barely slept a full hour at night. The only thing that calmed me was when I repeated Psalm 27. And the Christmas holiday would soon be upon us.

Sweet Jesus, how will I make it through that?

Chapter 21

I got to the cane fields, whip in hand, trying to ready myself for work. But the fields were empty. Where were the slaves; still eating breakfast? I stood there waiting. Not a single slave showed up for work.

It was Tuesday, the first work day after Christmas holidays. I'd dressed myself and stopped by the overseers' breakfast area. While eating, I'd made small talk with other overseers about how quiet Christmas was, and what a good change-of-pace it provided us all.

In my heart, I thanked God that Gavin had come by with food from his great house, and we'd both eaten Christmas dinner together.

"What the Hell's going on? Where are the slaves?" Overseer Mark Roberts asked when we got to the fields. He'd hurried up to me, looking around with disbelief.

"I don't know. I ... I don't understand," I said. Two other overseers joined us, mouths open, eyes wide.

"Vassell's going to kill them all," one said.

"This is not good. Let me go get Vassell," the other overseer said.

He turned around and hurried toward the great house. Not long after, Vassell stomped toward us, hair uncombed, shirt partially buttoned, whip in hand.

"Where are they? Where are the bastards?"

"No one showed up for work," Mark said.

Vassell growled, spun around, and stomped toward the breakfast area. We followed closely behind. There were no slaves.

He marched toward one of the slave huts. I followed him, alone this time. He burst through the door. Three women stood and stared Vassell dead in the eyes, quiet defiance oozing from their pores.

"Get your asses to work." No one moved. They continued to stare Vassell down. Their eyes said, 'Kill me; I'd rather die than work for you'. I'd rarely seen such bravery coming from women.

Vassell stomped his way to two other huts with me following closely behind. Same look from men and women, 'Kill me; I'd rather die than work for you.'

"Find out what the Hell is going on before I shoot them all!"

He spun around and darted toward the great house. I stood there, trying to pull my thoughts together. Then I headed to Miz Ada's hut.

The late December morning was bright and cool, with stunning sights of crops as far as the eyes could see. Bright yellow colors of ripened sugar cane and deep green Indian corn blessed my eyes. An opulent pasture of guinea grass also adorned the landscape. Lines of coconut and mango trees surrounded dozens of slave huts.

I sighed and kept walking; *beauty and strife; they just shouldn't go together.* Soon, I knocked on the wall next to the door of Miz Ada's hut.

"Yes ... who?" She yelled.

"It's Mas Sean. Have a minute?" A hand parted the burlap that served as a door. A head appeared. It was Zoya's.

"Come in, Mas Sean," she said, opening the curtain.

Slaves usually met you outside the hut, not invite you in. This was new. I entered the hut and saw Miz Ada standing by the back door. She walked up and stared at me, her eyes narrowed.

"What you want, Mas Sean?"

"I come to ask what you want. No one showed up for work this morning." Before she could answer, Zoya stepped in.

"I tell you what we want. Queen free us; massa won' set us free."

"Zoya, you know the Brits stopped the slave trade, but they didn't free the slaves yet. But that is coming; you must be patient."

"Patient? Time longer than rope and time run out."

"Okay. What is it you really want?" She didn't answer. She just kept ranting.

"People say Queen make us free, but massas goin' to kill all black man and save women and children and keep them slaves. If black man don't stand up, white man shoot him like pigeon."

"You know I'm one white man you can trust. What you just said, it's a rumor."

"Rumor? What that?"

"A rumor is something you hear that's not true." Miz Ada stepped in.

"Massa must pay us for work. We rather die than be slave, too much beatin,' too much torture. Bring you' gun and start shooting. We no work without pay no more."

"I understand. How much pay you have in mind?"

"At least 2/6 pence a day," Miz Ada said.

"I'll talk with Massa Vassell."

I walked out of the hut toward the great house. I barely saw the scenery this time, as I practiced what to say to Vassell and how I'd try to get through to him.

I climbed the steps to the verandah and knocked on the door to Vassell's living room. A house slave opened the door, let me in, and turned to get her master. Vassell walked in, took a seat on the settee, and stared at me. I started talking. I needed to make this short and to the point.

"Slaves all over the island are demanding pay for work," I said. Not invited to sit, I kept standing. Vassell sprang to his feet.

"Pay for work? Those stupid beasts are my property." He slapped his chest with a hand.

"I bought them, I own them, I can work them and I can hump their women. They're mine; I won't pay them shit."

I stared at him. I stayed focused and took deep breaths. *Keep calm, Sean. Don't get dragged into the hysteria.*

"They want 2/6 pence per day, at minimum."

"Tell them to go straight to Hell! The nerve. I'll shoot them all."

I continued to stand there, staring at him.

"You heard me. Straight to Hell. I'll kill them all!"

I turned, walked out the door and headed up the path. Miz Ada's words haunted my thoughts, 'We rather die than be slave ... bring your gun and start shootin.'

I remembered Olumbo sharing a Maroon saying with me; 'freedom or death, no other option.' *Sweet Jesus, the slaves are now using Maroon tactics. It's war!*

Chapter 22

I sprang out of bed, my brain in a fog. Sweat rushed down my arm pits. A horn blared in my ears. *What ... what's that horn? I know, someone's blowing a conch shell. What time is it? Must be before dawn. It's still dark outside. But there's light everywhere – where's that light coming from?* My mind took me from confusion to panic. I took deep breaths and reached for calm.

Soon, I stared through the window. Light blinded my eyes. Flames erupted like flashes of lightening.

I struggled to pull my pants over my hips. I finished dressing in a rush and bolted out the door, my thoughts whirling.

Sweet Jesus, the cane fields are on fire. The conch shell must have stopped blowing, because all I heard now were yells from other overseers.

"Field on fire, douse the flames!"

I grabbed two buckets and rushed to a water tank. I ran to the fields, put one bucket down, and flung water from the other into the flames. Then I grabbed the other bucket and did the same.

Heat, noise, and mayhem took over. More screams erupted behind me and I spun around.

Vassell 'flew' down the path from the great house like a villainous bat, whip over his shoulder, rifle in his hand, insanity on his face. He pointed the bayonet at a group of slaves who had just gathered around.

"Get to putting out the flames or I'll kill you all," he said. The slaves stared at him, unmoving.

He dropped the gun, grabbed the whip from his shoulder, and bolted toward them. Slave men stood in front of the women as Vassell whipped away. I rushed to the scene.

"Let me talk with them." He paused. He snorted. He stared at me, then at the slaves. He finally stomped away.

"Help me put out the flames, and I'll keep talking with Vassell about paying you. There's nowhere else for you to go," I said, staring at the group of slaves, the flames roaring away behind me.

The group of slaves, and others, grabbed whatever they could get their hands on to catch water. I rushed around with them to fight the flames for what felt like an eternity, till nothing but black smoke surged through the air. I stared at the mess. Half the cane fields had been burned to a crisp.

Finally, I turned my back away from it all and broke into fits of coughing. The other overseers and I spent the rest of the day assessing the damage. Vassell was nowhere to be found; relief washed over me.

That night after I cleaned myself up and prepared for bed, an urgent knock on the door startled me.

"Who is it?" I yelled.

"Gavin; let me in." I opened the door and he darted past me.

"Most of Toco Plantation been burned to the ground, Laddie," he said.

"We lost half the cane fields here too," I said.

"Most of our fields, gone. Two house slaves dead, too. Half the great house is gone, Sean."

"How'd you lose house slaves?"

"Field slaves refused to help put the fire out. Chambers beat two house slaves and forced them to go into the flames with buckets of water. They didn't come back out."

"Dear God in Heaven!" That was all I could muster.

"How'd you get by with such little damage?"

"Vassell threatened to shoot or beat the slaves. I made him stop, and I talked to them. They helped me put the fire out."

"Talked to them? What a concept. We didn't know how to do that at Toco," Gavin said. Then he paused and continued.

"Got hold of yesterday's *Cornwall Courier*. In addition to HMS Sparrowhawk, the HRM *Blanche* has also arrived here with 300 soldiers and a number of artillery men. The paper says they have two field-pieces and rockets. It's all-out war, Sean."

"Our slaves have refused to return to work since Christmas, unless they get paid. If we don't negotiate with them, they're ready to fight or burn us out."

"I read that they're already burning us out in Westmoreland, St. James, Falmouth, Lucea, Savanna-la-Mar, and Black River. Hundreds of slaves from the sugar estates, cattle pens, and in the urban areas, are getting ready to fight. They think Britain freed them, but we refuse to," Gavin said.

"And the planters refuse to negotiate with them for pay. I tried to reason with Vassell; he wouldn't listen. All he did was yell that he owns them and can do whatever he wants with them. Cruel, pompous, ass!"

"The slaves are no Maroons when it comes to bush warfare, but they're preparing to fight to their deaths. They're saying they'd 'rather die than be a slave.' Can't say I blame them. Too much abuse. We've turned them into trapped animals."

"We became animals when we were starving to death in Ireland. We didn't have the strength to rebel, but the slaves do. Where the Hell do you think this will end up, Gavin?"

"Not going to be pretty. Slaves won't stop till they're free; Britain will eventually have to free them."

"You think Britain will free them?"

"I do. But in the meantime, let me try again to talk some sense into Chambers' head," Gavin said. He rushed back out the door.

In the weeks that followed, the overseers and I worked hard to clean up burned-out areas of the cane field. Devastation surrounded me. Soot and smolder ravaged my eyes.

The bright yellow of the ripened sugar cane ceased to exist in half the fields. It was replaced with clumps of burned cane roots. All guinea grass had disappeared, as far as the eyes could see.

The smell of smoldering Indian corn floated through the air. Coconut tree trunks dotted the landscape, their burned branches hanging to the ground. One day, I glanced up at sounds of wings flapping. A flock of crows hovered overhead, looking for bodies of man or beast.

With Zoya's and Miz Ada's assistance, I talked a few slaves into helping. Vassell went from tantrums to threats. But most slaves refused to budge, no pay, no work. Then Vassell tried to starve them out, "no more food for those bastards," he said. That didn't work either.

The slaves had their own small provision grounds, and whatever they didn't have, like boars' meat, they secretly traded for, with the Maroons.

I reached out to Olumbo, one way of secretly supporting the fight for freedom. He kept his promise to help. Boars' meat came in abundance from the Maroons; the slaves had all the food they needed. It was all-out war; crippling news for the plantation.

Fierce fighting erupted between local British forces and over 500 slaves. Newspapers, other overseers, Zoya, Miz Ada, and Olumbo, kept me up-to-date. We hunkered down at Havendale.

Friday morning came and I sprang up in bed to an urgent knock at the door. It was Gavin. I opened the door and he rushed in, brandishing that morning's *Cornwall Courier*.

"Sorry to wake you, Laddie. Just read that the first round of fighting went to two bands of inadequately-armed slave men, who challenged the St. James militia under some Colonel named Grignon."

Gavin opened the newspaper and started reading, "'The Colonel refused to remain at the post. He retreated the whole body of his men to Montego Bay, which enabled the freedom fighters to cut the road from Montego Bay to Savanna-la-Mar.' He closed the newspaper and stared at me, "You believe this shit?"

"Dear God, it's all-out war. Grab a seat. Want some pineapple juice?" Gavin sat at the dining table without answering, still armed with his newspaper.

I hurried to the kitchen and returned with two cups of juice. I took a sip. Gavin slammed the paper on the table and he opened it once more.

"Listen to this."

The freedom fighters lost their two leaders, Johnson and Campbell. Johnson was killed so close to the white people, they could not carry his body away. Campbell was killed the next morning. His supporters made a rough coffin and buried him. But the freedom fighters held their own, and there were reports of activity along the Great River into St. Elizabeth.

Gavin paused, slapped the paper shut and took a sip of juice. "We'll make it through this, Gavin. But we must stay calm." Two days later, the *Courier* wrote,

The tide has begun to turn under pressure from the St. Elizabeth and Westmoreland militia regiments and the British soldiers. The forces are augmented with marines and an additional 100 soldiers from Kingston. A large force has also been held in Kingston, to deal with any insurrection there and elsewhere. The General has also called on the Accompong Maroons to cover nearby areas.

I thought of Olumbo. The Maroons in his village refused to help the Brits; would the Accompong Maroons help them fight off slaves?

Vassell soon called another brief meeting, during which he read words from the newspaper to us. "'Unlike the Maroons, the freedom fighters are not skilled in bush warfare, and only a small number of them have firearms or are trained to use them. Most are armed with machetes, sharpened sticks and wooden clubs.'"

He looked up from the newspaper and grinned, reveling in the fact that the slaves might be defeated.

"Yes, but I hear slaves are fighting bravely, attacking armed militia men and soldiers," I said.

"I also read that they're breaking up into small groups, with bases in the forests. They're moving quickly from place-to-place. They're setting most plantations on fire," another overseer said.

"According to the *Courier,* the government is extending martial law another 30 days," I said.

"Jesus! When will this end?" Vassell asked, before ending the meeting and sending us home to rest. Like anyone could rest with everything going on.

Several days later, I saw Olumbo hurrying toward Miz Ada's hut. I walked up to him.

"Hey, Irishman, I see you survive burning. More worries comin,' though," he said, as I approached.

"What do you mean?"

"General name Cotton; his men bottle up slaves who rebel, take Montpelliers in the Great River Valley, and push rebels on to Belvedere and Greenwich," Olumbo said.

"What will that mean for the rebels?"

"They break up into small groups and hide in forests. Not good. We act like we don't see them. Other Maroons not so kind, 'cause of peace treaty."

"Good God!"

"End is near. Start gettin' slaves ready for harder times," Olumbo said.

"Talking about hard times; I need your help. Vassell still trying to starve slaves out to force them to continue working without pay. You know how I feel about starvation tactics."

"No worries, man. I already bring meat and river fish so slaves not starve. I send more tomorrow. And don't worry, Maroons from my village refuse to turn fightin' slaves in."

"Good. One way or another, we'll help them fight for freedom. I got cloth, tools and salt to trade with you. How are Asha, Ode and the boy?"

141

"Papa good. Asha walking 'round like princess in fancy dress from cloth you give her. She ask for you the other day," Olumbo said, a mischievous grin on his face. "And my boy good. He ask for his Mama a lot, though."

"I'll send more fancy cloth for the princess."

Olumbo walked into Miz Ada's hut, after a short knock on the door frame had her inviting him in.

I turned and headed to my quarters, my mind whirling with thoughts about the future. I must come up with a bigger plan to get through this. White planters will only retaliate with more violence. That was all they knew; beat them, maim them, control them.

But better days had to be coming. I could feel it.

Chapter 23

Another pounding on the door had me springing up in bed, yelling, "Who is it?" *Jesus, I wake in a panic many mornings, now. I'm exhausted and my head aches.*

"It's Zoya and Miz Ada."

"One minute," I yelled, dressing quickly and opening the door. The women stood there, staring up at me, fear in their eyes.

"What happened?"

"They capture three of the rebel leaders. And we hear that Daddy Sam Sharpe jus' give himself up," Zoya said.

"Come in. Don't let anyone hear you." Moving aside, I allowed the women to hurry past me. I invited them to sit around the dining table, and I sat in front of them. Miz Ada started talking.

"Thousands of us protesting cruelty and slave labor. Why we not deserve pay for work?"

Zoya slammed one fist on the table, "No matter how much they capture and kill our leaders, we not stop fighting. They will never break we spirit. We want freedom, and we plan to get it."

Miz Ada stood, paced back and forth, then flung herself back in the chair. "Now they blaming the Baptist preachers and gettin' ready to turn on them. They hate the preachers 'cause they teach us to read 'bout God, and that we should be free. White man just see us as beasts of burden."

"We hear white man gettin' ready for revenge. They goin' to kill everyone who take part in rebellion," Zoya said.

"They can't just kill people. There has to be trials —" I finally got a word in, but Miz Ada cut me off.

"They control everything. Trials don' mean nothing. And how we goin' to survive when they tryin' to starve us to death, like they did your people in Ireland?"

"No one will starve to death if I have anything to do with it. I found a way to get boars' meat and river fish to you. Between that and the provisions you grow, we'll be able to survive hard times till things get better. In the meantime, I need you to encourage your slave brothers to help us get the fields back together, so we can move on. Remember, you have nowhere else to go, and I'm still talking with Vassell about paying you for work. If we stick together, we'll make it through this."

"You good man, Mas Sean," Zoya said. The two rose and headed out the door.

Later that day, Gavin arrived, shoving a copy of the *Cornwall Courier* at me. Sitting at the table with Gavin across from me, I read the front page.

The rebellion has been crushed; whites are about to launch a reign of terror. Through court martials and civil courts, whites will start rapid convictions, hangings and savage floggings. Fourteen whites and three browns have been killed. Twelve whites and three browns have been wounded. Fourteen free persons and 750 slaves are facing convictions for alleged participation in the rebellion. Field slaves are in the majority, but a large number of participants are mechanics, drivers, and other skilled workers.

"Zoya and Miz Ada were right. Read the second page," Gavin said.

I turned the page and read out loud:

The Colonial Church Union, which was formed by planters and Anglican ministers of religion, are presenting a general petition to the Legislature for the expulsion of all sectarian missionaries. They want to prevent the dissemination of any religious doctrines, except for those of the English and Scottish churches.

I looked up at Gavin, my eyes wide, then I lowered my head.

"Listen to this. 'A few Baptist churches have already been destroyed, including one in nearby Falmouth.'"

I stopped reading. I slammed the paper down on the table. "It's like Ireland all over again. They're using the church to stay in control."

"Whites are terrified of the black majority, Sean. They're using the old tactic, 'teach them a lesson, terrorize and brutalize them so you stay on top.'"

"Slaves are expecting this; they refuse to back down. They're still chanting 'we rather die than be slave.'"

"Yeah, and it looks like England is about to take their side," Gavin said.

"What you mean?"

"Haven't you been reading the papers, Laddie? There've been political fights between the Whigs and the Tories. Riots just devastated Derby and Bristol. Yesterday, I read that the military was called out to prevent the burning of aristocratic properties. More destruction is expected as the English working class create havoc. They're demanding their own rights. And Britain's working class is also fighting for the abolition of slavery in Jamaica," Gavin said.

"Yes! Yes indeed!" I jumped out of my chair and pumped the air with one fist. "Freedom is coming, Gavin! I prayed for God to show us another way. Who would think he'd send us the British working class."

"Exciting news, Laddie. Jamaicans who can read must have passed this news around. No wonder slaves are refusing to back down."

In the weeks that followed, Olumbo and his people became even better trading partners, continuing to keep the slaves fed. But despite Zoya's and Miz Ada's pleadings, slaves refused to work without pay.

So, the other three overseers and I worked hard to clear burned-out sections of the cane fields. We also struggled to keep slaves calm, since news had spread that rebel leaders were captured, and that hundreds of rebels were now being tried.

But things got worse as whites sought revenge. They tarred and feathered another preacher in Falmouth. The Courier also reported that eleven Baptist churches had been destroyed, including those at Salters Hill, Falmouth, Montego Bay, Rio Bueno, Brown's Town, Lucea, and St. Ann's Bay.

I set up two meetings with Vassell in the midst of this mayhem. He flatly refused to negotiate any kind of pay for work, despite the fact that the second time I met with him, I had support from our three other overseers.

"Don't stop beating their asses. They'll come around. They'd rather die than be a slave? Good. I'd rather kill them than pay them."

Things had spun out of control; fear was beginning to gnaw at my gut. Gavin pounded on my door early one Thursday morning.

"Come ... come with me, Sean. They tried and convicted 580 rebel slaves and most of them have already been hung. They're hanging their leader, Sam Sharpe, today. I have one of Chambers' horse carts. Let's go."

Sitting next to Gavin in the two-seater horse cart, heading to the town square next to Montego Bay's court house, I stared at the devastation around me.

Burned stubs of sugar cane filled the fields; soot and charred fences showed up, everywhere. Rows of red, green and yellow crotons and clumps of flowering hibiscus leading to great houses had disappeared.

Verandas stood around charred sticks that were once wooden eaves. Slave children milled around, seeming lost and abandoned. And once more, crows hovered overhead, cawing expectantly.

Memories of Ireland during the famine threatened to haunt my senses. I quickly turned my eyes to the road ahead. As the cart got closer, slave men and women hurried along, on foot, in the direction of the town square. Then, in the distance, I saw a huge throng of slaves gathered around.

"That's the town square. Slaves are there to witness Sharpe's execution. It's going to be a rough day," Gavin said.

He pulled the cart up to a tree and I jumped down with him. He tied the reins around the tree trunk. I turned, walked toward the crowd next to Gavin, and pushed my way closer to the front.

The crowd erupted. A black man marched toward the middle of the square, flanked by two guards. Arms shackled behind him, the man, of medium height, had a fine, sinewy frame, and a broad, high forehead. He wore khaki pants that hung just over his ankles, a loose, blue, prison shirt, and black sandals. He had huge, piercing eyes that surveyed the crowd, from one side to the other. He stood erect, his head held high, courage and nobility in his stance. He seemed unmoved by the closeness of death.

"Did you know he was a Baptist preacher with his own church and congregation in Montego Bay?" Gavin whispered. I nodded.

The crowd immediately quieted down and stared ahead. Anger and tension thickened the air. The guards held Sharpe by the arms and walked him up the steps to a platform. Sharpe addressed the crowd in a clear, unwavering voice, like he was preaching to his congregation.

"Brothers and sisters, I have broken the law.

Now, I depend on salvation from the Redeemer,

Who shed his blood for sinners upon Calvary.

The missionaries had nothing whatever to do with the uprising.

I planned it, I organized it, and I executed it.

Freedom to you all, brothers and sisters,

I go with your blessing,

In the name of God Almighty!"

Sharp's reference to the crucifixion of Jesus by the Roman authorities had significance. Relating this to his own execution had resonated with the slaves gathered to watch his demise. *Demise? What the Hell am I thinking? This is a God damned lynching!*

The crowd yelled, 'Amen.' They soon quieted down. An eerie stillness tainted the air. A tropical dove flew overhead, cawing furiously. The executioner shoved Sharp's head into the noose. He tightened the rope.

Sharpe's body suddenly hung lifelessly above us all. I held back vomit. I shoved back tears. Sickness stabbed me in the gut. The crowd erupted into chants of freedom and defiance.

"No more slave - we die first.

No more whip, no more starvation.

We done ... we slave no more.

Hail, Daddy Sharpe! Hail, Daddy Sharpe! Rest in peace."

My ears stung. Insolence and determination fortified the air. I whispered the words of Psalm 27; "The Lord is my light and my salvation, whom shall I fear? The Lord is the strength of my life; of whom shall I be afraid ..."

By the time I was through, I knew, without a doubt, that Britain was about to free the slaves. The British working class would see to it. The time had come.

Chapter 24

"Sweet Jesus, I don't believe it! It's Quaker Tomas!" I said.

"Who?" Gavin asked.

"Over there, that's Quaker Tomas. I worked with him at a food kitchen in Ireland during the famine."

I pointed at the Quaker standing behind three men at the market. I hurried toward the man who'd caught my eye. Gavin scurried along next to me.

"I don't believe it — it's really you," I said, holding my hand out to the Quaker. It was like I'd run into an angel from above.

"Good God ... Sean! What you doing here?" He asked, shaking my hand over and over and slapping me on the shoulder.

"Came after burying my mother. What you doing here?"

"Here to help African Jamaicans adjust. Freedom is coming for them all."

"What? Dear God, finally! They've been fighting like animals for freedom; many of them have died fighting for the cause. This is the best news I've heard in a long time. How did this happen?" I wanted to hear what he knew, compared to the newspapers.

"The Baptist missionaries sent one of their men, William Knibb, a white Brit, to England. Knibb talked with the government about the hangings and Baptist church burnings. He pleaded for the slaves. He told them African Jamaicans had a right to religious teachings, to worship God, to learn to read and write, and to be free."

"Thank you, Lord," I raised my head and arms up to the sky.

"Soon after that, a Governor sent a dispatch about the number of rebels the planters had executed, the number of churches they'd burned, and other atrocious state of affairs. And an article published in the London *Extraordinary Gazette,* took Brits through it all. British and local newspapers reported that, through their martial and civil courts, the plantocracy and their military had launched a reign of terror, with trials in the morning, and savage floggings and hangings in the evening. After reading this, several societies began to press the government so hard for immediate emancipation, freeing the slaves became front and center in Parliament."

"Absolutely amazing," I said.

"That's not all, Sean. The British working class were already riled up about their own working conditions. They proceeded to pillage and riot for both themselves, and for the abolition of slavery in Jamaica. Britain now has little choice but to free the slaves," Quaker Tomas said.

When, in God's name, will this happen?" I asked.

"In a couple of weeks. Keep quiet about it till the official announcement is made."

"What about Ireland. They need you there, too."

"Had to bury too many of the dead. Almost lost my mind. Brits got me out and sent me here. Someone else has been sent there."

"So sorry, Laddie. Glad to see you, though. Forgive my manners; excitement got the best of me. Meet my friend, Gavin Ryan. Gavin's an overseer at the plantation next to mine." Gavin smiled, said hello, and shook the Quaker's hand.

"Another Irishman; indeed. Never thought I'd run into any here. Good to meet you, Gavin. So, Sean, you're an overseer here too? How's that working out?"

"Long story. Will tell you all about it when we have more time. Where you living?"

"Right here in town, not far from the plantations. Which one you work for?"

"Havendale."

"You're a brave man."

I laughed. "More like crazy."

"Here, take my address. Stop by and see me soon." The Quaker scribbled his address on a piece of paper he'd pulled from his breast pocket, and handed it to me.

Running into Quaker Tomas was a blessing. And the news about the abolition of slavery had my mind working overtime. I needed to focus on getting whatever assistance I could from the Quaker, so newly-freed slaves at Havendale and at Toco Plantation would be able to survive as free people.

Vassell and other planters would start planning reprisals; I just knew it. They would moan that Britain had abandoned them. They would blame emancipation for their economic woes.

But the slide in sugar production had started many years earlier. Jamaican planters had been facing strong competition from European beet sugar, and sugar from Mauritius, Brazil, Puerto Rico, Fiji, and Cuba; these countries still relied on slave labor.

And I read in the Courier that, in order to meet the demand for cheap food to feed its rapidly growing population, Britain had removed the preferential tariff on West Indian sugar. This opened the market to international competition, and tons of cheaper foreign sugar now entered Britain.

According to the Courier, several of the West Indian and British financial houses had gone into bankruptcy. So, planters were even more angry now, because they had to sell their crops on the open market, often at a loss. And most newly-freed slaves would probably not want to work on the plantations.

"There are reports of an outbreak of cholera and small pox on the island, Sean," Quaker Tomas said, the next time Gavin and I ran into him at the market.

"What? Where'd you hear this?" I asked, trying to push down fear.

"Just got a report from Britain's Anti-Slavery Society. They're the ones who sent me here, remember? I was going to try and get a message to you."

"Is it all over the island? What areas?"

"Mostly in the cities, Kingston and Spanish Town. Population is dense in these areas, and sometimes there are many living in one small room, passing diseases around."

"Dear God, I'm seeing the fever again in Ireland."

"Not the same. People are not really starving here. Blacks have the strength to fight off disease. Not sure about whites, though. You be careful."

"Good point," I said.

"Go home and lay low. Talk with Vassell about keeping the plantation as isolated from newcomers as possible. We don't want disease spreading to other areas."

"We can get our hands on meat and fish, enough provisions to survive for a couple of weeks. Thanks for the information. You should lay low, too; be careful. I'll stop by sometime," I said, before Gavin and I headed out.

Vassell did not take the news about cholera well.

"We're in the middle of a God damned drought, and now this? The Gods are punishing us, I tell you. Why the Hell did we have to mess up the sugar trade? How much more of this will we have to take?"

I focused on getting him to understand what needed to be done to keep disease away. I also went to Toco Plantation, and Gavin and I briefed the owner on how to handle things. I urged him to spread the news.

Just when I thought things were under control, I awoke one morning sweating like a pig. I tried to get out of bed and got knocked back down, pain in my body feeling like Vassell's three-horse cart had run me over.

I laid at the edge of the bed, panting, trying to gather more strength to rise. Then I heard a knock at the door.

"Come in," I said, my voice a weak croak.

"Sweet ancestors, what happen'?" Zoya asked, staring at me laying there, looking like death was knocking at the door.

"I feel sick."

"Sweat all over you. You can stand?"

I struggled to stand and dropped back down on the edge of the bed. Zoya hurried to one corner of the room, grabbed my pants, shirt, and an old white rag. She dipped the rag into a basin of water on the corner table and hurried back to me.

"Take off you' shirt. I wipe you with cool rag. I help you put clothes on. Then we go."

"Where ... where we going?"

"Straight to Miz Ada's hut. She rub bush medicine all over you."

I struggled out of my shirt and Zoya wiped my face and upper body with the cool rag. Then she said.

"Hold up your arm. I put your shirt on. I help put your pants on, too." Like a child, I followed her instructions, too weak to resist.

Several minutes later I staggered to Miz Ada's hut, one arm over Zoya's shoulders. Her arm wrapped tightly around my waist, she kept me steady as I stumbled along.

Havendale had not yet come to life on that early Sunday morning. I was grateful, because I knew I looked wretched. The obeah woman's hut soon came into view, and Zoya yelled, "Miz Ada I need your help."

"Aah! Come this way, Child." Miz Ada rushed over, grabbed me by the waist on the other side of Zoya, and the two women dragged me through the door of the hut. They heaved me on to a cot.

I laid there, moaning, feeling like I was knocking at death's door. *Sweet Jesus, not the fever. I thought I left it behind in Ireland. Don't let me die here from the fever,* I thought, my mind going in and out of consciousness.

The women yanked every piece of clothing from my body. I winced and tried to rise.

"Stay still, Mas Sean. I take real' good care'a you," Miz Ada said.

Her hands rubbed liquid all over my body; it smelled like real strong bush. But I actually felt my body cooling down. Miz Ada then grabbed an old white sheet and a big piece of burlap.

"Help me, Child,'" she said to Zoya.

Miz Ada rubbed another liquid on my feet, especially on the sole. The two women wrapped my body in the white sheet, and then the burlap. They left my head out.

Thank God! I was starting to think I died and they were getting ready to bury me without a coffin, just like I did my mother.

"What you doing?" I asked, almost disoriented.

"Gettin' you to sweat-out the fever. Here, drink this," Mis Ada said, handing me a vial of dark-green liquid. Zoya raised my head from the cot. I opened my mouth, swallowed the liquid, knitted my brows and smacked my lips. It tasted awful. I handed the empty vial back to the obeah woman.

"Taste bad, but heal real good," she said. Then she paused and issued more instructions.

"Zoya, pass that old rag over there. Dip it in the basin in the corner." Soon, a cool, wet rag laid on my forehead and wrapped around my head. Fumes from the soaked rag crept into my nostrils and I felt like it crawled all over my face and deep into my head. Soon, I felt nothing.

I must have laid there, in and out of consciousness, because I kept feeling myself swallowing more foul-tasting bush medicines and chicken broth. I also felt Miz Ada's hands all over me as she unwrapped me, rubbed me down with remedies, wrapped my naked body back up, and wrapped more wet rags around my head.

My body sweated so much, I heard the obeah woman tell someone to wash and hang-dry the sheet and burlap, so she had a change of cloth each time she unwrapped me.

I finally opened my eyes one day, feeling really good. I stared around. I was still in Miz Ada's hut, wrapped-up like a mummy.

The room was larger than the average slave hut. It was neat and well-kept. There was another cot next to the one I laid on, and at the other end of the room, I saw a small straw bed, well spread, on a dark-brown, polished, wooden platform. Two wooden boxes sat upside-down, on each side of the bed.

One corner of the room had a hemp line with a few pieces of clothes hanging on it. Another corner had a rough-looking wooden table and two old wooden chairs. Next to the table was another wooden box with clothes.

I tried to move and couldn't. I groaned.

"Aaah, the Irish man come back to life," Miz Ada said, moseying over to me.

"How long I've been here?"

"Three days. Fever gone. Feelin' better?"

"Feel like a new man, Miz Ada. What you do?"

"Don' you worry 'bout that. Had to heal you. Dead Irish man no use to us."

"The fever. What was it?" I asked, fear threatening to wash over me once more.

"Dengue fever. Make you feel real' bad, but easier to heal than others."

"Thank God. For a minute, I thought you were about to bury me alive."

"We not ready to bury Irishman yet. He too kind to us," the obeah woman said, staring into my eyes, smiling mischievously.

"Vassell knows I've been sick?"

"Yes, Zoya tell him. Come, I help you get clothes on. I walk you to your quarters," Miz Ada said. I felt really good.

"Thank you, Miz Ada. I won't ever forget this." I dressed myself and headed out the door, telling her I could get to my quarters on my own.

As I ambled along, I thought about Miz Ada. No wonder slaves loved the obeah woman and depended on her to heal their wounds. That woman acted like an angel.

In the days ahead, there were no reports of deadly disease at Havendale, and we were thankful. I kept us isolated, and was able to convince our slaves to stay put until we got news that the threat of disease had passed.

They agreed; fear had made them obedient.

Chapter 25

I sprang up in bed to midnight cries and the loud blowing of conch shells.

"The monster is dead ... we slave no more!" I heard, over and over.

Rushing to urgent knocks on my door, I opened it to Zoya and Miz Ada, jumping up and down and prancing around like Maroons moving to the rhythm of the drums.

"We free ... we free, Mas Sean!"

"What ... what's happening?" I asked, wiping sleep from my eyes.

"Brits jus' abolish slavery for good! For good, Mas Sean!" Zoya yelled.

"Where'd you hear that?"

"At gathering at Mas William Knibb church," Miz Ada said.

She grabbed my hands and had me prancing around with her, outside the door, in the dark, a big, round moon shining down from above. I had little rhythm, but I didn't resist.

"Thanks, Mas Sean, for everythin' you did to help free us. Everybody up and dancing in the streets. We gone," Zoya said, and they danced away in the dark.

I closed my door and knew there would be no more sleep that night. Slaves screamed joyfully and horns blasted through the night air, forcing crickets and tree frogs into a longer retreat.

Light streamed by my windows and I peeked through. Men and women joyfully danced by with torches raised high and children prancing happily behind. Drums pelted the elements as feet stomped the earth. Maroons must have arrived to celebrate with their brothers and sisters.

I could stay put no more. I quickly dressed myself and left my quarters. I wanted to stomp the earth with them, but I remained quiet, following along and watching. Afterall, it would get ugly if Vassell saw me stomping the earth with his newly-freed slaves.

Never, in my life, had I seen African Jamaicans so joyful, and it was like pumpkin soup to my very soul. Nothing and no one, would stop these strong, passionate and determined people now.

In the weeks that followed, freedom celebrations erupted all over the island. But I laid awake at night, wondering how I could help newly-freed African Jamaicans survive. I must meet with Gavin and Quaker Tomas, and plan next steps to provide resources and support.

How would they pull through? They knew nothing but forced labor, the sting of the whip, and mental beat-downs. They were always told they were nothing, but they stubbornly insisted they were something; they were human beings who must fight for freedom and regard. And they fought like panthers; many had fought to their own deaths, but they didn't die for nothing. Like the Maroons said, 'freedom or death, no other option.'

Memories of my visit to Olumbo's Maroon village soon came rushing back. Those people were proud, independent and determined. Maroons had waged bush warfare for their freedom, and had protected that freedom with every bone in their bodies.

The slaves were no Maroons, but the look on Daddy Sharp's face as he walked to the gallows that day; the look in his piercing eyes, told me these people were no victims. Sharpe had been a slave, too, and he had led the fight for freedom of his brothers and sisters. There would be challenges, but freed African Jamaicans would make it.

I kept appealing to newly-freed slaves to work parts of the field that had been saved, but they refused to.

Vassell had withdrawn into an eerie silence; I didn't know what was coming next. He knew his attempts to starve slaves back to the fields did not work, but he didn't know why.

And Maroons kept showing up in the shadows of night to trade meat and fish, thanks to Olumbo. Zoya and Miz Ada brought food for me and the other overseers at night. The overseers continued to get paid, and we worked the fields as much as we could. But there was just not enough labor. And the summer rains were almost here, with the mosquitos swarming.

The *Cornwall Courier* wrote continuous stories about the abolition of slavery.

Sam Sharpe, other freedom fighters, and the British working class, had reset the timetable for freedom. Jamaica had been a searing picture of a society in which property was put before the human being, and violence became the first resort in maintaining authority. Now, African Jamaicans stand free to pick up the pieces of their lives, and move on with faith and courage

Vassell called me to the great house a day later. As I approached the house, not knowing what to expect, I saw two men repairing verandah heaves that had been damaged during the burnings. Another man worked the burned-out garden in front of the verandah, tilling soil and planting crotons and hibiscus. I walked next to a wooden ladder that held one of the men, and knocked on the half-closed door.

"Come in," Vassell yelled. I entered the living room and saw him sitting on the settee, sipping a cup of tea. "Want tea?" He asked.

"No, thank you."

"Grab a seat over there."

He pointed to an arm-chair across from the settee. He was strangely quiet and composed, but I expected a torrent of rantings from his lips at any minute.

The rantings never came. Instead, he asked that I take his small horse cart and pick things up at the market. He wanted one whole chicken, two pounds of boars' meat, one bag of sweet potatoes, and so forth.

I grabbed pencil and paper from the table next to the arm-chair, and wrote down the list of goods. I said goodbye and headed out toward the horse cart, which was hitched to a big lignum vitae tree at the side of the house.

I was perplexed. Why wasn't Vassell ranting? What in God's name had been going on? I needed to know, soon.

I pulled the horse cart up to Toco Plantation's gates and asked the guard to get Gavin. A few minutes later, Gavin walked briskly toward the cart.

"Heading to the market. Take the ride with me?"

"Could use a ride this morning, Laddie. Been up nights listening to joyful freedom celebrations. Have news for you, too. Give me a minute," he said, turning and hurrying back to the fields.

Several minutes later, he returned, grabbed the side of the cart, heaved himself up, and plopped down next to me. I pulled the reins and we headed to town.

"Our people are finally free, Gavin. They're still celebrating in the streets at Havendale. I'm so thrilled for them."

"Me too. They deserve every second of happiness they're feeling. You haven't heard the other news, then?"

"Which news? There's been a lot of news lately."

"This one is big! Britain announced that slave owners in Jamaica will receive compensation amounting to a total 6,616,927 pounds," Gavin said.

"Holy Christ! What for?"

"Get this; for 'the inconvenience and loss they are expected to suffer when they no longer controlled the forced labor which had been the mainstay of their lifestyles.'" My mouth flew open.

"You mean their cruel and opulent lifestyles?"

"You got it."

"No wonder Vassell was so smug this morning. He's getting a shit-load of money."

"Aye, Laddie."

"What about the Africans they brought here and maimed and abused? They're the ones who did all the work in the cane fields.

There are ten times more of them than whites around here. What the Hell will they get?"

"They'll get freedom. That's it."

"But they have no guidance, no training to pull themselves up out of oppression. I don't believe this. What the Hell is Britain thinking?"

"There's more coming their way too, Sean."

"What now?"

"The Brits have decreed that freed slaves will become 'apprenticed laborers' for a number of years."

"What does that mean?"

"According to British government, as apprenticed laborers, they must, by law, receive pay for work, food, clothing, lodging, medicine, and medical care," Gavin said.

"Whites are going to manipulate that. We've got to find a way to help them survive."

"I have a thought."

"What is it? Tell me, now."

"I overheard a conversation Chambers had with Vassell yesterday. They might take the money and run."

"Take the money and run?"

"Think about it. If they're getting all that money from Britain, why should they stay here and deal with things?"

"You're right! I'm getting a feeling here," I said, my mind racing.

"Remember us talking about saving to buy our own place? This might be our chance, Sean."

I paused; my mind raced even faster.

This Irish man is a true genius.

Chapter 26

Gavin and I met to talk about our plans to support newly-freed African Jamaicans. We also talked about money we were able to save, and how to make sure we stayed disciplined and focused on our plans. We passionately discussed the state of affairs in Jamaica. Before this visit, I was able to get my hands on some rum so I handed Gavin a calabash cup.

"Here, rum."

"Geez, thanks Laddie. I really need a drink."

We sipped our drinks quietly for a moment, then I said, "Let's go to town tomorrow and talk with Quaker Tomas about getting resources to help freed African Jamaicans adjust. The Quaker is well known, and can quickly get needed help from the Brits."

"Agreed. He'll need to help figure out how to move the island out of the hands of the plantocracy. The damned planters are still ruling the country, and they're going to make things hard for blacks."

"They've already started. Let's talk about that later. What do you think needs to be done to move things along without too much suffering?"

"Brits need to take over running the country, and let the planters take their money and run. It's the only way, Sean."

"You're right. Like what was done to put the abolition of slavery front and center in Parliament, we'll need to get word to the British government about all the cruel shenanigans the planters come up with, and you bet they're coming," I said.

"They're already here. But once we get Brits to take over, it's critical that we push for local representation in their government. And by local, I don't just mean mulattos and other high-colored Jamaicans. Ex-slaves need to be represented too."

"Definitely, Laddie. We have our work cut out for us. Let's get with Quaker Tomas as soon as possible."

"The good news is, we seem to have escaped disease. The Minister of Health's office thinks we're now clear, after losing thousands in the densely populated areas," Gavin said.

"Glad that's all behind us, especially after the dengue fever scare I had. I tell you, Gavin, if it wasn't for the obeah woman, I think I'd have been in deep trouble."

"Glad she took care of you, Laddie. By the way, did she predict your future? I hear she's good at that too."

"Predict my future? The way I felt, I didn't think I had a future." Gavin laughed out loud, but he became serious once more.

"Let's talk about what the planters are up to. You know that the Emancipation Act says freed slaves should continue living at the plantations and get the same food, clothing and medical care, right? One clause also says the planters should allow apprentices to live in their huts for a 3-month grace period, then work out some kind of arrangement with the massas," Gavin said, between sips of rum.

"I know."

"There was confusion about that clause, and the Jamaican Attorney General ruled in favor of the planters. If they stay in their huts, the apprentices will have to pay rent. Right away, every planter is asking for at least a third of weekly apprentice pay or telling them to move off of the premises. If they do not pay, they could be evicted with a week's notice."

"No, not eviction, Gavin. Remember what they did to our people in Ireland?"

"After the week, if they can't pay the rent, they could be arrested and put in prison."

"But the planters can barely pay them on time. How's that going to work? These people have just been set free; they have nowhere to go, and no education. And now they're being treated like tenants-at-will? When will they be free to live normal lives?"

"It's the same old 'massa' mentality. They think the apprentices would prefer to stay on the plantations because of their African traditions."

"What you mean?"

"They think they'll want to stay in the place they were born, with their provision grounds and the graves of their ancestors. They have nowhere else to go," Gavin said.

"Yah? Well, I hear most of them are grabbing on to their new freedom. They're squatting on Crown lands in the mountains or on abandoned estates. Many with trades are leasing, or trying to buy small plots of land, to build modest cottages, where no one can evict them."

"I know. But whites are working with the government to keep control and make life intolerable."

"What are you talking about?"

"Any African Jamaican found carrying produce without a written permit could be arrested with the assumption the goods were stolen. And they put a Trespass Act in place that permits the shooting of small stocks like goats and pigs, exactly the sort of animals that smallholders would have. But horses and cows from the plantations are exempt," Gavin said.

"Now that you say it, I read in the papers that landlords are constantly moving workers' cottages to make sure they can't benefit from permanent crops like coconuts and breadfruit, which they planted. People are having to pull down and rebuild their cottages at their own expense. So now, they build shabby little huts. They don't maintain the huts because they know they may have to tear them down at any time. I knew planters were vindictive, but this is ridiculous."

"Right now, the missionaries are on the sides of freed slaves. And with a few Quakers here too, life should get better for them."

"We need to decide how we can buy a place of our own," I said.

"This may be the time. Sugar has gone way down in value, and that means land is also losing value. We may need to strike while the stew is hot."

I got Vassell to agree to pay three shilling per week to our apprentices at Havendale, and they started working the fields once more. I explained that it might take time for them to get paid because of the working capital and negative sugar trade problem. They still agreed to work. They trusted me, and I didn't want to let them down.

The next time I got my hands on the Courier, there were reports of reprisals on the apprentices who stayed to work the plantations. Planters were angry and bitter.

Reports said that since apprenticeship, thousands of apprentices received brutal lashings, and thousands received other punishments by tread-mill, chain-gang work, or some other device.

Those sent to the workhouses got lashed with cat-o-nine tails and chained by the neck to other men, or forced on the treadmill that was used to grind cornmeal, which fed the prisoners. They were flogged if they couldn't quickly 'catch the step' of the treadmill.

I got sick in the gut when I read this.

But at Havendale, I managed to keep Vassell at bay. And some nights, I thought about how different things might have been if there had been men strong enough to stand up for our rights in the old country.

Planters had not learned, even though their plantations had almost been burned to the ground during uprisings. Just like slaves had carried the marks of the whip on their backs, planters in Jamaica carried with them the tensions and anxieties of living in a fortified society ruled by fear, and now by feelings of British abandonment.

Things had to get better, though. There was no way in Hell, they could get any worse.

Chapter 27

"Chambers is gone, Sean. He abandoned the plantation," Gavin said, rushing into my quarters after I'd opened the door to another urgent knock. He looked like he'd just jumped out of bed and quickly dragged yesterday's clothes on. He paused, brushed disheveled hair from his face, and stared at me. Fighting off sleep, I could muster only one word.

"What?"

"Two days ago, after he beat the apprentice, Andi, close to death, four big apprentice men suddenly surrounded him. One grabbed his hand with the whip, stared into his face and said, 'We no more slave. One more lash and we go to hangman noose for beatin' you to death!'"

"Dear God, I knew it would come to this. How do you know he's really gone?"

"Talked to two of his house slaves. They said he'd been packing his personal things for the past two days. They also said he'd been talking with Vassell."

"Come to think of it, I haven't seen Vassell in the last two days. Thought he may just be laying low."

"Oh Boy!"

"Grab a seat over there. Let me get dressed, then we'll walk to the great house and check on Vassell."

It was a nice morning, the skies a bright blue. There wasn't a cloud in sight. Only a few people had stirred on the plantation to start their day. A balmy morning breeze rustled the hem of my loose cotton shirt as I hurried along, Gavin next to me.

I got to the great house, mounted the steps to the verandah, and knocked on the door. Footsteps approached briskly. The door opened, and Vassell's housekeeper, Ella, stood in front of me.

"Ella, we here to see Massa Vassell. You know Mas Gavin," I said, looking at Gavin and then at her.

"He gone, sah. I was comin' to see you this morning," she said.

"Where'd he go?" I asked.

"Don' know, sah. Don' think he comin' back."

"Why you say that?"

"All day yesterday he was packin' up his clothes and such, grumbling and yellin' at us to bring him this and that. He mumble somethin' 'bout leaving this God damn' Hell hole behind."

"Did he leave a note, Ella?" I asked.

"No, sah."

"All right, you stay here with the other house apprentices. Don't let anyone into the house. I'll come back soon and let you know what to do next."

"Okay, Mas Sean." Gavin and I walked away as she closed the door behind us.

"Back to my place, Gavin. Let's talk about things there."

We hurried back to my quarters in silence, my mind racing. A pot of tea and a plate of fried cassava had been left outside the door. Zoya must have just left, because the tea was still hot. I picked up the food and headed inside, Gavin behind me.

"Grab a seat. I'll get us two cups."

I put the food on the dining table and headed to the kitchen for cups. Returning, I poured tea into the two cups and Gavin removed the cloth covering the cassava. We quietly ate and sipped tea. Gavin broke the silence.

"You know what this means?"

"Oh yes! This could be the chance we've been waiting for."

"We could put together, buy these two plantations, and do what we planned with them. This is our chance to give the apprentices the freedom they've earned and deserve, maybe even empower them with land ownership," Gavin said.

"Aye. No time to waste. You think those two cruel cowards owe money on the properties?"

"I once heard Chambers talking to one of his friends about owing money to Planters Bank here in Jamaica." Gavin paused and his eyes popped open.

"That's it! Most whites on the island use that bank to finance their land. Let's go talk with them."

"Hold it! Remember Quaker Tomas? He has a lot of contacts on the island. He can help us."

"You got his address, right?"

"He lives at 5 Queen Street in town. We'll take Vassel's personal horse cart. Let's go."

Gavin and I headed to town in the cart, the horse picking up a spirited canter as we moved along.

The sun shone brightly, and I could feel the promise of a warm, tropical day. I glanced around. Lignum vitae, thatch palm, fan palm, coconut and breadfruit trees, loomed large. And they were lusciously green.

We took a short gallop along the coastline, and beauty washed over my senses, as it always did. The ocean laid there, sporting different shades of turquois. White sand reached out on the shore like puffs of clouds on a clear day. Sea grape trees leaned over crystal-clear waters, surrendering to the weight of fruit almost ready for picking and devouring.

I glanced at the other side of the shore. Poinciana trees stood in full bloom. Their stunning red and yellow flowers were like healing powers to my soul.

Beloved Ireland, I don't plan to return to your shores just yet. You're in a better position to recover than these folks. Freed Jamaicans have nothing; they need me more right now. I knew there were challenges ahead, but I needed to make things work here.

We got to the town center. I pulled the reins and headed toward the Quaker's house. Turning on to Queen Street, I slowed the horses down as we approached number 5.

Pulling the cart up, I hitched the reins to a tree in front of the small, old, white, wooden house with its shingled roof. The house looked like it was in need of some repairs.

Gavin and I walked three steps up to the small verandah, and I knocked on the door. A man's voice yelled, 'Coming,' and soon, we heard footsteps approaching. Quaker Tomas opened the door.

"Sean, good to see you, Old Chap. You just caught me. I was about to leave on an errand."

"Glad we caught up with you. Really need your help. Can you spare a few minutes? Remember my friend, Gavin?"

"Of course. Come in, you two. I have fresh lemonade. Want some?"

The Quaker walked us into a room with a small dining table to the left, and a bed with two wooden crates on each side, serving as tables. The crate to the left side of the well-made bed had a large, black bible on top. The walls stood bare, except for an old, frameless picture of the ocean hanging above the bed.

"Thank you," I said, sitting at the table. Gavin sat next to me and our host quickly joined us with three cups of lemonade. He put a cup each in front of us, and then he sat down.

"Now tell me. How can I help?" I got straight to the point, not wanting to make him late for his errands.

"Vassell and Chambers have both abandoned the plantations. Gavin and I want to buy both properties."

"Interesting. They left the island?"

"Yes," Gavin said.

"There have been reports of planters abandoning their properties and going back to England. The price of sugarcane has hit rock bottom, labor has been in short supply since the abolition of slavery, and the value to properties have crashed. Planters are running scared," the Quaker said.

"Let them run. We want to buy both properties. Can you help?" Gavin asked.

"Are there mortgages?" Quaker Tomas asked.

"We think they're under loans with Planters Bank here on the island," I said.

"I know the managing director of the branch here in town. Let's pay him a visit and see what can be worked out. You available on Thursday?"

"We'll make ourselves available. What time should we meet you?" I asked.

"Ten in the morning. I'm heading in that direction today, anyway. I'll stop by the bank and make an appointment. He's a Brit; his name is Mark Edwards. He's a good man."

"We want to talk with you about getting more resources for freed African Jamaicans. We also want to discuss how to help move the island from plantocracy and into the hands of the British government," I said.

"Funny you should say that. I just heard that Britain is considering exactly that. Let's talk further about this when we have more time."

Gavin and I thanked the Quaker and headed home. My spirits leapt up to the skies. My heart filled to the brim with hope.

I must tell Gavin not to discuss our plans with anyone but the Quaker and the bank. I trusted Quaker Tomas, and he seemed to trust the bank manager. Brits were known to stick together; I had no intention of having our efforts sabotaged by greed and jealousy.

Chapter 28

"Good to see you again, Mark. Brought two friends from Ireland to meet you. This is Sean O'Sullivan and Gavin Ryan. Sean and Gavin, this is Mark Edwards, managing director of the bank," Quaker Tomas said.

"Pleasure to meet you, Mr. Edwards," I said, shaking hands with the man I felt very happy to meet.

"Same here," Gavin said, also shaking Edwards' hand.

A middle-aged Englishman, Edwards had piercing turquoise eyes, a sharply-straight nose, and dirty blond hair that laid neatly cut around his face and ears. He wore a dark gray cotton suit, white shirt, and a light-blue-and-gray bow tie. He had a thin, narrow gold ring on his wedding finger. He seemed dull and all about business, but I'd seen him perk up when he saw Quaker Tomas. He obviously had great respect and affection for the Quaker.

"Irishmen indeed. How long you both been here?"

"Close to three years," I said. Quaker Tomas got straight to the point.

"Sean and Gavin are head overseers at Havendale and Toco Plantations on the west side of town. Unfortunately, they just discovered that both owners have abandoned the plantations. They're interested in buying both properties."

"This is happening all over the island, owners cutting and running back to England, leaving us all to pick up the pieces. Very sad," Edwards said.

"Indeed. But Sean and I are not going anywhere. We're prepared to buy both properties," Gavin said.

"We're aware that sugar is on the way out, and that property values have plummeted. Seems to us it's a good time to buy," I said.

"What do you plan to do with the properties?" Edwards asked.

"We plan to grow produce that are now in great demand for export, like bananas, ginger, arrowroot, and pimento," I said.

"Sounds like a good plan. You both seem to have given this a lot of thought. Let me pull up the files for both properties so we can discuss further. Give me a few minutes."

"While you're doing that, I must go to another appointment. Sean and I go back a long way. We've both experienced more challenges and devastation than I could ever explain. He's a hard worker; a good man. I recommend him highly. Take care of him and his friend, please," The Quaker said.

He rose, shook Edwards' hand, bid us goodbye, and headed out. Gavin and I glanced at each other. What a stroke of luck; this was more than we could ever have asked for.

As we waited for the managing director to return, I looked around. We sat around a huge, mahogany desk, cluttered with files and papers. The office had a mahogany shelf in one corner, a small table in the other with a tray, a teapot, and a couple of metal cups. The door to the office was ajar, and I could see a bustle of activity in the main area as employees, all white, worked to address the needs of people in two lines.

"Let's see what we have here," Edwards said.

He'd returned with two big, old files, sat down, and began leafing his way through them, one at a time. He made occasional murmurs of, 'Mmmmm.' He finally closed the second file and looked from me to Gavin.

"Gentlemen, I think we could work something out."

"Great. I assume there are mortgage balances on both properties?" I asked.

"Yes, but not huge amounts. Vassell and Chambers have owned the estates for over 20 years and have paid the mortgage down considerably."

"How much will it take for us to pay off the mortgage and take over the properties. As you know, property values are less than 60 percent of what they once were, what with Jamaican sugar no longer dominating the market and Britain in a state of economic upheaval," I said, making sure Edwards knew we were on top of things and aware of what the land may now be worth.

"And things will be even more difficult, with a dwindling supply of labor after the abolition of slavery. Ex-slaves no longer wish to do plantation work. They're leaving in droves for city areas, and setting up small huts on crown land," Gavin said.

"You're right. Given all this and your relationship with Quaker Tomas, I will work out a deal for you both. Give me two days; I'll also need to talk with the higher-ups."

"We could be back here next Tuesday. What time is good for you?" I wasted no time.

"How about two in the afternoon?"

"Perfect. Gavin and I will be here then."

We shook hands with Edwards and walked out of the bank toward the horse cart. I unhitched the reins, climbed up and took my seat, with Gavin next to me.

We headed back home in silence, trying to process what had just happened. My mind raced here and there, anxious, cautiously optimistic. Gavin finally broke the silence.

"It's about to happen, Sean. We're finally going to have our own properties."

"Easy, Laddie. After facing death and destruction in Ireland, I've learned to be very cautious."

"You mean you learned to be negative. Don't do it, not about this. We will make it work."

"You're right. I need to be optimistic. Sweet Jesus, could this really be happening?"

"Better believe it!"

"We'll have to share all details with Quaker Tomas. His help will be needed to make more things happen."

"Once we own the properties, we can share everything with the Quaker, not before. He'll help us even more then, if he can. He's here to do good for the people."

"You're right, Gavin. Oh my God, my heart is pounding."

"Mine too. Like the ex-slaves would say, 'we're on our way, my brotha.'"

"Aye. Damned right."

I jiggled the rein and the horse galloped along, faster.

Chapter 29

As usual, a knock at the front door woke me up. After asking for a minute and quickly dressing myself, I opened the door.

"Morning Sah. Olumbo say he want to see you, urgent he say. I bring him," Zoya said, standing outside the door, Olumbo by her side.

"I come to talk with you, Irishman. Real serious," Olumbo said.

"Of course. Thanks for bringing him, Zoya." She nodded, turned, and headed back toward her hut.

"Come in, man. Want some tea?" I asked. Olumbo looked at me like I had three eyes. He'd probably never been invited into a white man's house.

"Come on in; it's all right." He walked gingerly into my quarters and quietly looked around.

"Sit at the table. I'll get the tea." I quickly returned to the table with two cups of tea and handed him one. I sat down in front of him and took a sip.

"What's going on?"

"I hear Massa Vassell gone," he said.

"Damned Coward! Yes, we think he went back to England."

"What happen to Havendale now? You goin' back to Ireland?"

"Oh no, I'm staying here."

"New massa coming?"

"I plan to be the new massa."

"What you mean?"

"I'm buying the place." Olumbo stared at me, incredulous.

"What 'bout Toco Plantation? I hear their massa run too."

"Buying that too, me and Mas Gavin."

"The other Irishman who work there?"

"Yes. We working as a team to buy both properties."

"That's jus' the news I wanted to hear. New free people been worried. Want me to tell them?"

"Not yet. Just tell them to stop worrying, that I say all will be well. Try to stop them from leaving. Tell them I'll meet with them in a few days to talk about what's going on."

"Okay. But meet soon. Some already plannin' to walk away."

"I will. Drink your tea, man. It's all right." I saw that he hadn't taken a sip of tea. Then I seemed to surprise him with a question. "How's Asha?"

His eyes narrowed. "Asha real' good."

"Can you take me back to visit your folks after I talk with our new, free people? They call them apprentices now."

"Yah, let me know when. I never forget what you did for my son. I visit again real' soon."

"Before you go, I want you to know there's even more hope for your ex-slave brothers and sisters. Gavin and I are working with someone high up with the Brits, to get resources that will help folks adjust to freedom. I worked with this person in Ireland to feed the sick and starving. We saved many lives by serving them cups of soup. Anyway, this person is also going to help to remove the planters from governing this island."

"Remove planters? Who replace them?"

"Probably the Brits, until Jamaica is ready for self-government."

"You trust Brits?"

"I wouldn't say so. But the British working class is watching the government's every move. They were the ones who pressured the government to abolish slavery and to end the abuse of Jamaican slaves." Olumbo looked me deep in the eyes; it was like he looked into my very soul.

"Before I leave today, I ask Zoya to pull everyone together so I can tell them not to worry and stay put. I tell them you and Mas Gavin workin' on plans that will be real good for everyone. I not give no details 'bout what we discuss."

I put one hand on his shoulder and stared him in the eyes.

"Great idea. Thank you. Also, thanks for the friendship and support. Mean the world to me."

"You good white man, and I want what's best for everyone 'round here."

The following Tuesday, Gavin and I got all dressed up and took the horse cart to our appointment with the bank's managing director. After close to three hours of negotiations, we drove back home with big smiles on our faces and hope in our hearts.

We had bought Havendale and Toco Plantation at deeply discounted prices based on what was left on both loans, and on the financial and social conditions on the island and in Great Britain. As partners, this left us with enough working capital to begin planting, but not enough to pay wages right away. But we had a better plan that we hadn't yet discussed with anyone.

Excitement wrapped around me like a comforting, warm, bath robe. I now had the power to help people who had suffered. I would make up for the times I was helpless, hungry, and unable to make things better. Praise the Lord. Now, I could fulfill my purpose.

Gavin and I pulled the cart up to my quarters, and I invited him in for a drink of rum. We sat at the dining table and clicked our cups.

"Here's to us, and to a future of making money and helping those less fortunate make their own money," I said.

"Here, here."

Gavin and I took long sips. Afterward, we reviewed plans we'd already made for the properties, making sure there were no misunderstandings. As always, Gavin and I were on the same page.

"Let's pay Quaker Tomas a visit tomorrow and thank him for his assistance. We can also share details of our plans with him, and talk more about changing the island's politics," I said.

"Good idea, Laddie. Something tells me he'll be able to help us all, especially the apprentices."

During our visit with the Quaker, he got really excited as Gavin and I shared our plans for the properties. After congratulating and complimenting us, Quaker Tomas stared at me, and then at Gavin.

"You've come a long way from starvation and death in Ireland to this beautiful place of conflict, and now hope. I want to help with your mission; it will be so fulfilling."

"We were hoping you'd feel that way. I'm so very pleased, Quaker Tomas," I said.

"I know people with money in England who are extremely supportive of the abolition efforts, and want to help in any way they can. They will be happy to help the apprentices if we call on them."

"We'll definitely need their assistance. Would you also start planting the seed about removing the cruel and oppressive plantocracy?" I asked.

"Seed already planted, my friend. Britain is working to turn Jamaica into a Crown Colony. Please keep that piece of news quiet." My eyes flew open.

"That is great news! Let's also work on getting local people into the government agencies. African Jamaicans will need strong representation."

"Absolutely! Exciting times ahead, Bloke."

"Gavin and I will announce what's going on at the plantations, to our apprentices, tomorrow morning. We've set up a meeting at eleven in the morning; we'll treat them to lunch. Will you attend?"

"Happy to. Nothing would please me more than seeing the looks on the faces of ex-slaves when you make those announcements. I'm thrilled! You're about to make a difference in the lives of people who have suffered, like your people in Ireland did. I'm proud of you both."

On our way back to the plantations, Gavin and I stopped at the Montego Bay United Baptist Church for a meeting with Pastor Mullings, the church's head. Mullings was very popular with local African Jamaican church goers, and he had a strong influence on other pastors in surrounding areas, such as Hanover, St. Ann,

Trelawney, and of course, St. James. I had sent Zoya and Mis Ada to the church yesterday to request an appointment with the pastor, so he was expecting us.

After welcoming us, Pastor Mullings led the way through the church hall, and then to his office. A short, stout, middle-aged, African Jamaican man, he had hair graying at the temples. He wore a loose, short-sleeved, white cotton shirt, black pants, and black boar-skin shoes. Around his neck hung a large, silver cross on crisp, black ribbon. He had a brisk gait.

The pastor invited us to sit around a small wooden table in his office, and we explained our plans for the plantation. His serious manner changed to sheer delight.

"I've been praying for a blessing for my brothers and sisters who've been set free with no support from the government. And here you come, with the most amazing plan I've heard in a very long time. Thank you, Lord!" He said, looking up at the ceiling. "You are the blessing God has sent me. Of course, I'll assist. Blessings to you both!"

"Thank you. We hope this will have a big impact on the lives of our people," I said.

"My brothers, not only will my church help, I plan to pull all other churches in surrounding areas into the project. God will bless us all."

Gavin and I rode back to the plantations, our spirits soaring. I dropped him off so he could prepare his people for the event the next day. As the horse cart approached the great house at Havendale, I saw a team of men and women assembling tables and preparing the clearing in front for the upcoming event. They were led by Zoya, Miz Ada, and two house apprentices.

I hitched the cart to a tree nearby, rolled up my sleeves, and joined the preparations. Smells of curry, pimento, and garlic soon wafted by. The team of cooks that prepared meals during slavery, had already got busy preparing for cooking early the next morning. Olumbo and his people had agreed to provide extra pounds of boars' meat, cassavas, and pumpkins for the event, in exchange for tools and cloth. We worked till late that evening, and I retired in the great house for the first time.

Sleeping in the great house really had me off balance. The house came with terrible, brutal memories, like Vassell's tantrums at his weekly overseer meetings, his cruelty to the house slaves, and young concubines that he bedded and flogged.

As soon as I made my announcements and we'd celebrated, I planned to have Miz Ada come in with burning sage and other herbs she used to drive out evil. I'd feel better about the place after that. After all, Miz Ada was my 'angel' too. I might even ask Pastor Mullings to visit and bless the place.

But tonight, I'd have to make-do with a nice dinner and bath, provided by the well-trained ex-house slaves, who were now apprentices. By the time bedtime came, they'd handed me a cup of herb tea that would make me 'sleep real good'. The tea began to work the minute I laid my head on the pillow and closed my eyes. A good night's sleep will prepare me for tomorrow's events.

* * *

I held my face up to the blue yonder. A beautiful day surrounded me, with not a single cloud in the brilliant blue skies. In the distance, two blooming Poinciana trees filled with red flowers that shaded the earth with glory, stared back at me. Around the clearing stood huge mango, plum, and tropical almond trees, filled with fruit. Just thinking about allowing apprentice children to fill their bellies with fruit made me smile. I glanced up again, as a tropical dove flew by, cooing melodiously. This would be a day I'd never forget.

Soon, Gavin stood next to me behind a long, wooden table in front of the throng of anxious Havendale and Toco Plantation apprentices. More than 100 men, women and children stood there, waiting for the news we'd promised. As I looked around, my eyes stopped and stared at two special guests.

Olumbo and his sister Asha, stood close to the front of the throng. Olumbo had his Maroon drum, which hung around his neck with wide, boar-skin straps. And Asha stood there looking her best, wearing a summer dress made from the blue and yellow cloth I'd given her. I was thrilled to see them both.

I saw Miz Ada leading Quaker Tomas and Pastor Mullings to the front of the crowd. I stood, looked around at the throng in front of me, and shouted, "Greetings, free people of Jamaica, welcome!" The crowd quieted down and stared at me. They were so quiet I could have heard a leaf drop.

"As of today, I refuse to call you apprentices. You are Jamaicans; you are free Jamaicans," I yelled. The crowd erupted, "Ya, ya, we free Jamaicans!" Then they quieted down and continued to stare at me.

"Before our announcements, I want to welcome and introduce you to a few special guests. In front of me is Quaker Tomas, a man I worked with in the past under tough and cruel conditions." I pointed at the Quaker in the audience. He turned around and waved his right hand. I continued talking.

"And standing next to him is Pastor Mullings, a man of God that you all know." The pastor also turned and waved his right hand at the crowd.

"I'd also like to welcome two Maroons I call friends. They are Bene Olumbo and his sister Asha Olumbo," I said, pointing in their direction. The crowd shuffled, trying to get a look at the guests I'd just introduced, then they quieted down.

"We're here today to give you special news. Mas Gavin Ryan and I have just bought Havendale and Toco Plantations. But we have no plans to run the properties like plantations. Evil and cruelty will live here no more. We will manage both properties in partnership with every single one of you standing in front of us."

The crowd erupted once more, cheering, pumping their fists in the air. They soon quieted down and stared at me, looking eager to hear more.

"Starting tomorrow morning, Mas Gavin and I have contracted with a team of surveyors to divide Toco Plantation into half acre lots, to be sold to all of you who want a home of your own."

I opened my arms, like an embrace to the throng in front of me. The eruption grew louder now, with Olumbo slamming three pounds on his drum and everyone jumping up and down, pumping their fists in the air. Olumbo pounded once on his drum, and the crowd quieted down and stared at me. Gavin took over.

"You may be wondering where you'll find the money to buy a lot of your own. We have a plan for that. Our two special guests over there, Quaker Tomas and Pastor Mullings, are going to work hard to help with funds you may need for a deposit."

The crowd erupted once more. One pound of Olumbo's drum, and they again quieted down.

"You will be encouraged to build a home on your lot for your family, and to plant provisions for personal use, and for export. We will arrange for you to pay us twenty five percent of your earnings from export. This will help pay for your half acre of land," Gavin said.

"And we are going to ask you to work at Havendale half-day every day. We won't be able to pay you for the first year, because we will be short of working capital till the crops are produced and exported. But your earnings for that first year of work will be applied as payment for your piece of land. After that, we will begin to pay you, and then you can start paying us each month for your lot. And one last thing, the fruit trees here belong to all of us. Feel free to pick and eat fruit. In fact, let your children climb the trees, fill their bellies, and enjoy themselves," I said.

Olumbo pounded the drums and the throng erupted once more into cheers, chants, and dances. They were happy, no, ecstatic was more like it. There would be no quieting them down, anytime soon. Gavin and I stood there and watched them celebrate, our hearts filled with love and satisfaction.

With all the awful work I did in Ireland to help the starving, I never got a sense of fulfillment. I only got sadness and a gut filled with pain and nausea. But today, this sense of satisfaction would stay with me till my dying day. I watched happiness on the faces of people who'd known nothing but brutality and near starvation. Like Pastor Mullings said, a true blessing had been sent to us by God. If we didn't share the blessing with those who deserved it, God would surely strike us down.

Olumbo finally pounded his Maroon drum again, and everyone slowly quieted down.

"Let us celebrate! Eat, drink, and be merry! A new day is coming for us all!" I yelled.

The drum pounded; the crowd erupted. Soon, the throng formed lines at food tables, with Zoya, Miz Ada and three others directing them.

Gavin and I walked over to Quaker Tomas, Pastor Mullings, Olumbo and Asha. We walked them to the table up front. One woman served us plates of food and drinks. We said little, as we enjoyed curried goat, roasted boar, boiled cassavas and pumpkins, dumplings, roasted breadfruit, bread pudding, and pineapple juice.

Olumbo and Asha rose, excused themselves, and joined the crowd once more. The drum pounded a happy refrain. Hips, arms, and legs moved to the rhythm with gratitude and sheer jubilation.

For the first time in my life, I truly felt the blessings of God flowing down on me, like rays of light on a day filled with warm breezes and sunshine.

Chapter 30

I opened my eyes early morning to the sound of people milling around outside. I quickly dressed myself, washed up, and walked into the kitchen. Sabra, who I now proudly called housekeeper, stopped me at the door.

"Long line outside since five this mornin,' Mas Sean. Everybody excited and want name on list for land. I so excited. Want some tea?"

"Yes, on the tea. Bread with jam too? I'll eat quickly, then go outside and talk with folks."

I plopped myself on a chair around the dining table and quickly ate what Sabra served up. Opening the front door, I stepped out on the verandah. Cheers erupted. Zoya rushed over to me.

"Couldn't keep crowd away, Mas Sean. Sorry. You put names for land on list to keep crowd quiet?"

"No worries, I'll take care of it. Go inside and help Sabra bring out the small kitchen table, a chair, some writing paper and a pen. Go on, hurry."

I turned to the crowd and raised my arms. They quieted down.

"It warms my heart to see you so excited about our plans. Can't wait to work with you and build our community. Today, you will all be put on the land list, every last one of you," I yelled.

More cheers and whooping filled the air. By the time the crowd quieted down, the table stood ready so I could take names.

"Before I take names, please remember that nothing can be done till the surveyors finish their work dividing up the land. They start that work in two days. While they're doing this, we need you to get to work planting the banana fields so we have a head-start. The quicker we start planting, the faster we can start reaping. The banana stalks arrived late yesterday. We'll also be planting ginger root and pimento

183

in the fields, and you can grow those on your lots later on to make your own money to help pay your bills."

The crowd shuffled around. I could see they were happy yet anxious. They wanted assurance; they wanted their names on a list. I didn't blame them.

In the hours that followed, I sat and wrote names. Each person smiled and said, "Thank you, Mas Sean," or "God bless you, sah," or "We work real' hard, sah." The line got longer, as news got to Toco Plantation and everyone there rushed over and joined in. Gavin also arrived.

"Let me write names now, Laddie. Long line ahead," he said.

I rose, gave him the chair, and slowly paced back and forth behind him on the verandah. Then I looked around. It was a heavenly morning, the sun rising in the east with brilliant rays of orange and yellow, which spread across the skies like beams from a huge diamond just held before light.

No more beauty and cruelty. In this place I now owned, there will be beauty and kindness.

When Gavin got through writing names, everyone still milled around, no one wanting to leave. Gavin rose and I raised my arms. Everyone suddenly went quiet, all eyes on us. Gavin spoke.

"Go back to your huts, now. Start preparing to work the banana fields tomorrow morning at seven. That includes those of you from Toco Plantation. Like in the old days, we will have breakfast for you in the clearing close to the fields here at Havendale. Lunch will also be served. Go take care of your families, and make arrangements for someone to watch your children while you work the fields." It was my time to speak, once more.

"We're making arrangements for each of you to meet with Quaker Tomas for assistance with your land deposit. Those of you who are church members, please talk with Pastor Mullings after church for the next three Sundays. See how the church can assist with your deposit. See you tomorrow morning in the fields."

After the crowd disbursed and the housekeepers cleaned-up the verandah, Gavin and I sat down to discuss future plans. Sabra brought us two glasses of pineapple juice, which I enjoyed while breathing in the cool, fresh, morning air.

"People are very lucky to have us at the helm, Laddie. Things are getting challenging out there," Gavin said.

"I know. Lots of news flying around, making our folks nervous. But once they start building their houses and farming their own land, they'll settle down."

"Other landowners are demanding huge rents for their huts. They're charging eight shillings and four pence per week for what looks like small pig pens. And they're only paying one shilling and eight pence per day for wages. It's unreasonable."

"They're still angry at Britain for freeing the slaves, and will do anything to oppress them. They can't beat them with a whip anymore, so they try to beat them in the pockets."

"Yesterday, I read that some landlords are refusing to employ their own tenants. And some locals who can buy land are being scammed with false deeds. They've had to turn to the missionaries for help," Gavin said.

"It must end soon."

"They're evicting people now, just like they did to us in Ireland."

"The word 'eviction' makes me sick in the belly. Can't the government do something to stop them?"

"They're no better, Sean. They govern on the sides of the planters; they're the plantocracy, remember? Britain has ordered them to stop the evictions. Now, they just restrict the amounts of Crown lands available to former slaves. Most crown lands are now going to whites."

"Aye. I heard that the planters paying fairer wages are doing better with production. But they're also charging excessive rents. They're charging separate rent for each family member."

"That's insane. Some even offer irregular employment on purpose. They think if they increase the hardship, laborers will be forced to work harder. No whip, so hit them in the pocket and in the head," Gavin said.

"We must ask Quaker Tomas to help get pressure put on the Brits to make the island a Crown Colony, as soon as possible."

"African Jamaicans are fighting back, though. Smallholders continue to scrape whatever they can to buy land. They're starting to build small communities. The missionaries continue to help; this makes whites even angrier. They think former slaves should only aim to be field hands, nothing more," Gavin said.

We finished our pineapple juice and spent the rest of the time planning for better days at Havendale and Toco. These were good times for our people, and in turn, they began to act positive and hopeful.

In the weeks that followed, the surveyors completed dividing Toco into half-acre lots. Our people worked like mules to plant the fields. Quaker Tomas got funds and loans from friends and from the Anti-Slavery Society, so he helped many with deposit money. The churches helped others.

People knew they needed to feed themselves and their families at dinner time, so they continued to live off provisions they'd planted behind their huts. They traded for meat with the Maroons, but several raised pigs and chickens. And they fed me and my housekeeper too. I could always count on dinner being delivered by Zoya or someone else, most evenings.

After Gavin and I opened up the fruit trees to all, ample supplies of breadfruit, mangos, plums, tropical almonds, and pineapples begged for everyone's attention. I loved watching the children chatting away while enjoying mangos and plums, or skillfully hanging off the limb of a tree while tossing ripe fruit to those below. The planters' belief that 'you have to beat them to get them to work' was based on fear and control. There would be none of that in our new community.

One day Gavin and I took a walk along the edges of the fields toward Toco, and my heart pounded with joy. Banana trees stood green, lush, and bolstered by wooden sticks, as huge bunches threatened to weigh them down. Pimento and ginger root grew almost wildly on the west side of the fields, and occasional pastures of guinea grass were easy on the eyes. The Indian corn, just beginning to spear, boasted a deep green.

I stared off into the distance, as the sun slid slowly into the horizon, leaving beams of orange, yellow and gray in its path. God had blessed us with beauty and abundance.

Gavin and I quickened our pace toward Toco. He, too, had moved into the great house, and plans were for him to keep an eye on the building and farming that was about to begin. We had lost our overseers to other plantations and were happy they walked away. I just didn't think they would adjust to this new lifestyle of hard work, fueled by kindness and respect; they were too used to the old ways.

As I looked around at Toco, I saw nothing but flat fields of divided lots, some with an old slave hut and provision ground still in place. The great house stood in the distance. Gavin said he was more comfortable living there after moving furniture around and giving a few pieces to his people.

"Get Miz Ada to use her herbs on the place," I said.

"Great idea, Laddie. I'll have her stop by in a couple'a days."

"We should give this community a name," I said, still looking around in awe.

"How about the two of us coming up with two names. We could have everyone vote on the one they like most. Might be fun."

"Olumbo and the Maroons love to celebrate their accomplishments. How about a celebration to open up our new community? We could announce the chosen name then."

"Indeed! Please invite Olumbo and his sister. I love watching people dance to the rhythms of the drums. I still don't know how they move their bodies like that."

"Comes naturally. Asha tried to teach me when I visited the Maroon village, but I couldn't stop my body from jerking from side-to-side like a chicken in heat. My legs and hips kept going into all kinds of weird directions." We both laughed so hard, I doubled over with a belly ache.

Chapter 31

Walking slowly next to Gavin, I looked around, my mouth wide open. I stood staring at a village, at a community. Except for the great house, nothing around took me back to the horrifying memories of the old Toco Plantation.

Small cottages appeared, as far as the eyes could see. Some got built around old huts, while others stood in front of the old huts. The cottages, modest and built of Spanish wall or board that the new homeowners had cut from forest trees, already had roofs made from wood shingles. Some roofs boasted new thatch.

I looked up at the clear, blue skies overhead, and my heart sang a joyful tune. Birds flew by, chirping melodies. A throng of green, yellow and orange butterflies flitted around a flowering bush.

"Most of the cottages have two to three rooms, one or two bedrooms and a living room or hall. They're doing a great job," Gavin said.

"I'd love to take a look inside a few of them sometime. I'll ask Zoya to show me around her cottage. It's exciting, Gavin."

"It sure is, Laddie. All people needed was a chance. Look how hard they're working to make things better for themselves."

"Aye. And the government is not lifting a finger to help."

"Do you know that a few influential people in Kingston have asked the government to assist with developing other villages? Their appeals have fallen on deaf ears."

"I read that people are trying to take over abandoned estates and turn them into villages. African Jamaicans are going to develop communities, by whatever means they can. I wish we had the money to develop more communities," I said.

"Me too. People are refusing to work on the plantations due to low wages and horrible treatment. The planters are suffering, and they're angry."

"They'll get no sympathy from me," I said.

"Yesterday, I read that freed Jamaicans can now register to vote. But whites aren't making it easy."

"I know. They can only register to vote if they own real property worth six pounds, pay thirty pounds in rent, or pay three pounds in taxes. Most folks aren't able to meet those requirements."

"The problem is there's no one in the government to represent them. The newspaper reports that in order to become part of the Assembly, they must have an annual pay of three hundred pounds, and paid-off properties worth three thousand pounds," Gavin said. "Whites are hindering African Jamaicans from moving forward."

"I'm afraid more rebellions may come. Britain needs to move faster with the Crown Colony designation."

"Things will change. The British working class and African Jamaicans will see to that."

"Folks will die fighting rather than take more abuse," I said.

"Let's keep our eyes and ears open."

"We allowed our people to open doors for themselves and their families. Anything more we can do to keep their trust will help protect us all, if there is another rebellion."

After our walk that day, Gavin and I sat down to lunch at his great house. Then we spent the rest of the afternoon planning for banana cutting, and reaping ginger root, pimento, and arrow root, all for export.

"After this crop, we'll be able to pay wages," Gavin said.

"Our people will be happy. Now they can finish building their homes, and they can plant more crops for export on their own land. They'll become small holders; that's what the government is calling small farmers."

"Did you come up with a name for the village?"

"Not yet – been so busy. Will think of something tonight."

"Good. I'll think of a name and give it to you so Zoya can float it around."

Zoya giggled when I told her the name I'd thought of, 'Pimento Bay.'

"Love it, Mas Sean."

"Good! Let's see what Gavin comes up with; I want you and Miz Ada to take a vote; everyone must be included. Then we'll have a name for our village."

"Feel so proud to have me own home. Couldn't do it without you, sah."

The plan to have workers do half-day's work, then go home to work on their houses and plant their land, worked well. Gavin and I arranged for them to arrive at 7 in the morning and work till 1 in the afternoon. But they insisted on coming to work one hour earlier, at 6, so they could put in close to a full day's work. We called it shared labor. We fed them lunch before they left in the afternoon, and I heard them working all hours at night on their homes and land.

Soon, the village was a sight to behold, with spanking, new cottages and back yards that were fully tilled and lushly planted. Front yards flaunted colorful clusters of crotons, thatch palms, and hibiscus. Some cottages had layers of rocks and coral on both sides of walkways leading up to the front door. Toco had become a beautiful, inviting village, a community built with pride and care.

"Mas Sean, we want to name village Pimento Bay. Most like that over Sea Breeze Village," Zoya said, standing next to Miz Ada. Their eyes gleamed in the sunlight.

"Pimento Bay it is," I said.

"We plan celebration. We put together lots'a food."

"Okay. Mas Gavin and I will provide the drinks."

"You invite Olumbo? We love dancin' to his drums," Zoya said.

"Absolutely. Everyone acting like Maroons, dancing and celebrating every chance they get."

"We have lots to celebrate. We real' grateful, Mas Sean," Zoya said.

"Talk 'bout grateful. We want to build church in village so we can praise God for blessings. That all right?" Miz Ada asked.

"Very all right," I said.

"And later, we want to build school. You hear what just happen?" Miz Ada asked.

"What?"

"They build a school name' Mico Institution. It's for our people," Zoya said.

"Oh yes. I read in the newspaper that the school was built at the bequest of a Lady Mico, 'for the benefit of African slaves made free and engaged in the work of teaching.' That's a real good thing, ladies. Things are really looking positive and promising."

"Yah man. And if we have our own school, our children can learn to read and write. And maybe we can learn too."

"Sounds like a good plan."

In the weeks that followed, we reaped and sold, for export, our banana, pimento, and ginger root crops. Our people were also able to sell, for export, the first round of ginger, pimento and arrowroot from their personal planting grounds. So, they declared that it was crop over, and planned a big celebration in the community to celebrate both crop over and freedom from slavery.

The celebration was like nothing I'd ever experienced. The smell of delicious food wafted through the air and drinks flowed. Gavin and I christened the village 'Pimento Bay,' to loud cheers and whooping.

Men and women dressed up in the most colorful, extravagant costumes made of dyed burlap. They wore yellow, blue and red head dresses made from long fowl and bird feathers. The revelers moved without shoes, but their calves were wrapped with strips of yellow and blue burlap. Under the burlap, painted legs and feet made them look like they were wearing boots.

Moving their hips and legs through the dirt roads of Pimento Bay behind the throbbing drums of Olumbo and two other Maroon drummers, they grinned and stomped the earth in a parade of gratitude and glee. Gavin and I moved our bodies behind the throng of revelers, trying hard to catch the beat and laughing as we jerked our bodies from side-to-side like startled chickens.

"Will we ever be able to move our hips and behinds like they do?" Gavin asked, breathing hard and struggling to keep up.

"Not in this lifetime," I said, swishing my behind from left to right.

I would never forget this day. If it lasted forever, I would have been one happy man.

Chapter 32

Havendale, or should I say Pimento Bay, had finally quieted down, so I had time to read the newspapers during breakfast each morning. Today's headline was about a march and protest happening close to town. I flung the paper down and hurried to see Gavin.

"Big protest in town this evening. Let's show up. We need to know what's going on," I said. Gavin motioned me to sit on the verandah and called for his housekeeper to bring us two cups of tea.

"Saw that, agree we should go. Know what triggered the protest?" Gavin asked.

"No, I threw the paper down and headed here. You know something?"

"Remember the roads leading to Savanna-la-Mar? The poor use those roads a lot. Well, the government just put toll gates there."

"Sweet Jesus. Anything to mess with poor people."

"According to the papers, protestors tore the toll gates down and when they went to trial, hundreds of them showed up. Things got so heated, the toll gates had to eventually be removed."

"Been hearing some of our people talking about two men, George Gordon and Paul Bogle. Apparently, they're the ones now leading protests and demanding rights and justice for African Jamaicans," I said.

"Those two are leading the protest tonight. I read that they're both pastors. They're also getting ready to lead revolts in a place named Morant Bay, in St. Thomas parish," Gavin said.

"Why there?"

"They're both from that area, which has suffered tons of injustices." Gavin took a long sip of tea, then he picked up his newspaper and said, "Listen to this," and started reading.

Things are happening rapidly on the island as African Jamaicans take advantage of their new-found freedom. Nineteen unprofitable sugar estates have been turned into free villages, as well as some abandoned coffee plantations in St. Andrew, Manchester, and Metcalfe. Villages are also springing up in Trelawny, St. Thomas-in-the-Vale, Clarendon, St. Catherine, Portland in the foothills of the Blue Mountains, and all around us here in St. James.

Gavin paused and looked at me.

"Aye. They're also coming up in remote areas across the island. But whites have made sure the better lands are denied to small, black landowners."

"African Jamaicans just see this as a minor set-back; it will not stop them. Whites are pissed."

"Too bad."

"Check this out, Sean," Gavin said, burying his head back into the newspaper and reading out loud.

Many older villages have grown into prosperous market towns. One is Old Harbour, which once had only two taverns, two houses, a post office, a pound, a blacksmith's shop, and a police station. It is now the scene of a flourishing Saturday market where all sorts of ground provisions, baked products, meat, poultry, and haberdashery are sold. Porus is also having the same economic boom, catering primarily to freed blacks.

Gavin stopped reading, raised his head from the newspaper and smiled.

"Great news, Laddie. When things settle down, you and I should take a few short trips to explore those bustling new towns," I said.

"Always up for an adventure. In the meantime, onward to that protest tonight."

"Freed Jamaicans will forge ahead, no matter what. Zoya told me many now have constant employment with the Commissioner of Roads, including two of her cousins."

"Makes sense. Roads need to be built so people can get to new villages. I hear they're also getting jobs with other companies on the island, like the Rio Grande Copper Mines. Those companies offer good, timely pay," Gavin said.

"Good for them. I love the sound of that."

"And Quaker Tomas told us that ex-slaves also work as carpenters, teachers, servants, masons, and some do task work. African Jamaicans will just weather the storm and keep moving."

"He also said others grow provisions for sale, some split shingles, and others clean pastures. Bottom line is, everyone's finding ways to push forward."

"Let's walk to the fields. I'll meet you here around five this evening." Gavin said, changing the subject and rising from his chair. We headed out.

That afternoon Gavin and I rode into town. About a mile before we got to downtown Montego Bay, I pulled the horse cart to a sudden stop and sat there, staring at a sea of African Jamaican protestors in front of me, as far as the eyes could see. There were no disturbances; people just waited, chatting away.

"Can't ride any further. Let's hitch the cart here," Gavin said.

"Aye." I jumped down from the cart and tied the reins to a huge lignum vitae tree. Gavin jumped down too, and we inched our way at the edge of the bushes next to the crowd, for what felt like forever. Finally, we were about four rows from the front.

"Let's stop here. Not wise to draw more attention to ourselves," I said. We stood quietly and waited.

The crowd suddenly erupted and I looked ahead as two cultured-looking, well- dressed, African Jamaican men strode to the front of the throng.

"The one on the left is George Gordon. He's the politician who's been fighting for voting rights and other benefits. They say he's quite wealthy," Gavin said.

Gordon had a light brown complexion, wavy, black, mixed-race hair parted at one side, straight nose, medium height, and full lips. Dressed in white shirt, white ascot, black jacket and black pants, a small pair of wire-rimmed glasses accented his prominent face.

"I read that he was born to a white planter father and a slave woman," I said.

"And he's a leading critic in the newspapers, of that awful Governor Eyre."

"Can't say I blame him. Eyre takes the planters' side, every time."

"The people love him. I heard he has subdivided large pieces of his own land and sold it to poor blacks. All this, while Eyre and the planters are dead set on making it impossible for blacks to buy land."

"That must be Paul Bogle next to him. He's a fighter for justice, too. Those two are good friends. Bogle's a deacon at Stony Gut Baptist Church in St. Thomas."

Bogle stood thin and a little shorter than Gordon. He had medium brown skin, a small nose, neat black eyebrows over big dark eyes, and full lips. He wore a loose white shirt, brown jacket and black pants.

"Brothers and sisters, good evening to you all," Gordon yelled, his voice strong and deep. The crowd shuffled, stared ahead, and started to settle down.

"Quiet down so we can get started, brothers and sisters," Bogle shouted, looking around at the throng in front of him, his hands raised. Sounds of muttering and 'shh' reverberated, then everyone stopped talking and stared ahead. Gordon began to speak.

"I'm George Gordon, and standing next to me is Paul Bogle." Loud applause and fist pumping erupted. Gordon raised, then lowered his hands. The throng quieted down.

"We've been fighting for justice, and have made some headway. But there's a lot more to do. Eyre and the planters continue to try and keep us down. After we pushed for the right to vote, they say if we don't own large pieces of land, we cannot vote. But they make it impossible for us to get our hands on large acres of land. If we cannot vote, we have no representation," Gordon yelled.

The crowd erupted once more, yelling and pumping their fists in the air. Bogle held both his hands up, then lowered them. Everyone quieted down again, and Gordon continued.

"Heard about the Master and Servant's Act the Governor just put in place? Know what that's all about? Planters can now reduce wages and provide irregular employment. People never know when they'll be paid or when they'll be laid off. And they fine us for small things, so sometimes we have no money left to take home to our families. Yet they still try to force us to work the plantations. The Brits have freed us. We're no longer their slaves."

The crowd erupted once more and I didn't think they'd ever settle down. But they did. They wanted to hear more.

"You hear the latest? Planters are working with the government to import cheap labor from India and China, 'to fill the gap'. Let's see how long that lasts as the white man launches more cruelty," Bogle yelled. The crowd shuffled and grumbled, then they settled down.

"I just attended a meeting of the Assembly. Ah, the Assembly; you've heard of them. They're now arresting us if we use abandoned estates. All this, while stopping us from leasing land for cultivation, or pricing Crown lands so high, we can't afford them. And they just added an inheritance tax to the Franchise Act. We cannot move forward under these conditions," Gordon yelled.

"And listen to this! The Assembly just added a 10-shilling stamp tax, 'as a great discouragement of the exercise of the Franchise, by the humbler class of freeholders.' They actually admitted the reason for the tax is to keep us down. We will fight! We will die for the right to vote!" Bogle yelled. More shouting and fist pumping erupted, then everyone quieted down once more.

"They can whip us to death no longer, so now they're taxing us to death. Planters pay much lower duties on imported goods, than do we, the poor," Gordon said. Before the crowd could erupt once more, Bogle yelled.

"Duties on food and clothes are twelve times higher than before, and we're taxed on bread and salt; the taxes on donkeys are way too high. Our donkey carts used to run without taxes. Now they're being charged eighteen shillings per year, while plantation carts go untaxed. All this money is used to provide services to the planters, while our needs are ignored."

The crowd shouted even louder now. Men and women yelled and pumped their fists in the air. Gordon and Bogle had a tough time quieting them down this time.

"And one last thing, the cruel beasts are fighting to prevent our children and their parents from getting an education because, according to them, 'it would give the field-hands political and social ambitions and this would make them unfit for labor.' The God damned nerve!" Bogle yelled. More noise from the crowd. After they quieted down, Gordon shouted.

"Brothers and sisters, this is why we fight. And we won't stop till there's equal rights and justice for all. The fight will go on, with help from our Baptist and Methodist churches."

Bogle then yelled, "We are free! This is our country! We have rights, and I'll be damned if I'll stand by while they're taken away!" Noise from the crowd exploded with such force, I didn't think it would ever quiet down.

"Let's get out of here," I said. I turned and inched my way along the edges of the crowd by the bushes, Gavin following close behind. The crowd was so riled up, no one paid attention to us. I was grateful.

Gavin and I rode home that evening in silence. But soon, I could hold my tongue no longer.

"Those bastards are crippling the rights of free people. This is outrageous!"

"They'll stop when blacks rise up and kick their asses for good, like the Maroons did."

"Unbelievable! The nerve of those fools, thinking they control the world and everyone who's different must serve them."

I was so angry I had to take six deep breaths to calm myself. Gavin and I rode the rest of the way in silence.

The next morning, I read that in a meeting of landowners and attorneys held in Trelawny, the planters had declared, 'The people will never be brought to a stage of continuous labor while they are allowed to possess large tracts of land now cultivated by them for provision.'

I looked up, fighting back more anger. So freed blacks are fending for themselves like we weren't able to do in Ireland, and this was an issue? *Let them bring laborers in from China and India; we'll see how that works out.*

I stepped out on the verandah and got ready to head to the fields.

"Mas Sean, ah bring Pastor Mullings to talk with you 'bout building the church at Pimento Bay," Zoya said, jolting me out of my angry thoughts. Conflict and hope; those two also went together here.

"Pastor Mullings, pleasure to see you," I said, holding my hand out to the pastor. He came dressed in black short-sleeved shirt, khaki pants, and a pair of brand-new, brown, boars' skin shoes.

"Good to see you again, Sean." The pastor and I shook hands.

"Let's sit here. I have a few minutes before I head to the fields," I said, motioning him and Zoe toward two chairs on the verandah. I sat on the third chair and listened.

"Pimento Bay indeed. I love that name," the pastor said as he sat down.

"Mas Sean come up with that name, and we love it," Zoya said, after she'd cheerfully plopped herself down on a chair next to the pastor.

"You know almost everyone here attends my church, right? They're a wonderful, hard-working group of people, and sometimes we don't have enough seats in the pew for them. So, when they approached me about helping build a church at Pimento Bay, I couldn't have been more pleased," the pastor said.

"We've talked about this for a while now," I said.

"There's enough room in front of the clearin' to build a small church, Mas Sean," Zoya said.

"Yes, there is. Who will do the building? Where will the materials come from?"

"We've been taking special collections every Sunday at church, and also at our night services. We have enough to get going," Pastor Mullings said.

"And our men can build, Sah. Two of them are carpenters since plantation days," Zoya said.

"We've collected enough money to buy shingles and Spanish wall, board for flooring, and planks from the forest to make pews. We're more than ready to get started," the pastor said.

"And you will be the pastor of both churches?" I asked.

"I've been training my son to be a pastor. He grew up in my church. He's ready now to be Pimento Bay Baptist Church's junior pastor. I will give him all the guidance he needs."

"Pimento Bay Baptist Church; I like the sound of that. I'll discuss this with Gavin. I'm sure he'll agree. When can we get started?"

"Nex' week, Mas Sean. We ready," Zoya said.

My spirits rose to new heights. *Progress in the midst of hardship. No wonder I love this place.*

That evening I walked to Gavin's house and gave him the news. Filled with joy, my kind and caring friend would have done anything to keep our people happy.

"Grab a seat, Laddie. Let's have a chat. I have dinner in the kitchen; care for a bite?"

"Thanks, but I already ate. How 'bout a drink?"

"You bet. Rum and pineapple juice?"

"Aye."

I took a seat as Gavin hurried inside. He returned with two glasses, handed me one, and sat next to me. I took a long sip.

"Aah, this is good."

"My favorite drink. Glad you like it too. You still keeping up with what's going on out there?"

"Another rebellion is coming, Gavin; I can feel it."

"Living expenses get higher and higher. Some blacks are homeless, unemployed, and resorting to stealing food and picking wild fruit. They're punished with floggings and imprisonment."

"Strap yourself in. Another talk with Quaker Tomas is overdue. Britain must take governing away from the plantocracy, sooner, rather than later."

Chapter 33

"Can we count on you to keep everyone calm as things get more difficult out there?" I asked, sitting at the dining table at the great house, Gavin next to me. Zoya and Miz Ada sat on the other side of the table, staring at me.

"We try, sah. But people angry 'bout all the bad treatment we still getting. When they goin' to take their boots off our backs?" Miz Ada said.

"You know Mas Sean and I are not part of that, right?" Gavin said.

"We know, sah. But we brothas' and sistas' suffering. You hear what happen' at Florence Hall in Trelawny?" Zoya asked.

"That's not far from us. What happened?" I asked.

"They try to evict a man from his property; he was part-owner. The whole village come out every night and march. They march to police station in Falmouth and burned the wharf down. Six people dead, and over a hundred takin' punishment," Zoya said. The word 'evict' made me cringe, like it always did.

"They refusing to let us lease land. Those who squatting or have some kind'a lease, refusing to pay additional rent they now bein' charged. They attackin' lawyers and surveyors. More people goin' to get killed," Miz Ada said.

"And they askin' for deed on land. When our people hand over deed, they tell them deed not good. False papers all about the place. People bein' tricked. How we suppose' to survive like this?"

"There are no false deeds here, so don't ever worry about that. Please spread this word to the others," I said.

"What you know about the two men, Gordon and Bogle?" Gavin asked.

"The two of them fightin' for us. They help people buy land and lend money to small farmer. They even give cattle to people so they can pay tax and vote," Zoya said.

"They tryin' to work with Governor, but Governor still tryin' to keep us down," Miz Ada said.

"Some'a our people walkin' round half-naked, sah, 'cause of high duty on cloth. They can't put clothes on their backs," Zoya said.

"That's why they say we violent. Some would rather be dead than live like this," Miz Ada said. I didn't like the sound of that. Gavin shifted in his chair.

"Let's take care of each other. You have a right to be worried; we're concerned too. Please spread the word that everything is okay here. Mas Gavin and I will call a meeting with everyone tomorrow afternoon to assure them that we care, and to let them vent their concerns," I said.

"Okay, sah. We do what we can," Miz Ada said, glancing at Zoya. They both rose and walked out the door. Gavin sighed; we discussed plans for the meeting. Afterward, we headed to the fields.

The next afternoon after field work and lunch, Gavin and I stood in front of our people at the clearing where the church would be built. Everyone gathered in front of us, waiting. As I began to speak, they all quieted down.

"I'm proud to stand in a place where you'll soon begin building your own church. And I'm proud of all of you standing before me. Mas Gavin and I wanted to let you know that we'll stand by your side during good times and bad. We're aware of all the awful things happening out there. Rest assured that we, too, despise the behaviors that cause you distress. We promise to do all it takes to ensure your lives here are secure," I said. I paused and Gavin began to speak.

"Our missionaries are pleading with Britain to do whatever it takes to stop the cruelties. Britain will take action."

The crowd shuffled. The looks on their faces said they couldn't count on the Brits for help. I understood that mindset very well. Gavin and I took a few questions; we allowed those willing to speak the chance to vent. We listened quietly and commented where we could, all the time encouraging them to hang on.

I walked home that evening, uneasiness washing over me. *They blamed the potato famine on us in Ireland. I must hold out hope that they won't blame the conditions in Jamaica on free blacks,* I thought.

The *Courier* soon reported that the Governor's Office had received a copy of a letter, which had been sent to the acting Secretary-of-State for the Colonies, by the Baptist Missionary Society. In the letter, they described the challenging conditions on the island.

The Governor's office sent a response to Britain, claiming that the accusations had been 'exaggerated and distorted; that the problem of poverty was to be blamed on the low moral character of the people and on their willingness to squander money on such things as fancy church clothes.'

I could not believe my eyes. The Governor, Eyre, did admit that economic conditions were bad and growing worse. But he maintained that 'laziness was the major problem with African Jamaicans.' *Sweet Jesus, they're doing it again. They're blaming black people's suffering on themselves, just like they did to us in Ireland. Trouble is coming.*

* * *

I expected a rebellion, but I got a flood.

Rain pounded the roof of the great house for two days, not easing up and coming down in torrents. If this water kept coming, we'd lose all our crops; there would be starvation. On the second night of the rains, I dropped to my knees and prayed to God for a break in the clouds. I repeated Psalm 27, over and over. After barely surviving the potato famine, I knew what horrors could be unleashed on us.

Everyone at Pimento Bay had to stay inside, trapped, as water flooded the earth. But I awoke that Friday morning to sounds of people moving around outside. I kept my ears peeled. The rain had stopped. I rose, hurriedly dressed myself, and yelled, "One minute," to a pounding on the door. I rushed over and flung it open.

"Everyone's out, Laddie. We need to save the banana crops," Gavin said. He stood at the door, wearing long rain gear with a hood tied tightly under his chin, and high, black, water boots.

I grabbed my water boots from the left side of the door and hauled them on. I slapped a big, old khaki hat on my head and bolted out the door. Gavin and I hurried to the fields. We were met by Haji, the young black man who'd been supervising our field work.

"We digging ditches along lines of banana trees to move water along and away from roots before nex' downpour," he said, hurrying past us. Then he yelled, "Bananas grow good in water, but we don't want roots to rot."

"Good job, Haji," I yelled back. I glanced around and saw Zoya, Miz Ada and three other women hurrying toward us, carrying what looked like big buckets of water on their heads.

"What you got there?" Gavin asked.

"Mosquito fish, sah. Some'a us have ponds full of them," Zoya said.

"What you going to do with them?" Gavin asked.

"Puttin' them in ditches 'round banana root, sah. Mas Haji say it fertilize root – save crop," Miz Ada said.

Gavin and I moved out of the way and hurried behind the women. I stared ahead, wide-eyed. The roots of all trees and plants were at least six inches under water.

"Thank God we planted tall-variety bananas; the roots should be deep inside the earth. Maybe we can save them," Gavin said.

We both grabbed shovels and started digging ditches next to every single man in the community. Women followed behind. As water drained from the banana roots and moved to the ditches, they threw in buckets of mosquito fish. We'd embarked on a labor of survival and love.

We'd been digging for hours and barely finished, when the skies opened and another torrent had us running for cover. Gavin and I bolted toward the great house's verandah, me motioning everyone behind to follow us. We were soaked to the bone.

I went inside and returned with bottles of rum. I took a swig, handed the first bottle to Gavin who held it to his head, swallowed, and then passed it around. By the time the rain eased up, everyone had warmed their insides before hurrying off to their homes, some talking real' loud, others giggling.

Rain poured all night, but next morning I awakened with rays of sunshine seeping through gaps in the curtain overhead. I breathed a sigh of relief. Hopefully, this was the end of the flood waters. Now we needed to ensure the fields dried out, so we could assess the damage.

In the days that followed, we cleared ditches so water would keep running away from the trees. We dug up crops of ginger and pimento. We moaned as reality hit — most of those small crops were lost. People groaned over the loss of crops in provision grounds behind their homes. I helped them till the earth as soon as things dried out, so new planting could quickly take place.

I called an urgent meeting and announced that Gavin and I would suspend house payments until the next reaping. Everyone cheered. Then a voice from the crowd shouted, "Most small crops in field gone too, ginger and pimento. We take half pay till things get better." The crowd cheered and whooped.

I looked in the other direction as another man yelled, "We wait to build church. We use some of that money to keep us going." More cheers and whooping. Gavin leaned over, a big smile on his face. "We going to survive this, Sean. We really are going to get through this. We're one amazing team."

I couldn't stop smiling. He was right.

One afternoon as we worked to pull the crops back together, I glanced at the most stunning sunset in the distance, surrounded by puffs of light gray clouds and sprays of orange and yellow beams lighting the distant sky. It was a glorious evening, cooled by recent rains and wind. A nice breeze ruffled my hair, and I glanced up as fireflies darted around, lighting up the evening skies. Ah, the beauty of this place.

But this afternoon, my mind took me to other places once more. Could a flood wash away the stains of oppression? What would it take to heal the wounds of a people, who rose and struggled for survival after every beat-down? I searched my mind; wounds were deep, and they were scathing. I could only find one answer.

Jamaica must become a Crown Colony, with local representation in the Assembly to lobby for the rights of African Jamaicans. Then later on, they must prepare themselves for self-government. That time was coming, I just knew it.

Chapter 34

"Irishman, I come to help after flood. What you need?" Olumbo asked, walking up to me in the fields. His words were like blessings sent from God. And this time he approached in daylight, without fear of being captured. These were really good times.

"Any food stuff you can trade with us would be much appreciated. Flood didn't wash out your crops?"

"No man! We in the hills, 'memba? Water run down and flood you."

"Ah yes. What you got? We need everything."

We got whole heap of boars' meat and provisions, breadfruit, yam, and cassava. And you may soon be able to get rice." He said this with a twisted smile on his face.

"We need all of it. Wait a minute, rice? Who's growing rice?"

"Whole family of Indians farmin' rice downhill from Maroon Village."

"Indians? Arawaks?"

"No. Indians from India that white man bring' here to work fields. You know our people don't want plantation work no more. Too much bad treatment."

"Interesting. So how they get land to grow rice on?"

"Look like they capture crown land. They run from plantation real fast. Let's see how long it take' before white man throw them off of land. Maybe we get some rice before then," Olumbo said, same twisted smile on his face.

"I know they also brought laborers here from China, and parts of Europe, too."

"Yah. Chinese all over market sellin' things. Few Germans there too. They run from plantations the minute contract finish. Too much wickedness," he said.

"Brits, they never learn. Not everyone is here to serve them. They're not Gods."

"Gods would treat us better. They too wicked to be Gods. I only help Irishman, not Brits. How we get food to you?"

"I go with you in a horse cart."

"Bring big horse cart. We'll have whole heap of food. Park downhill and wait for my men to bring food. Cart can't go uphill."

"Okay. I take three men with me to take food downhill and load up cart."

"No. My men bring food downhill and your men load up cart." I almost forgot; no one allowed near Maroon villages unless they were well trusted.

"All right. We meet you tomorrow morning 'round eight?"

"Sound good. And Irishman, Asha say you trade us with what you have now, and we get the rest later when things get better. That good?"

"That good. Tell Asha thanks; she's a lifesaver. Can I come visit soon?" I'd been wanting to see Asha.

"Yah man. Let's get your people eatin' and planting first."

The next morning, Gavin and I drove the large horse cart to the foothills that led up to Olumbo's Maroon village.

The morning came with cool breezes and the sun rising brightly in the skies in front of us. Tropical doves began to coo melodious refrains as the crickets and tree frogs halted their chirps and retreated for the day. Lush tropical trees rose to the skies, flaunting flowers and blossoms as a thank-you to recent rainfalls.

Mango and plum trees grew abundantly, bowing their heads with yellow and white blossoms. Poinciana trees bloomed, their red and yellow flowers forming stunning shelters overhead.

Magnificent maypole trees rose elegantly to different heights in the distance, surrounded by luxuriant mahogany and lignum vitae trees, swaying in the wind.

"Sean, to your right, Indians," Gavin said. I glanced at the clearing to my right.

A group of eight Indians, four adults and four children, sloshed around, working a field that was still soaked from the rains.

The women wore colorful sari frocks in reds, yellows and blues, and the men wore big, beige pants and loose shirts in beiges and browns. They all wore floppy hats to shield their faces from the sun.

Most waded around in what looked like water boots. Big, burlap bags hung over one shoulder or rested on a hip. They sloshed around, grabbing handfuls of seeds from the bags and flinging them in front, and from side to side.

"Jesus, that looks like back-breaking work," I said, slowing the cart down so we could get a good look.

"It sure does. And everyone is doing it, man, woman and child," Gavin said.

"Just think about it. They'd rather do that than work the plantations. That says a lot."

"Hey, Irishman; over here," Someone yelled. We had already passed the rice fields and had headed toward more forest. I slowed the mules, looked to my left and saw Olumbo, waving us over. He had three men next to him, holding baskets of food on their heads and hanging from their arms.

I turned the cart around, came to a stop, and Gavin and our three men jumped off. We relieved Olumbo's men of their loads and packed them into the cart. I handed Olumbo two bags with cloth, salt, and a few tools. I patted him on the shoulder.

"Thanks, my friend. You've probably saved a few lives at Pimento Bay. We'll never forget the kindness of your people," I said as I mounted the cart.

"Yah man! We plan that visit real soon," Olumbo said. I whipped the mules into a trot, and then a slow gallop.

We'd been traveling in silence for a short while, listening blankly as our men babbled away in patois in the back of the cart. Then Gavin spoke.

"After seeing those poor Indians working like mules to grow rice on land that doesn't belong to them, I remember reading that the

211

planters had also brought indentured laborers here from Germany and a few other European countries, most of them, Jews."

"Aye, I also read that they brought over four thousand Jews here years ago, to increase the number of whites on the island, always worrying that blacks outnumbered them."

"To make sure the Jews stayed, the *Courier* says the planters granted them freedom to worship. All this, while they abuse their black majority and give them no rights," Gavin said, shaking his head. "I heard Jews left the plantations the minute their contracts ran out. They worked hard and became tradesmen, before they set up their own businesses."

"The Jews always resented being laborers. I bet they were treated like Hell on the plantations. Nothing close to how blacks were treated, though."

"Planters have also been bringing white indentured servants here from Scotland and England; some came here from Ireland too. Like the two of us, most of them bolted to escape famine and other hardships. Good thing we got here earlier. We got good jobs the minute we walked off the boat."

"Yeah, we were lucky. But would you believe this? There are also reports that the government has been giving Jews financial assistance, hoping they'll become small farmers when they leave the plantations. And again, black people are given nothing but oppression."

"I know. But none of those people wanted to stay on at the plantations. According to the *Courier,* some of the Indians tried to return to their countries after their contracts ran out, but there was so much red tape, it was hard for them to leave," Gavin said.

"Indians are having a tough time. Most of them don't speak English. They're Hindus or Muslims and they've had religious issues. White man didn't make it easy for them to worship, like they did the Jews."

"And I hear the government has also been throwing the Indians off of Crown lands. Poor people are just trying to survive. Let's see how long those in the rice field we just passed, will last."

"It looks like Chinese laborers are having an easier time surviving," I said.

"Yeah. They're very industrious. I see them all over the market selling their wares, and some have already started taking over the grocery shops."

"Sugar plantations will soon disappear. Great decision we made to plant bananas. That crop even survived the flood. I don't think sugar cane would have pulled through," I said. Gavin nodded and changed the subject.

"Our people talking again about building their church."

"Let's try to hold them off till we reap the next crop. We'll have enough money to help them then."

We pulled into the gates of Pimento Bay, and a group of men ran from the fields to greet us. I slowed down and guided the cart to our community kitchen.

Men held on to the sides of the cart and trotted next to us. They got to work unloading our loot. A team of women, led by Zoya and Miz Ada, soon began to prepare the boars meat for curing or cooking.

Afterward, I drove the cart up to the great house's verandah, hitched it to a tree, and invited Gavin in. He plopped himself down on a chair and I hurried inside to pour us two glasses of pineapple juice. I returned to the verandah and handed Gavin one of the glasses.

"We'll be fine now. We made it through an awful flood, and there'll be enough food in our pots for a while," I said.

"Here's to Pimento Bay," Gavin said, holding up his drink. We clicked glasses.

"Happy to be alive and healthy, my friend," I said, as I stared off into the sunlight. I felt truly blessed.

Chapter 35

After fighting the flood with every muscle in our bodies, the banana crops thanked us with relish. Never had I seen banana stalks soar to such heights and bear so abundantly.

I walked the fields before our men and women started reaping, and silently thanked God for his blessings. Huge stalks hovered overhead, some bowing their heads under the weight of fruit. Our men had made v-shaped wooden sticks to hold up over-loaded trees. Tree trunks boasted a healthy green and bright yellow.

I looked up and marveled at the stunning wave of lush green leaves, looming high against bright blue skies. There wasn't a cloud in sight, and three birds flew by, singing a sweet harmony as fresh morning breezes rustled the leaves.

During this time of reaping the work will be back-breaking, but our bellies will be full and kindness will prevail. I closed my eyes and soaked things up. The sun warmed my skin and brought my senses to life.

"Time for reapin,' Mas Sean," I heard behind me. I turned around. Zoya and Gavin approached.

"You ever seen such a beautiful day? Can't wait to get started, Laddie," Gavin said.

Before we knew it, swarms of men, women and children converged on the fields and started reaping the crops. The children reaped all ginger and pimento that had survived the floods, while the adults worked the banana crops.

Two ships had already docked in port to collect loot in the area. Gavin had announced that everyone would be let go at one in the afternoon, so they could eat lunch and go home to harvest backyard crops that had survived.

The next day, Gavin and I rode into town to shop. I stood there, stunned. Main Street had turned into a bustle of vendors aggressively selling their wares.

I walked into the market, Gavin by my side, and looked around. Vendors stood side-by-side, their goods displayed in large heaps in front of them. They yelled as Gavin and I passed by, "Hey sah, want some breadfruit? Real good and fresh."

Indians sold rice and the most beautiful cloth I'd seen on the island. A few Chinese men had mounds of merchandise in front of them, from tools to pots and pans. And a few white merchants sold wares too, two looking like Syrians.

Now I knew what the papers meant when they described the bustling markets in Old Harbour. Gavin and I shopped away, needing to repay Olumbo and his people for their kindness after the flood. And I wanted to replenish the great house with food and drink, since the flood had depleted all my supplies.

Staring at the hustle, bustle and abundance around me felt like sunshine after a storm. I was one happy man.

Soon, I rode the small horse cart to the foothills of Olumbo's Maroon village, the cart loaded with supplies. I was alone. I had sent a message to him with one of the Maroons I'd run into at Pimento Bay. As I pulled the cart up and got ready to tie it to a tree, Olumbo and three other Maroon men emerged from the bushes.

"Tie horse over there, Irishman. Less chance anyone will see it," Olumbo said. I took his advice and watched, as his men unloaded the cart and got ready to trudge uphill with big bags of loot. I'd never known people strong enough to carry so much weight on their heads and shoulders; and uphill, too. A remarkable sight.

"You comin' to visit, Irishman? Papa and Asha askin' for you," Olumbo said. "Ready to trudge uphill with me?"

"Yes. Was hoping you'd invite me. Have something special for Asha, and for the family too."

"Yah man. Cart safe right there. Let's go."

I grabbed the two bags sitting on the floor of the cart next to the driver's seat, and scurried along next to Olumbo. He snatched one bag as we trudged uphill through the forest. All this, while he batted away bushes, making way for us to move along. Still, no cleared path to the Maroon village; no one could find it unless they were led by a Maroon.

"You still got traps set around the village?" I paused to take a breath as we moved along.

"Lots'a traps. No one must invade us. Stay close to me."

I gladly obeyed. Life was too darned good right now for me to lose a limb, or be impaled.

Twenty minutes later, we moved closer to the village; delicious aromas of food and baked goods wafted through the air. Sights of huts and cabins soon came into view. Many had fresh thatched roofs; some walls looked newly white-washed from the recent pouring rains, and the back-yard gardens loomed lush and green with herbs and provisions. The flood waters had been good to them, too.

I walked next to Olumbo to his family's cabin, saying hello to Maroons strolling by and curiously giving me quick stares. Olumbo knocked on the wall next to the open door, and a woman said, "That you, my brother? Come in." It was Asha, and before Olumbo could respond, she rushed to the door, hugged him, grabbed me by the arm and led me inside.

She moved so quickly I barely got a good look at her. But, beautiful as ever, she wore a short, loose burlap frock and black sandals. Her hair had grown longer, and it hung down her back, tied at the ends with a hemp twine.

"Glad to see you, Irishman. Was hoping you'd come today," she said. She sat me down in a chair around the dining table and yelled, "Papa, we have a visitor. Come out, will you?"

Mr. Olumbo soon walked toward us. Opening his outstretched arms when he saw me, he flashed a big smile. Dressed in a loose, burlap top that one threw over the head, he wore a pair of khaki pants and brown, boar skin sandals. He looked strong and healthy, and he had grown a short, salt and pepper beard. I glanced around.

The cabin, neat and nicely furnished as I remembered, had a wood-framed settee in one corner of the living room, and two lounge chairs in front with a small wooden table in the middle. A colorful Arawak rug laid neatly on the floor. Clearly, these people took pride in their homes.

"My dear Irishman, Sean. How good it is to see you once more. We worried about you, but I see you survived the flood," Mr. Olumbo said. I'd decided not to call him by his first name, though he asked me to. This mature and gracious man deserved a lot more respect.

"Oh yes, thanks to the kindness of you and your family, we made it through and saved most of our crops. We are forever grateful to you," I said.

"We're the ones who are grateful. Because of you, my grandson was saved. Now he's back with his mother without any fears—"

Asha interrupted. "How's Uma? I miss him so." Her eyes threatened to tear up.

"Uma is doing really well. He misses you too, I'm sure, but is happy to be back with his Mama. I must bring him to see you sometime."

"We'd love that. Asha took such good care of him when he was here; she was like a second mother to him. What we would give to see him again," Mr. Olumbo said. Then he paused and continued.

"As usual, we have food and drink. Would you allow us to break bread with you? It's almost lunchtime."

"Of course. It would be a pleasure. I brought you something," I said, watching Asha's eyes light up. "This is for you," I handed her one of the bags I'd brought.

"Thank you ... thank you so much!" She smiled, a twinkle in her eyes.

"You're welcome. And this is for you, Mr. Olumbo. There's enough to make shirts for both you and Olumbo." I handed the older man the other bag.

"Oh, I love it. What a wonderful bracelet. It's made by the Arawaks. I'll wear it with pride," Asha said, pulling the bracelet I'd bought her at the market, from her bag. Then she pulled the cloth from the bag and unfolded it. "I love this too. I can wear the bracelet with it once I get the dress made. You have such great taste, Irishman. Thanks again."

One woman arrived and set the table, and another put bowls of food in the middle.

"Want a drink? I have rum and coconut water. Real good," Mr. Olumbo said.

"I'd love a drink. Thank you."

The four of us sipped our delicious drinks. Then we dug into servings of cured river fish sautéed in fresh coconut milk and tropical seasonings, fried cassava cakes, boiled dumplings, plantains and pumpkins. What a great reminder of how much I loved local foods; the seasoning tasted like nothing I'd had before.

After lunch, the two women cleared the table and brought us bowls of fresh pineapples and plums. As we began to eat our fruit, Mr. Olumbo spoke.

"Glad you came to visit, Irishman. I want to warn you about something, so you can begin preparing yourself and your people."

He paused, looked me in the eyes, and continued. "You're a different kind'a white man. You came here from pain and hardship. So, you know, firsthand, what our people have been through."

"Lots of pain and hardship, Mr. Olumbo. I buried dozens of my people who starved to death during the potato famine. Also had to bury my mother; I wasn't even able to put her body in a coffin. I have to be kind. There's too much cruelty in this world."

"So sorry for your suffering, my friend. The people at Pimento Bay can't stop talking about your kindness and caring. They love you and your partner. But not all African Jamaicans have been lucky enough to be cared for by men like you both. Many of them are still suffering at the hands of those in charge of our island," he said.

"I know. They've tried everything to keep freed blacks down. But they're failing. African Jamaicans are strong and they're thriving, despite all the setbacks."

"We Maroons had to kick their backsides for our own freedom. That's the only thing that worked for us. Other African Jamaicans have learned this. They're getting ready to launch another rebellion."

"What? Where? How do you know about this?"

"Government ask Maroons to help them squash uprising. They still holdin' article 6 of peace treaty over our heads like a big stick. Most Maroons will not help, but you never know with some of them," he said.

"But the peace treaty said you should help squash slave rebellions. There are no more slaves."

"To them, we always slaves. You know 'bout a place named Morant Bay?"

"That's somewhere near Kingston, in an area called St. Thomas, no?"

"Yes indeed. You ever hear of a man named Paul Bogle?"

"My people talk a lot about him and the other freedom fighter, Gordon. I attended a rally they both held in town. They're smart, and they're determined to keep fighting for justice."

"You were at that rally? You're a brave man. Remember freedom fighter, Sam Sharpe? They're taking over his movement."

"They're back in Morant Bay, then?" I asked

"Yes, and we think the rebellion will be there, but it will affect everyone on the island. Read your newspaper every day, so you can see what's going on. And remember, we're here if you need us."

"Thanks so much. I'll keep my ears wide open."

"I let you know when I get news," Olumbo said.

I laid in bed that night staring up at the ceiling, my thoughts whirling like wind from the storm we'd just survived. *Another rebellion to worry about. As long as whites keep abusing African Jamaicans, they will always rebel. And I don't blame them, one bit.*

Finally, I closed my eyes and prayed that one day, rebellions would be a thing of the past as people are given their rights and made to feel respected. That day would only come, after plantocracy became a thing of the past.

Chapter 36

Early Sunday morning, sounds of loud chatter and hammering jolted me out of a deep sleep. I listened closely. Thank God, it was happy chatter. I rose, pulled myself together, dressed, and rushed out the door. The sounds came from the clearing, so I hurried there. As the clearing came into view, I saw masses of people scurrying about as I approached. A deep voice broke into my perplexed thoughts; I spun around. It was Clifford, Pastor Mullings' son.

"Mornin' Mas Sean," he said.

"Morning, Clifford. Thought you were preaching this morning."

"Yes, sah. But right after sermon, the minute I announced that we had enough money to begin building the church here, everyone shouted 'Amen and thank the Lord.' They bolted to the place where they stored supplies. They each returned with arms full of tools and supplies, and the men started building. Hope you not angry, sah; I didn' get a chance to tell you and Mas Gavin. Plans were for me to let you both know after church service, but folks got really excited."

"Angry? Oh no; how does one get angry at such enthusiasm. Flood waters almost did us in and we had to delay building the church. Everyone was more than ready to get started." I glanced to my right and saw Gavin approaching.

"I wondered what the racket was all about. Good God, they started building the church. It's good commotion," Gavin said.

"Sorry, sah. Never knew they'd start buildin' before I got the chance to tell you," Clifford said.

"Ha! No worries, man. Those are some happy people working away at their dream to serve God, with a roof over their heads. How could anyone be angry at that?" Gavin asked. I could always count on him to be on the same page with me.

"All right sah. Now that I know everything good, I return to main church to help get things in order for evening service. Good day to you," the young pastor said. I watched him walk away, and in the distance, I saw him hop on to a horse cart that must have been waiting for him.

Gavin and I stood around watching the activities in front of us. What a community; pride washed over me. Everyone came out, man, woman and child helping to build their church.

Some men hauled heavy materials to the site while others sawed wood, and some positioned planks and hammered nails into them. Women and children hauled lighter materials and handed nails and tools to the men. It looked like they'd been rehearsing a long time for this day.

"You busy this morning, Sean? Why not come by my place for breakfast. Cook is making a big Jamaican breakfast," Gavin said, moving me out of my reverie.

"Perfect. A good breakfast will make the soul even happier this morning. Besides, I have a bit of news to share with you."

"Good. Let's go, Laddie. Next Sunday, we lend a hand with the church building. Let's relax today."

We got to the verandah of Gavin's great house, where Cook had set a table for him to have breakfast and enjoy the morning breezes.

"Grab that seat; let me get another chair," Gavin said, hurrying through the door.

I sat and looked out at the garden. Another sunny, tropical morning had mango and plum trees swaying in the wind, and clear, blue skies boasted lush puffs of white clouds.

Gavin soon emerged with a chair, followed by Cook, carrying two bowls of food. Cook bid me good morning, put the bowls on the table, and hurried back inside for more food. Gavin put his chair next to mine so he, too, could enjoy the view.

Cook returned with another place setting and more bowls of food on a tray. Everything smelled delicious. *I must get a cook to make me food like this.* I'd been too busy building a community and fighting floods to focus on certain luxuries.

House slaves no longer existed, but Chambers' cook had asked Gavin if he could stay on and work for pay. He did almost everything. He kept the great house tidy, cooked, helped with the gardening, and took clothes to the washer woman every week.

"Dig in, Laddie. Cook made us one 'helluva' breakfast. This food could grow hair on your chest."

I helped myself to dumplings, sweet potatoes, fried plantains, cassava cakes, boiled green bananas, greens and salted cod, and brown stewed chicken. It was breakfast and lunch, all in one, with fresh pineapple juice and hot tea.

After I'd filled my belly, Cook returned and began to clear the table. Gavin and I moved to two lounge chairs on the other side of the verandah, carrying our cups of tea with us.

But the mood of the morning was about to change when Gavin asked, "Sean, you said you had news to share. What is it?"

"Aye. A few days ago, I went to Olumbo's village for a visit —"

"Really; how'd that go? Were you able to find the village by yourself?"

"Seriously? No way! They still have traps all around the village and I've come to be protective of every limb on this body of mine. Olumbo led me there. I'd gone to give him the supplies we owed his people for helping us through the flood." Gavin guffawed.

"You're a wise man to watch out for those limbs, Laddie. How is Olumbo's family? Did you see the beautiful Asha?" He egged me on.

"The family is great; the village continues to thrive. And Asha is even more beautiful." I took the bait this time.

"You like that girl, don't you?"

"What's not to like?"

"Why don't you start dating her?"

"Thought about it. Still want to keep all limbs the Lord gave me. Have a feeling I could lose a very important one if I try to date Asha and things don't work out. They're Maroons, my friend; they don't play around."

Gavin guffawed once more. The mischievous rascal then said, "Big old coward." We both laughed and took another sip of tea. I stayed silent for a few minutes, before I got serious.

"Gavin, before I left the Maroon village, Olumbo's father told me that another uprising was heading our way."

"Not surprised. Been reading the *Courier* and things are brewing on the other side of the island, in Morant Bay."

"Exactly. Mr. Olumbo says the two freedom fighters we saw in town, Bogle and Gordon, are more aggressively taking over Sam Sharpe's fight. They're hammering away for political rights and justice."

"Can't say I blame them. Bogle and Gordon are talking the language of African Jamaicans. They reject any form of oppression by the white minority. They're educated men, who clearly believe that rights of the many must be protected against the power of the few."

"Aye. I've been doing more reading too, and it seems things are really challenging in Morant Bay; worse than in other parts of the island. Gordon is pushing back against the lack of medical attention for poor blacks there, and against unsanitary conditions and the horrible treatment of those in the local prison," I said.

"Yeah, the papers say Gordon had been elected to represent the parish of St. Andrew, where he condemned the treatment of poor blacks, and criticized fraud and corruption in high places that go unpunished. All this, while free blacks are punished for petty crimes. He's taking that fight to Morant Bay."

"It's the usual, Gavin. Whites still resent the fact that blacks have been set free. They're doing everything to prevent them from living a decent life. What the Hell is wrong with them?"

"What's wrong is that they see black and brown people as inferior, unfit for self-government, and only here on this earth to

224

serve them. So, they put laws in place that work against blacks. And they turn around and wonder why no one wants plantation work."

"And don't forget all the taxes and property laws Bogle and Gordon talked about at the meeting we attended." I looked up and saw Cook coming out the door.

"Sunday *Courier* here, sah. I forget to give you earlier," he said, handing the newspaper to Gavin and walking back into the great house. Gavin opened it, read quietly, paused, and then he gasped.

"Oh my God. Check this out! 'Paul Bogle and his followers now have their own unofficial court system in some parts of the island, including Morant Bay. They did this because of the intolerance and bias against blacks in the judicial system.'"

"What? How can they get away with that? Keep reading."

"Look at this," Gavin said, leaning over to me with the newspaper. "'They have selected their own judges, clerks of the courts, and police force. They issue summonses, try cases and levy fines.'"

"Good God, they can do that?" I asked.

"It's right here, Sean. Check this out. 'The courts have been linked to the local churches, so disobeying the court's authority could mean expulsion from the church.'"

"That's absolutely brilliant! These people are no fools."

"This will be one heck of a fight. We'd better muscle-up," Gavin said. He was right.

Sometime later, I read that Bogle had begun giving his followers military training; he was talking about using force to bring down the oppressive system, if necessary. Meetings were called all over the island to discuss the unbearable conditions free blacks had been forced to bear.

Petitions got passed around. Many signed the petitions, and hundreds, who couldn't write, marked them with an 'X'. Soon, the papers reported that a representative was actually sent to Britain to lay the matter before the Secretary-of-State for the Colonies.

Gavin and I kept reading and exchanging information, hoping for some good news. But the government stubbornly refused to acknowledge the seriousness of the situation and the need to address the issues.

Governor Eyre passed around thousands of copies of a letter he claimed had expressed the views of the Queen of England. The letter basically said blacks should continue to work hard at the plantations when needed, and that this would allow the plantations to thrive and be able to pay them higher wages.

According to the newspaper, Gordon and Bogle would not let up. They soon brought to the attention of the Assembly, that the treadmill, an instrument of torture that had been banned after full freedom, was being used once more in the prisons.

Meetings Bogle and Gordon called in Morant Bay, under much duress from local government, ended with the decision to send a delegation to the capital, Spanish Town, to place grievances before the Governor.

Bogle and a group of men walked over 40 miles to Spanish Town, with the letter. But Governor Eyre refused to meet with them or hear their complaints.

Tensions ran high, according to the newspapers, and several unfair court cases ended in disaster as crowds dragged and beat policemen on the steps of the courthouse. Other policemen were captured, beaten, and threatened with death in Morant Bay.

I had worked with a fellow Irishman to build a community where everyone felt cared for and protected. But, in this area, only two men worked to make a difference in the lives of freed African Jamaicans.

Most African Jamaicans had no one on their sides, as they struggled to survive, support themselves and their families, and move ahead with their lives. Britain's plans to remove Jamaica from the claws of plantocracy must come, sooner, rather than later.

Chapter 37

Another crop over celebration appeared on the horizon. This one would really be special, despite the troubles around us. We had barely survived devastating flood waters, but this year's celebration was even more remarkable because our people had built a Baptist church, on property, with their own hands.

I could not believe how quickly they'd built the foundation of the church. Looking at a solid foundation, I remembered the entire village working and chatting away about making sure it could 'stand up to any hurricane coming our way.'

With the foundation up, I listened from my bed as our people worked night after night, through wee hours of the morning. They laid flooring, put up walls, built seats with planks of wood almost as heavy as those they'd used to build the foundation. It had been a labor of love, and I thought, for sure, that days in the fields would be a struggle.

But they worked even harder in the fields, anxious to plant new crops so we could 'make more money and make up for what we lost to flood waters.' They'd hurry through lunch and head home to work their own grounds.

Day in and day out, this had become a drill and no one had to remind them of their responsibilities. I'd learned a few lessons from the experience, and the most important one was that respect, caring and sharing could be fuel for hard work and results.

"Mas Sean, we plannin' big crop over celebration, and guess where we having it this year?" Zoya asked, hurrying toward me with a bucket in one hand and tools in the other. She'd been working the fields all morning, and it was almost lunch time.

"Where?" I asked, the excitement in her voice playing with my senses.

"At Pimento Bay Baptist Church, sah! It be celebration we never forget." She glided past me with a huge smile on her face.

"Pastor Mullings agrees with that?"

"Yah man!"

I just loved the way African Jamaicans said 'yah man'; that's when I knew they were really excited. No more 'yes massa, no massa;' 'yah man' was just fine with me. And I always smiled, because the way they said 'man' sounded like 'mon.' 'Yah mon.'

"You sure the pastor gave his blessing on that?" I was dying to hear more.

She giggled. "Not only he give blessing, you ever see pastor Clifford dance?"

"Haven't seen that yet. What's that like?"

"That man can move his hips and legs like a real heathen. He young, you know. All them young girl in church watchin' and hoping."

I smiled and egged her on. "He interested in any of them?"

"No, sah. Is all 'bout the Lord with Paster Clifford. But I sure take a good look when he movin' his behind to the choir at his Papa's church," she said, before innocently moving on with her chores.

I laughed till tears filled my eyes. *I wonder if the young pastor could teach me a few moves, so Asha will look at my behind one day.*

"Hear 'bout the big celebration coming our way?" Gavin said. He must have walked up behind me. I turned around.

"Just heard about it from Zoya."

"Whole village brimming with excitement over it. They planning a big feast in the clearing outside the church, too."

"Great! Let's get boars meat, a few chickens, and some seasoning at the market tomorrow. Important that we support their accomplishments."

"Let Zoya know so she can pass the word around. I'm really looking forward to this, Sean. We all need to lift our spirits."

"It will be like a warm bowl of boars' head soup for the belly. God knows, we need it. Hear anything new about the uprising?"

"Same things we been reading in the papers. People talking more about it, now. They're saying this one will be worse than Sam Sharpe's revolt."

"Not surprised. Everyone's tired of dealing with the petty, vindictive, and subversive laws and behaviors of the plantocracy. African Jamaicans are not putting up with it anymore. Can you blame them?"

"No blame from me, Laddie. When I think back about how our people took the abuse and were too starved to fight, my heart aches. Enough is enough! Looks like the only thing that get's through to these cruel bastards is what the Maroons did, kick their backsides."

"Let's focus on the happiness coming our way right now."

Before going home that evening, I headed toward the clearing at Pimento Bay. There had been a few afternoon showers earlier, and wet grass crunched under my shoes as I moved along.

I glanced up and saw a few dark-gray clouds moving toward the horizon. The sun was setting, and bursts of colorful rays embellished the skies ahead. Very little breeze fanned the air around me, but I was grateful; no mosquitos buzzed around.

As I approached the clearing, I stared up at the spanking new church building looming ahead; what a sight to see. A simple shingle roof soared up to the skies in the shape of an upside-down v.

As I got closer, I stared at a neatly-built, black, wooden cross perched on top. The sturdy outer walls, a gleaming white, showed four steps leading up to a smooth, wooden, back door, painted black.

I walked around to the front, mounted the steps, pushed one of the double doors open, and gazed ahead. My eyes followed a long aisle, which led up to a dais with two long tables, six chairs, and a wooden lectern standing neatly in front. To the side of the dais stood two rows of wooden chairs, for a choir.

My eyes took me on a slow voyage, up and down the aisle. Sturdy, polished, wooden pews sat to the right and left. At the back of each pew, wooden pockets spread across to hold bibles and hymn books.

I looked down; the floors boasted a gleaming, polished, dark red clay. My people had done an amazing job, and I was overcome with pride.

* * *

I walked into Pimento Bay Baptist Church at ten that Sunday morning. Celebration time had arrived. The building stood filled to capacity; above capacity, really, as people stood against walls on each side, and at the back, in rows.

I looked ahead, and at the left of the platform stood two rows of a choir, everyone dressed in light blue gowns over white shirts. Preacher Mullings and his son Clifford, sat at tables in the middle of the platform. The second table up front had two empty chairs.

I surveyed the room once more. Bedecked in their Sunday best, everyone had hair neatly coiffed, and wore frocks and shirts without a wrinkle.

The young girl children had satin ribbons of all colors tied into bows around their braids. Most pews had bibles or hymn books stuck in the wooden pockets in front.

I noticed a couple of fascinating things. Each person had what looked like colorful, feathered head dresses either in their hands, or on the floor next to them. And in the front row sat Miz Ada, close to the aisle.

Silent, happy chatter filled the air. A voice behind suddenly jolted me out of my reverie.

"You ever seen anything like this?" Gavin asked, as he approached and stood next to me.

"Never! This is one joyful day."

Soon, I saw Zoya rising from a seat in the front pew. She hurried toward us, dressed in a bright yellow frock with short sleeves and frills around a hem that fell just below her knees. Her hair brushed neatly back into a bun, she wore a pair of light brown sandals.

"Come, Mas Sean and Mas Gavin. We have two seats for you up front," she said.

Zoya had told us earlier that the preachers expected us to give short speeches before the service began. So, Gavin and I followed her to the platform, mounted the steps, and took our seats.

Miz Ada walked up to the platform from her seat in the front pew, and positioned herself in front of the choir. She too, was dressed in blue and white.

The choir rose, she held her arms up, and they broke into a rousing rendition of the hymn, 'What A Friend We Have in Jesus.' They sang it with passion and tenderness; never had I thought people at Pimento Bay could sing so beautifully.

After Miz Ada moved her arms fervently and brought the song to an end, young Pastor Mullings gestured for me to take the lectern.

I stood, walked up to it, and I yelled, "Pride - that's what I feel today as I stand before you. I am proud of you all!" The crowd erupted into cheers and whooping; they soon quieted down.

"I've seen every man, woman and child here today work hard over the past months to keep our village going, to plant and reap our crops while building their homes, and finally, to build this beautiful church. You are a true example of love, passion, teamwork, and ambition. As we celebrate together in this loving church, my heart and soul are filled with love and respect for every single person in front of me. So, let us worship, eat, drink, and celebrate till we drop. We deserve it all."

The crowd erupted into cheers once more. I turned and returned to my seat.

Gavin rose, a huge smile on his face, and walked up to the lectern. He gave another spirited speech of love and unity, the crowd cheering and whooping, over and over.

Afterward, the choir belted the hymn, 'How Great Thou Art.' The older Pastor Mullings took the stage and belted out a message of God's love and forgiveness during these difficult times, 'as the fight for justice and respect continue all over our island.'

Young pastor Mullings proudly welcomed his throng of worshipers, read and expounded three verses from the bible, and begged for love and kindness during difficult times ahead.

A remarkable event soon took place. Miz Ada marched to the lectern, raised her hands high, stared at the crowd, and slammed her eyes shut.

She screeched like a possessed being, words that I failed to understand. She stood there, shaking, her eyes rolled back into her head, a trance-like state taking mastery over her. Goose bumps roamed up and down my flesh and I shuddered.

"Brothas' and sistas,' no more worrying 'bout killing and rioting. We shall be unshackled once again. Another emancipation is about to rain on us, like gushin' showers before bright rays of sunshine. Those who chained us about to set us free, once again. Freedom is pounding at the door, and it's about to break through. And when we truly free, we will thrive; we will be a force in this world."

Miz Ada kept her eyes slammed shut, she stood strong, she trembled, and she continued.

"Many will flock to our shores seeking tranquility from our beauty, from our rhythms, from our prowess and determination. Calm you'self, brothas' an sistas,' change is a comin.' It will be sudden! It will be glorious! It will be massive!"

Miz Ada's voice echoed up and down the hallways, her body like a possessed medium. Her message carved a coupling with every soul standing in front of her, their hands held high, their eyes slammed shut, their bodies swaying from side to side in the mystifying aura of Pimento Bay Baptist Church.

No cheering and whooping followed Miz Ada's message. Everyone, including the two pastors, stood for minutes, eyes slammed shut, arms held high, bodies swaying from side to side, chanting, 'Amen; yes Lord; thank you, Jesus; send it our way, Dear God!"

My body refused to halt the tremors galloping up and down my spine. Miz Ada finally lowered her arms, opened her eyes, and strolled back to her place in front of the choir.

By the time speeches, preaching, and predictions came to an end, everyone sang and clapped as the choir burst into hymns, thanking the Lord for all his blessings. I swung my body from side-to-side to the rhythms, rocking in a state of jubilation and gratitude.

The choir continued singing, hands in the air, and danced their way down the steps and isle behind Miz Ada. The two preacher men followed, and so did Gavin and I.

Glancing behind, I saw the throng moving down the aisle, from the front pew on down, clutching their head dresses.

We got outside and the crowd kept dancing and singing, till everyone had exited the building. I looked up. It was a beautiful morning. Blue skies reigned and there wasn't a single cloud above.

Soon, I heard it; the sound of Maroon drums peppered the air. My spirit moved joyfully away from worship, and landed smack on a wave of celebration.

Olumbo and his two men pounded away at the drums, stealing all tempo from the choir. By then, everyone boasted big, feathered headdresses of light green, aqua, purple and orange, as they moved passionately to the tempo.

"Come on Laddie, feel the rhythm. We in Jamaica. Dance till you drop," Gavin said, grinning, moving next to me like tomorrow would never come, and trying to catch the tempo. He gyrated closer to me.

"Laddie, Miz Ada just predicted the next freedom call, Crown Colony for Jamaica. That woman is magnificent; she's a prophet," he said. I nodded and moved with the rhythm, tremors still frolicking up and down my spine.

The dancing and whooping continued for hours, up and down the streets of our village. People sat on corners, taking a break and gobbling down food.

Gavin and I joined the food line when we got to it, at the other side of the clearing. We followed suit, sat on two rocks on one side of a road, and enjoyed our food.

"We always wondered how African Jamaicans withstood the cruelties of slavery. Now we know," Gavin said.

"Olumbo said his father taught him to feel the rhythms of the drums in his heart and soul when things got tough. He claims Maroons who were born on the plantations but had escaped slavery, would tell him, 'Close your eyes, listen to the rhythm of the drums. It will get you through the cruelest day.'"

"I believe them, Laddie. It's like the rhythm wraps itself around their souls and refuses to let go. They were born that way."

"Not a bad way to be born."

We rose, threw our banana-leaf plates into the bushes, caught our version of the rhythm, and pranced our way to catching up with the revelers ahead.

Chapter 38

"Rebellion at Morant Bay, Mas Sean! Five of we men gone," Zoya yelled, pounding on the front door of the great house. The celebration abruptly over, I quickly dragged my pants on, hurried to the door and opened it. Zoya stood there, staring at me, terror in her eyes.

"Gone? Where?" I asked, trying to rid my senses of sleep.

"They gone to join Bogle and his men. It going be war, sah."

"Zoya, I need you and Miz Ada to keep everyone calm as we ride this out. Tell them to focus on what Miz Ada just predicted. Who are the men that left?"

"Surgi and his two big son Kafi, and Bahati; Ode and Isabis gone too. Them last two leave families behind, women and babies."

"Dear God! Try to keep everyone together. I'll stay on top of what's happening. The newspapers, Olumbo, and the Quaker will keep us informed. Go, now. Let me know right away if you need help."

I watched her disappear into the dim light of dawn, and I washed up and walked to the clearing to collect the morning paper. When I returned, I ran into Miz Ada walking away from the verandah.

"I leave some breakfast for you on dining table, Mas Sean. Don't worry, me and Zoya keep everybody calm. We watch over family Ode and Isabis leave behind. Goin' to be tough days ahead, but we get back to workin' fields. Things better if we stay busy and focus on future," she said.

"Thanks for everything. I'll keep you up-to-date with what's going on."

I waved the newspaper in front of me, opened the front door, and walked in. I sat at the table for breakfast, opened the paper, and started reading.

In the fields that day, a slave woman walked up to me, "Mas Sean, a white man in horse cart waitin' outside the gate for you. Gate man say he name Tomas."

"Quaker Tomas?"

"Yes sah."

I dropped everything, hurried to the gate and told the gate man to let the Quaker in. This must be urgent, for him to ride all this way to see me.

The Quaker drove a short distance through the gate and brought the mules to a halt. I jumped up on the cart and sat next to him.

"What's going on?" I asked, too anxious for small talk.

"Brits ask me to go to Morant Bay. Planters tried Bogle and are about to hang him. Very long ride; you go with me tomorrow morning?"

"Yes. Not too safe out there. Can we take my Maroon friend Olumbo with us?"

"Great idea. Think he'll agree to come?"

"He'll come. He's a loyal friend. He'll be here later today to see his son. I'll tell him we'll pick him up at the bottom of the hill tomorrow at 6 in the morning. That all right?"

"Yes. I'll get here around half-past-five. Take change of clothes. We won't be back for a couple of days."

I jumped down from the horse cart and watched the Quaker turn it around and head out through the gates. When I got back to the fields, I immediately found Zoya and told her to have Olumbo stop by to see me. I went looking for Gavin and told him what was going on.

"Okay, I'll stay here and watch over things. Olumbo will make sure you travel safely."

Quaker Tomas was on time the next morning, and so was Olumbo. We galloped along in silence for the first several minutes of the ride, me sitting next to Tomas in front with my loaded bayonet under my seat, and Olumbo in back of the cart with a machete wrapped in burlap, hidden under his seat. The Quaker soon started to speak.

"Last night I read that over four hundred demonstrators from Stony Gut, a town close by, just stormed Morant Bay. They sacked the police station and moved to the courthouse. The custos, Baron von Ketelhodt, called in a volunteer militia from Bath. He walked out on the courthouse steps and started reading the Riot Act. According to the paper, the crowd kept advancing. The militia fired a volley at them, killing ten people. The crowd went crazy, broke loose, regrouped, and returned with sticks, stones, machetes, and other objects."

"Aye. It's reported that they attacked the courthouse, set fire to the schoolhouse and other buildings, and broke open the jail."

We rode along, sharing more information from yesterday's *Courier,* which reported that over fifty prisoners had broken loose and joined the mayhem.

Members of the vestry and the magistrates had hidden in the schoolhouse and another house nearby, but they got driven out by fire, and attacked as they fled. Some got shot, others got chopped or beaten to death. Those who survived hid in a latrine and behind hedges. They found Baron von Ketelhodt dead, his head smashed.

"This news is not good," Tomas said. No words came from Olumbo. I glanced back at him. He sat there, staring ahead, the veins on his forehead bulging and throbbing.

"Sweet Jesus, the military is going to kill them all," I said, my head spinning.

"They may try to kill all them, but the rest of us won't stop till we get justice," Olumbo said.

Tomas kept talking about what he'd read in the newspaper. He cited problems in other parts of the island, with hundreds of marchers from Manchioneal being intercepted by a throng of black soldiers from Port Antonio. According to Tomas, they killed over a hundred people.

"Damned governor Eyre's the main problem, always ruling for planters. Need to get rid of him, fast," Olumbo said.

"For sure. He finally responded to the petition the people sent to him weeks ago, threatening consequences if the uprising continued. Things are out of control," Tomas said. I glanced at him as he jerked the reins. He knitted his brows so tightly, he'd become red-faced.

"People sick and tired of being treated like dogs," Olumbo said.

"Eyre declared martial law last week, but it caused more bloody fighting as people defended their rights to freedom. The papers say protesters, led by Paul Bogle, had captured the courthouses at Bath and Morant Bay," Tomas said.

"They say Bogle ask Maroons nearby for help, but they refused," Olumbo said.

"Why'd they refuse?" I asked.

"Damned article six of peace treaty we sign with Brits years ago say we should help crush slave revolts," Olumbo said. I turned and looked at him.

"I told you before. This is no slave revolt; these are free people."

"Tell that to fools in that area who call themselves Maroons, givin' us bad name. They're the ones who captured Bogle and hand him over," Olumbo said.

"One day later, he was court-martialed and now they're hanging him. Where's the God damned justice for freed people on this island?" Tomas asked.

"Britain must step in, now," I said.

"Brits should have stepped in a long time ago. But then again, we both know what sometimes happens when they step in. Olumbo, Sean and I have been through some horrible times in Ireland," Tomas said, glancing back at the Maroon.

Olumbo said, "We not starving here, we fighting. They can kill some of us, but the rest just waitin' to rise up and fight like beasts."

We'd been riding and talking for over four hours, when I took over the reins so the Quaker could close his eyes and get some rest.

Zoya had packed food for me to take on the trip, and Tomas had also brought sandwiches. We stopped to take care of the horses and rest them. The three of us ate before continuing the journey.

We agreed that we'd watch out for the men who'd left Pimento Bay to join the rebellion. If we found them, we'd make space in the cart and take home anyone willing to ride back with us.

By the time we approached Morant Bay in St. Thomas, sunset had surrounded us. After making three stops to tend to the horses and ourselves, we'd been traveling for almost 12 hours.

As we approached the town, I immediately saw unrest. People roamed the streets, talking and shouting. The air felt tight with anxiety and agitation.

Tomas pulled the cart to the side of the road and stopped. Crowds of people walked by, chatting and yelling. I listened closely.

"Lawd Jesus, they goin' hang Paul Bogle tonight," one man yelled.

"They goin' hang Gordon, too. What we goin' do?" another man said.

"Gordon in Kingston. He sick," a woman said.

"No. They send warrant for him, so him give himself up," a man said.

"They say Eyre himself show up to arrest him and take him to Morant Bay," another man said.

"But him have witness. They don' listen to witness? He wasn't in town during the rebellion," the woman yelled.

"They refuse to listen to witness. They won't let lawyer or preacher talk to him. We no get any justice," a man said.

"You no hear? They try him in one day and find him guilty. They goin' hang him with Bogle. Only way to stop this is to kill whole lot'a white man," another man yelled.

By then, my stomach had tied itself into a tight knot. Tomas and I stared at each other, speechless. Olumbo soon broke the silence.

"He right! Whole heap'a people goin' die before we get justice. Maroons already fight that fight."

I turned and glanced at the Maroon; he looked as serious as I was Irish. I knew, without a doubt, that if this continued, more war would erupt around the island.

Cool breezes wrapped around us as the sun moved down into the horizon. Tomas said, "Let's leave the cart here."

Olumbo and I hitched the horses to a tree in a small clearing. We must have been about half-a-mile from the town square, but the cart could go no further as crowds swarmed around us.

I said, "Got a better place to hide the gun? Walk into town toting a gun, and we're all dead."

"Hide it here," Tomas said, his hand opening some kind of crude locker under his seat. He grabbed the gun from under my seat and forced it into the locker.

"Give me what you got, Olumbo. We hide it here too," I said.

"Nooo, Irishman. I put what I got in holster under this big shirt. No one know it's there, till it's too late."

We meandered through the crowd to the town square. Finally getting close to the clearing, I saw two white men up front talking quietly. I stared at one of the men; his face looked familiar.

"Sweet Jesus, it's that horrid Governor, Eyre," Tomas said.

I recognized Eyre from pictures in the newspaper. Dressed in black pants and black jacket, white shirt, and a gray bow tie, he stood there, a scowl on his face. He finally looked out at the crowd.

"Who's the other man?" I asked.

"Don't know. Guess we're about to find out," Tomas said.

The other man stood tall and thin, with a balding head of gray hair. He wore a pair of gray pants, black jacket, and open-necked white shirt.

Next to Eyre and the other man, eight military men stood erect, four on each side, their bayonets cocked. I'd seen armed military men in the crowd, too.

"Cruel beasts ready to kill. See two noose hanging from that big lignum vitae tree behind them," Olumbo said.

"Sweet Jesus, I see them. And look, there are three whips hanging from another limb," Tomas said.

I stared at the whips. They looked brand new, with thongs neatly braided around wooden handles. At the end of the long thongs, flexible pieces of what looked like wire wrapped around, for louder 'cracks' and greater pain.

There would be a show of cruelty for the crowd of African Jamaicans to see and hear, if Eyre had anything to do with it. 'Teach them a lesson,' Vassell used to yell when he got ready to lash his slaves.

I glanced over at Olumbo, who had fallen silent. The veins in his temple throbbed, his teeth clenched, his jaw looked tight. Then he began to grind his teeth to hold down the rage in his eyes.

I looked ahead once more and saw a black man walking toward Eyre with a contraption in his hand that looked like a horn. He handed it to Eyre and walked away.

"What the heck is that?" I asked.

"They call it a speaking trumpet, helps crowd hear what's being said," Tomas said. Eyre raised the speaking trumpet to his mouth and shouted.

"Quiet, out there. You hear me, quiet!" The crowed continued to shift around and talk, but eventually quieted down and stared at the man in front, who had made their lives a living Hell.

"We're here today to bring justice to those who have wreaked havoc and death on our people, who were sent by the Queen to govern this island. Standing next to me is Ian Cummings, Mayor of Morant Bay. In the name of the law, we will be hanging the main instigators, Paul Bogle and George William Gordon, for treason. Several of their cronies will be whipped, up to 100 times, for the role they played in this disturbance."

The crowd erupted, yelling 'no, no,' pumping their fists and stamping their feet. The military men up front aimed their guns.

Eyre's screams of 'quiet, quiet,' fell on deaf ears. Fear ripped at my gut. *Sweet Jesus, don't let them start rioting. We'll all be dead.*

Eyre kept yelling, but no one paid attention. I looked behind me; the crowd soon began to quiet down. I turned back around and almost choked.

Two black men marched up and stood behind Eyre, each clasping the arms of Bogle and Gordon, whose arms were tied behind them with ropes.

A huge man walked up to the front and stood next to Bogle. The man looked like the Devil himself. Dressed in a big black 'shroud' that fell just below his knees, he wore black pants and black shoes. The hood of the 'shroud' covered his head, and it hung on his forehead, just over his eyebrows. His face? Barely visible.

Everyone around me gasped; no words could be heard, as the sun slid further into the horizon. An eerie silence filled the air, which had become so thick and humid, you could cut it with a knife. Beads of sweat gathered on my forehead and ran from my armpits, under my shirt.

"White bastards!" Olumbo said.

I glanced at him and then at Tomas, whose face looked twisted with rage. The Quaker clenched his fist. Sweat ran down his temples. Wet rings of sweat formed on the shirt under his arms. His face, red with horror, and, I swore, every blue vein on his temple bulged, like they would burst at any minute.

Eyre yelled again to the crowd, but no one listened. Men hollered and pumped their fists. Women screamed, held their bellies, and bawled.

I turned and stared at the spectacle in front of me, just in time to see the hangman hand one black cloth bag each, to the men whose hands stood glued to Bogle and Gordon.

The man holding Bogle covered his head with a black bag, bundled it around his neck and tied a string around it. He led Bogle up on a short wooden ladder, to the noose. The hangman then took over. He fit Bogle's head into the noose. Walking to some kind of pulley, he paused, then violently jerked the rope. Bogle's body shot up into the air. His body hung lifelessly in front of us, swinging from side to side.

The hangman took several steps back, as the man clutching Gordon's arm started to fit the black bag over his head. Same evil, horrid actions with the second noose, until Gordon hung next to Bogle's body. His chest heaved, his right arm jerked, then he hung still, the life wrenched out of him.

I covered my mouth to stop myself from retching. My gut tightened. Sickness overcame me. Tears fell and soaked the pockets of my shirt.

The hangman turned, walked away, and disappeared into gloom as the sun sunk into the horizon. Women wailed louder. Men hollered with rage.

My gut clenched harder. My throat got tighter. Burying the dead in Ireland was traumatic, but never had I watched anything as horrid as the life being snuffed out of two young, vibrant men, who did nothing but stand up for justice.

Eyre's voice, yelling through the speaking trumpet, jerked me away from one misery and landed me into another. Over the din, I heard him yell, 'lashes, 100 lashes ....' Before I could open my mouth, Tomas spoke.

"Let's get the Hell out of here. Enough!"

The three of us spun around and forced our way through the crowd, Olumbo in the lead. He shoved his right hand under his shirt and clutched the machete.

* * *

By the time we got home, news had already gotten to our people. They also knew about the punishment of other protesters.

The newspaper reported that whites had retaliated for their people, who'd been killed and injured. They'd burned hundreds of homes and crops of would-be protesters. They'd executed hundreds of blacks by court martial, shot others without trial, and killed some by 'other means.'

The morning after we returned from Morant Bay, Gavin and I called a meeting at the clearing just outside the church yard.

Olumbo attended; he'd stayed the night with Zoya and his son. I called him up front and he stood next to Gavin. We each gave updates on what we'd seen and read in the papers. Everyone listened. The air felt thick with discontent.

"Not everyone lucky to live at Pimento Bay, sah. Brothas' and sistas' suffering out there," one man yelled.

"White people only happy when they workin' us like mules and beatin' us to death," another man said.

"Yah. And governor wicked like the Devil. He workin' against us," a woman yelled.

"We tired of the abuse. We rather die than take any more," another man said.

"Understood. Let us keep building our community. Build a school. Educate ourselves. We won't have to take this abuse forever," Gavin said.

"We must educate our children so they can stand up for justice and get a noose 'round their necks?" A man asked.

"We educate our children so they win a seat in government. Then we have power," Olumbo yelled.

Gavin and I went back-and-forth with the audience, and we finally calmed them down. We listened when they got loud and passionate. And I could see that they knew we were on their side. Then a woman shouted.

"Mas Sean, we keep vigil at church for five men gone to Morant Bay. We worry. We want them home safe."

Everyone perked up. They all loved that idea. We ended the meeting and headed to the fields.

That evening, Quaker Tomas showed up at our gate. Always happy to see him, I suddenly got uneasy, my nerves queasy after the Morant Bay horror. Was he bringing more bad news?

"Good to see you again, Sean. Tough times around us," he said.

"Aye. Good to see you too."

He looked neatly dressed in a pair of khaki pants, white short-sleeve shirt, and black shoes. His hair, cut short, laid brushed back on his head. He looked tired.

"How's everyone here holding up? I'm here with news."

"Doing the best we can. What's going on?"

"Britain's nervous about the rebellions and hangings. They're talking about extending martial law if things get any worse."

"About time they got nervous. Eyre is evil. I swear, the planters must be paying him off. He's the reason why blacks are rebelling," I said.

"You're right. Let's hope the Brits step in. I know you're thinking things can get worse when they step in. We've both been there. But what other options do we have? Full-fledged anarchy?"

"At this stage, we'll take whatever we can get. Maybe they'll hurry the Crown Colony agreement along, now that their working class is rebelling in favor of African Jamaicans. I hear their situation in Britain is not much better."

I invited the Quaker to the house to share dinner. After we ate, talked, and I groused that we didn't find even one of our men in the crowd of revelers in Morant Bay, he said he wanted to get home before dark and he bid me goodbye.

That evening I entered Pimento Bay Baptist Church, a vigil in full swing for our five men who had walked for miles to Morant Bay. We had not heard a word from them since they left.

I walked to the front pew, sat down, and looked to my left. Families left behind by the men sat up front, singing loudly, their arms up, their bodies rocking from side-to-side.

I shuffled to my right to make room for Gavin, who'd walked up to join me. Soon, I held hands with Gavin and the woman sitting on my other side. We sang the hymn, 'It Is Well, With My Soul,' rocking from side to side, sopping up strength from fellowship with those around us.

As I moved my body to the hymn, I focused on Miz Ada's prediction, 'Change is a comin'. It will be sudden! it will be glorious! It will be massive!'

Chapter 39

Three men stumbled through Havendale's gates, their raggedly clothes barely hanging from their backs. Two, almost naked, had cuts all over their bodies. An older man limped behind the two, struggling to move his legs.

Dear God, Kafi, Ode, and Surgi, three of the men who had walked to Morant Bay to join the rebellion, hobbled toward me. I bolted toward them.

"You're back! Bahati and Isabis?"

"They dead. Military shoot them," Sergi said, tears streaming from his eyes over the loss of his son.

"Whe ... where are the bodies?"

"We go to get body, but they already bury them in grave with a lot of other dead people," Kafi said.

He, too, burst into tears. I walked up and held him around the shoulders. Soon, I heard a woman wailing behind me. She was Miz Suma, Bahati's mother. Gavin showed up and grabbed the woman around the waist. Holding her up, he tightened his grip as she held her belly and screamed for her son.

Every woman standing around began to cry. By then, Isabis' woman and baby had joined the group. The woman screamed and wailed, clutching her baby in her arms. She threw herself to the ground. Two women knelt next to her, holding her and the baby as they all wailed.

I fell apart. Agony gripped me by the throat and tears rushed down my face, drenching my shirt. I could no longer control myself.

A crowd had now gathered from the fields. Miz Ada and two men held the three men and walked them to the clearing. We followed closely behind. At the clearing, Miz Ada disappeared, leaving the men in Zoya's and the other women's care. She soon returned with a crocus bag full of bush medicines.

Three women laid the men down, stripped them of all clothes, and wiped them down with wet rags dipped in buckets of water brought to the scene by three men. Miz Ada went to work, with Zoya as her helper.

The men groaned with gratitude as the obeah woman rubbed bush medicines all over their aching bodies. It always amazed me to watch the obeah woman at work, especially after I'd experienced her healing touch.

Two men soon showed up with clean clothing, and helped the injured men into them. Four other men joined in. They heaved each man up, held him tightly, and walked him to his home.

Mourning washed over Pimento Bay like a black cloud over the next several days. But I thanked God that three of our men had survived.

That Sunday, I stood next to Gavin in the second pew of Pimento Bay Baptist Church, listening to the young preacher read scripture and shout honors to 'our two slain brothers.' I'd never forget that memorial service, filled with sadness, anger, and wailing so loud, my heart ached.

Afterward, I returned to the great house, struggling to cope, my heart full, my soul reaching for calm. I sat at my dining table and stared ahead, not knowing how Pimento Bay, or how the entire island, would recover from all of this.

Days later, Gavin and I took the small horse cart to market in town.

"Let's see if Quaker Tomas is home. He'll fill us in on what's been happening since the turmoil," I said.

"Good idea, Laddie," Gavin said as I made a left turn on to the Quaker's street. We hitched the horse to a tree outside the building, walked to the door, and gave a quick knock. I heard someone approaching.

"Who's there," the Quaker asked. I announced us and he quickly opened the door.

"Always good to see you, Sean, and you too, Gavin. Everything calm at Pimento Bay?"

"As calm as expected. We lost two of our men to the uprising. The village is in mourning," I said.

"So sorry to hear, Old Chap. How'd you lose the men? Most of the killing was in Morant Bay."

"They walked all the way there to join the rebellion."

"Sweet Jesus! Come in; grab a seat. Want some pineapple juice?"

"No thanks. Any news from England since the massacre?" I asked.

"Oh yes. I did get news—"

"Tell us."

"British working class riots erupted over the massacres of Bogle and Gordon. You're not going to believe this. They openly burned Eyre in effigy at Hyde Park."

"Good God! Burned him in effigy? They went that far?" Gavin asked.

"Yes indeed, 'change is a comin'. It will be massive!'" I yelled, quoting Miz Ada.

"Think about it. They're fighting for the same rights as African Jamaicans; an administration in favor of the many. They want the few to have less power," Tomas said.

"The Brits have condemned Eyre for the illegality and lack of justice of Gordon's trial, and for the barbaric and malicious punishment inflicted on so many people," Quaker Tomas said. "The working class has them under heavy pressure," Gavin said.

"What you think's coming next," I asked.

"The end of planter rule is coming fast, my friend. Trust me on that."

The Quaker sounded sure of himself. I stared at him; that reality shook my senses. Fifteen hundred people did not die in vain.

"Eyre will go down fighting," Gavin said.

"He's already started, that cruel, self-righteous bastard. He's screaming to the Brits about the terrifying spectacle of Haiti, claiming Jamaica will become a second Haiti. He's trying to appeal to white fear," Tomas said.

"Why am I not surprised. Eyre is the main reason we got to this horrible place," Gavin said.

"Like your Miz Ada predicted, 'change is coming. It will be glorious!'" The Quaker said.

"Talking about change, any news about what's happening in Ireland?" I asked.

"Good God, yes. So worked up, I forgot to tell you. The famine seems to be ending. It's now only confined to a small area of the country. With the blight affecting less crops, farmers have begun planting again."

"Thank you, Jesus," Gavin yelled. "Great news, Quaker Tomas, great news!"

I raised my fist with happiness, thanked the Quaker, and Gavin and I bid our goodbyes. We made our way to the market, talking about the state of affairs and verbally celebrating the wonderful news about Ireland.

Things bustled as usual at the market, but tensions made the air thick and uneasy. Everyone, blacks, whites, Syrians, Indians, Chinese, all chatted about the uprising and the current state of affairs. I got a feeling mayhem had brought all races together; another good thing to come out of this mess.

"You understand what they're saying? They're talking patois," I said.

"They sure are. Indians and Chinese knew no English when the planters brought them here, so they learned to speak like the masses," Gavin said.

I pointed to a beautiful piece of indigo blue cloth being sold by an Indian vendor.

"How much?"

"One shilling," the woman said. I gave her the shilling, took the cloth and stuffed it into my burlap bag.

"For Asha?" Gavin asked.

"For Miz Suma, mother of the young man who died in the uprising. A little something to cheer her up."

"Ah, you're a good man, Laddie."

"These people have suffered enough; a little kindness goes a long way."

Gavin and I headed home in silence, processing the news of the day. I broke the silence.

"I'm staying here, Gavin. I no longer plan to return to Ireland."

"Me too, Laddie. Ireland is well on its way to recovery. It will be just fine. Besides, this is our home, now. And our people are about to be truly free."

We both smiled and expressed hope for better days ahead.

That Sunday morning, I walked into Pimento Bay Baptist Church a little late. Instead of wailing and mourning, everyone sang and clapped, their bodies swaying from side-to-side.

As I headed up the aisle, the clapping got louder and I felt everyone's eyes on me. They had huge smiles on their faces. I walked to the front pew, stood next to Gavin and joined in with the clapping and swaying.

"What's going on?" I asked.

"Old Preacher Mullings just announced that the new tithes had produced enough for them to start building the school. He also reminded them that you and I had given 500 pounds toward building materials, hence the loud clapping as you walked up the aisle. These folks refuse to stay down for long, Laddie. One more time, they're rising from the vicious rubble of life, and shining like the sunlight coming through that window."

"Amazing! They always wanted that school. Our talk about fighting for justice with education hit home."

I tried to take some credit. But I knew better. African Jamaicans knew how to lick their wounds and keep going. Their resilient spirit had taught me many lessons. One lesson? Pick yourself up and keep going when thing got tough.

When the singing quieted down, young Preacher Mullings took to the pulpit. Everyone remained quiet as he delivered a spirited sermon of faith and deliverance.

But people did not stay quiet for long; shouts of amen and halleluiah soon peppered the air. The air brimmed with strength and determination. I, too, felt inspired and rearing to go.

At the end of the sermon, the young preacher yelled a rousing message of hope and defiance. "They will never keep us down. We demand justice. We deserve respect. We will fight for self-government. Let us educate ourselves and our children. It's the only way we will get the justice and respect we deserve."

The choir belted out a stirring rendition of, 'To God be the Glory.' Everyone rose, joined in with song, clapped and swayed. Gavin and I sang too, my heart overflowing with hope and courage.

Gavin leaned over. "If Vassell was still around, young preacher man would be tarred and feathered."

"Thank God for civilized men."

Rays of hope shone bright flashes of light into my soul, as I clapped and swayed with the bravest people I knew.

Chapter 40

"Jamaica is now a Crown Colony! No more plantocracy. The cruelty is over!" Quaker Thomas yelled.

"Thank you, Jesus! I couldn't ask for better news this morning," I yelled back.

The Quaker had come to see me and he delivered the news, still sitting on his cart. He jumped down from the cart, grabbed my hand, and we pranced around like two happy Maroons.

"It's over, Sean. The brutality is over," he yelled, eyes beaming, teeth glistening between a smile so big, I wished I could store it in my memory forever. After all the Quaker and I had been through, my heart embraced his excitement.

"At last, African Jamaicans can build better lives for themselves and their children. They can prepare themselves for self-government."

"This is about to hit the newspapers, Sean. Very important your people hear it from you before then," the Quaker said.

"Oh yes, happy to deliver this news. Know what I'll do? I'll have Miz Ada break the news with me."

"Why Miz Ada?"

"Because of her predictions last week, remember? She launched predictions for way into the future, after you and I are no longer around. She said that people would flock to Jamaica to enjoy its beauty and rhythms. And she predicted Jamaica becoming famous for its 'prowess.' Wonder what she meant by that?"

"Not sure. These people are strong and athletic; maybe that's where she was coming from?"

"Could be. The woman has mystical powers; she's been like an angel to us all."

"Great idea to include her when you break the news, Laddie. She will add credibility to the news. Now go; you have good work to do," the Quaker said.

He turned, heaved himself back up on the cart, waved goodbye, and cantered off, his head moving from side to side like he'd just caught a happy rhythm.

I summoned Miz Ada and Zoya to my quarters. Olumbo came along with them; he must have arrived early to see his son. This was good – I could tell all three at one time. And Olumbo always asked great questions.

I broke the news with happiness and enthusiasm. The women smiled, their eyes wary. And just like I thought, Olumbo peppered me with questions. Good, I could clarify things and give them hope.

"White man ask Maroons for help in case of rebellion, 'cause of Crown Colony news. What that mean?" Olumbo asked.

I grabbed him by the shoulders and stared into his big, brown eyes. "It means no more planter government. Britain will take over. They'll send their people to govern the island."

"Why their people better than planter government? All of them Brits."

"Governors will have to answer more to Britain. The British government will have to approve of how the island is being run."

"We want to govern our own country, but that cruel Eyre tell Brits we animals. They kill our leaders and refuse to give us any respect. We sick of it," Olumbo said.

"I understand. Think of it this way. Being a Crown Colony will help our people get the education they deserve, and prepare them for representation and self-government."

"Yah. But white man only think of us as laborers and servants. They think we can't make it without Europeans governin' us."

I could see he had given this a lot of thought. I didn't blame him for being conflicted. His people had been through Hell.

"Ah, but that's where education comes in. With education, your people will be more prepared to make the case for respect and self-government."

"Okay, Irishman. But we not puttin' up with any more abuse. If things get bad again, Maroons may have to go back to bush warfare."

"Give it a chance, man. You may be pleasantly surprised. Your people planning to help Brits round folks up if there's another rebellion?"

"No way, Irishman. And we tryin' to spread word 'round island that there should be no help from other Maroons."

"We need African Jamaican leaders to look out for us," Miz Ada said.

"I agree. Quaker Tomas and I plan to help get African Jamaicans into the new government, so they can represent your needs."

"How you' plan to do that?" Zoya asked.

"It will be a process, but with Crown Colony, there will be elections. And without planters and their tricks in the way, there should be fair elections so you can vote for people you think will do a good job representing you, like preacher Mullings, for example," I said.

"Ah see," Miz Ada said.

"Just be patient; Crown Colony leadership will work much better for African Jamaicans."

"We trust you,' Mas Sean. If our brothas' and sistas' get anything close to the treatment you give us, we be happy," Zoya said.

Gavin and I called a meeting at the main clearing right away. We delivered the news to an audience that shuffled quietly and stared at us, trying to process what we'd just announced.

As planned, Miz Ada stood in front of the crowd and took the meeting to another level.

"Brothas' and sistas,' ah told you change was'a comin'; ah told you it would be glorious, ah told you it would be massive! No more planter with whip on our back. Sharp and Gordon did not die in vain. We can learn to read. We can get job with pay. We can get ready to govern our self. An' later, we children can work to make Jamaica independent! We free, brothas' and sistas'! We finally free!"

The crowd erupted, whooping and shouting, "We free! We finally free! Thank you, ancestors, we finally free!"

Olumbo pounded his drums. People danced and stomped the earth like rejoicing Maroons. They danced and celebrated for hours. The air brimmed with hope, joy, and anticipation.

After that meeting, I read the morning papers every day.

A legislature has been nominated. Governors have been instructed that Her Majesty's government has the right to expect, in those to whom such great trusts are committed, that they will show themselves able to withstand the pressure of any one class, or idea, or interest, and that they will maintain that calmness and impartiality of judgement, which should belong to any governor of an English colony. As for the officials, their business is to consider the interests of the peasantry very closely and, without making themselves exclusively the representatives of those classes, to see that their interests do not suffer.

The *Courier* soon began to report on progress under Jamaica's new leadership:

Sir John Peter Grant, under the new constitution, has started laying the foundations for the development of an efficient, honest civil service. He's also working to improve the island's deplorable communications system. And he has plans to build a railway service, linking Kingston, Port Antonio and Montego Bay. This will lead to jobs for hundreds of Jamaicans. The new governor seems to be leading a mission on behalf of the Jamaican people.

In the weeks that followed, I went to bed to sounds of hammering, sawing, and loud chatter as every man, woman and child at Pimento Bay built their school.

The noise sometimes kept me awake, but I was not about to complain about ambition and determination. I knew everyone would show up on time to work the fields in the morning and their personal provision grounds would be well kept.

Early December came, with cool, refreshing breezes wrapped around us morning and night. The fruit trees had already blessed us with abundance, and now they stood lush, proudly moving their branches to the cool, tropical breezes.

Full or crescent moons shone down on us at night, and the days endowed us with glimmering sunshine and crisp, blue skies. On this beautiful morning, I walked briskly to the fields when a voice jolted me out of my thoughts.

"Mas Sean, we want to hire wives of Pastor Mullings and another preacher, to teach school. What you think?" Miz Ada asked, walking up to me. I turned to face her.

"Brilliant idea."

"We can't afford nobody else. They say they work for half fee for first year, more like ... what they call ..."

"Volunteering," I said.

"Yah man, that's it. You still think that all right?"

"Definitely. So, school-building almost finished?"

"Oh, yes, indeed!"

"I'll stop by and take another look this evening. I hear you working late every night."

"We anxious to finish so children get a better life."

"A better life. I love the sound of that."

Chapter 41

A sunny Monday morning had me walking briskly toward Pimento Bay's new school. I looked up at skies peppered with huge puffs of white clouds. Thoughts of the school made me grateful for progress. With better days ahead, I would stay positive and supportive, for our people.

The fruit trees had blossomed again; I glanced up at a big tree to my right. Huge breadfruits made the limbs bow with reverence. A mongoose scampered by, his bushy tail disappearing under a rock.

Ah, the mongoose. Thank God the Brits brought them from India to get rid of big rats that used to destroy the cane fields. The mongoose also devoured snakes, lizards and other critters. I was terrified of snakes and happy that the mongoose had rid the island of them.

But then I smiled, remembering fowls squawking and women bawling 'Mongoose,' at the top of their lungs, as those little beasts tried to steal their chickens. A Good Samaritan and a thief, all rolled into one small creature.

I approached the school and looked up at a sign, 'Pimento Bay Primary School,' proudly displayed above the front door. Pride washed over me. I heard voices and looked around at a remarkable sight.

Children of all ages gathered silently behind me, waiting to enter the building. The girls, dressed in burlap shifts that fell just above their knees, had dark green, home-made cotton belts cinched around their little waists. Each girl's neatly braided hair boasted dark-green bows.

The boys stood around in crisp khaki knee shorts, short-sleeved khaki shirts, brown hemp belts, and brown boar skin shoes. The children's faces looked cleanly-scrubbed, their complexions different shades of brown. They smiled with sparkling, white teeth, as they milled about, happy for the first day of school. I would never forget this beautiful sight.

"Good mornin,' Mas Sean," they all said, like a winsome choir, when they caught sight of me. I smiled from one ear to the next.

"Good morning, children. You look beautiful. I'm so proud of you."

They looked down with big, shy smiles. Two well-dressed women arrived. One tall, thin, attractive middle-aged woman had short-cropped hair and a stern face. The other woman looked in her 30s, with medium-length hair, smooth brown skin, and piercing eyes.

Gavin walked up behind me.

"That's old Pastor Mullings' wife," he said. "The young woman next to her is the wife of Pastor Thompson from St. James Baptist Church. They'll both be teaching the children."

The women let the children into the schoolhouse, and Gavin and I walked in behind them.

I stared around. Dear God, these people could be resourceful. The one-room schoolhouse, well-built, with a stage and pulpit, had wooden benches spread across the room, with a walkway in the middle.

The benches sat far enough apart to hold small, built-in, wooden desks with spaces in between, for the children to move in and out. Under each desk, a built-in shelf allowed the children to store books.

The two women ushered the children to their seats and motioned them of sit. Mothers and fathers stood against walls along the back and side of the room, smiling.

Staring at the front of the room, I saw the two Pastor Mullings walk up to the stage. The younger pastor took a seat, and his father walked to the front of the stage.

"Children, parents, and friends, welcome to you all. This is one special day, as we begin to educate our children and, in turn, ourselves. As African Jamaicans, we're used to fighting for our rights. You have now been given the right to learn and grow. Pimento Bay

Primary School is a symbol of freedom and empowerment. Open your minds, children! Learn everything in front of you. You know why? Education is the only way for us to move forward, now that we are free to do so. Say amen to learning."

"Amen," everyone yelled.

"Let us pray."

The children bowed their heads as the older pastor said a spirited prayer of gratitude and joy. Then he took a seat.

Young Pastor Mullings walked to the front of the stage. He looked around, slowly, with pride. He thanked everyone in the room for their hard work building the school. Then he shouted special thanks to me and Gavin for our 'spiritual and financial support.'

The room exploded with applause. Huge smiles of gratitude flashed across faces. What an honor it was to be part of this momentous morning, and to help make a difference in the lives of people who had fought like panthers for this day.

The clapping finally calmed down as the young pastor continued his message.

"In the next weeks, we will sing "God Save The Queen," every morning because we are now a British Colony, so we are bound by the rules of colonial powers. This is not a bad thing. It's just that we, the people, want more. And that 'more' includes representation in government, our right to govern ourselves, and someday, our right to be an independent nation. Children, this is where your education comes in. Take it all in; it will make you powerful. Always remember that power comes in two forms, physical and mental. Strengthen your mental powers and your future will be bright."

The young pastor paused, looked around at the crowd, and continued.

"We lost many African Jamaican leaders to the hang-man's noose. But they didn't die in vain, and the Brits have freed us from the cruel planters. And, we have a remarkable new, human rights leader now. His name is Marcus Garvey!"

The crowd shuffled; every man, woman and child looked ahead with pride and determination. They recognized the name, Marcus Garvey.

"Yes, Pastor! Hail, to Marcus Garvey," they yelled, fueled by passion, pride, and determination.

I'd read that Garvey was an African Jamaican man who grew up under the cloud of British colonialism. Yet he became well-read, got himself educated, had traveled and spread his message all over the world, and had returned to Jamaica to lead the fight for 'positive self-image after cruelty and subjugation.'

The young preacher continued to belt his message louder, jolting me out of my thoughts.

"Marcus Garvey is back to remind us that we are worthwhile. He's here to challenge us to grab on to our racial identity. We will not only teach you to read and write, we will teach you who you are, where you came from, and where you should be going."

The preacher paused, glanced around, and continued.

"We are heading toward a cultural and social awakening! This awakening will change your self-image to one of pride and racial equality. Embrace this change; it will project us onto the world stage. It will move our people into leadership roles in this beautiful country, our country!"

The young Pastor had obviously embraced the role of prophet, teacher, and preacher. My ears stung, as the crowd erupted into cheers and whooping. A cultural and social awakening, indeed!

That day as Gavin and I walked to the fields, he asked, "Where do they get such fighting spirits? How do they keep going?"

"Don't know, but I sure learned a lot from them," I said.

"Me too. To quote the words of our Maroon friends, with a few changes, 'it's onward and upward, no other option.'"

I nodded and turned around to the sound of a deep voice. Olumbo walked up to me.

"Irishman."

"What's going on, Olumbo?" I asked. Gavin greeted him, excused himself, and headed to the fields, leaving us alone.

"Big celebration comin' – Maroons' one hundred-and-forty-years independence from British, and Crown Colony freedom from planters, for our ex-slaves. I come to invite you."

"Congratulations! Great accomplishments. Glad to attend. When is it?"

"This Saturday. Meet me at bottom of mountain at ten in the morning?"

"I'll be there. Thanks for inviting me."

I watched him walk away, and I headed to the fields, smiling. Why did I get the feeling this would be a life-changing event for me?

Soon, I moved through the streets of Olumbo's village to the rhythms of Maroon drums, with Asha by my side. Oh yes, I was finally catching the beat.

I swung my hips to the music, almost like a Maroon. Asha grabbed my hand and moved next to me, gyrating to the beat of the drums. Wearing a short burlap frock and her hair pulled back into an ample braid, her beautiful face looked cleanly scrubbed. The woman looked almost as young as the first time I laid eyes on her. And boy, could she move those hips.

"Hey, Irishman, you want to be more than jus' friends with my sister?" Olumbo's deep voice echoed. *What in God's name am I hearing? Could this be?*

I glanced to my left and he moved next to me, powerfully swinging those hips, arms and legs to the rhythm like an African warrior. I glanced at Asha. She had a mischievous smile on her face.

"Yah man!" Was all I could muster as I kept moving. I was definitely in rhythm now. Nothing would stop me.

"Good!" Olumbo said. "I figure if she keep' waitin,' you never ask. You afraid of me, yes?"

"Been tryin' to gather the nerve," I said, almost speaking patois. *What the heck! I'm going all the way.*

I kept moving, the rhythm in my hips surging me forward as the drums pounded, and the balmy breeze wrapped itself around me. The afternoon sun embraced my skin and a warm glow took over my very soul.

Olumbo danced happily away, moving hips, arms, and legs like he could wrestle with a lion. My thoughts took me to a place of hope and gallantry.

Afraid of you? Aye, but it's time. I survived starvation, death, disease, hurricane, and rebellion. Go ahead; put me out of this fervor with Asha by my side. I'll die a happy man!

Printed in the USA
CPSIA information can be obtained
at www.ICGtesting.com
LVHW040026011123
762563LV00006B/842